THE WAKING

SPIRITS OF THE NOH

Also by Thomas Randall

The Waking: Dreams of the Dead

THE WAKING

SPIRITS OF THE NOH

THOMAS RANDALL

BLOOMSBURY

NEW YORK BERLIN LONDON SYDNEY

First published in the United States of America in June 2011
by Bloomsbury Books for Young Readers
www.bloomsburyteens.com

For information about permission to reproduce selections from this book, write to
Permissions, Bloomsbury BFYR, 175 Fifth Avenue, New York, New York 10010

Library of Congress Cataloging-in-Publication Data
Randall, Thomas.
The waking : spirits of the Noh / by Thomas Randall. — 1st U.S. ed.
p.   cm.
Summary: Just as Kara and her friends at the Monju-no-Chie school in Japan are
beginning to get over the horrifying deaths of two students, another monster emerges
to terrorize the school.
ISBN 978-1-59990-251-7
[1. Supernatural—Fiction. 2. Monsters—Fiction. 3. Schools—Fiction. 4. Japan—Fiction.
5. Horror stories.] I. Title. II. Title: Spirits of the Noh.
PZ7.R15845Was 2010   [Fic]—dc22   2009018251

Book design by Nicole Gastonguay
Typeset by Westchester Book Composition
Printed in the U.S.A. by Quad/Graphics, Fairfield, Pennsylvania
2 4 6 8 10 9 7 5 3 1

*This one's for every kid
who's ever been a part of
the Drama Club at St. Joe's*

PROLOGUE

Demons covered one entire wall of Yuuka Aritomo's classroom. At least, that was how other people would have seen her collection of Noh theater masks. Some were monsters, some evil spirits, and others merely distorted representations of gods, crazy people, and fierce warriors. Most of them were tragic figures, and many were hideous to behold, but Miss Aritomo thought them all quite beautiful.

A shiver went through her, a sudden feeling of dread that spider-walked up the back of her neck. She turned to stare at the shadowed corner of the art room, troubled by the certainty that something had just darted out of view. For a moment, it felt as though the masks were staring at her.

Stop. You're frightening yourself.

Alone in the room, the school so quiet, it was easy to get spooked, but this was something more than nerves. Something had made her uneasy. Something had flitted through the shadows in her peripheral vision.

No. Stop.

"You're a grown woman," she said aloud, and the sound of her own voice comforted her. She might be an adult, a teacher, but at heart she was still the little girl who had been afraid of her own shadow.

It's just the murders, she thought, and shivered again. Several students and one teacher had died on the campus of Monju-no-Chie school this past spring, and another girl had been drowned the previous fall. They hadn't all been murders, at least according to the police, but she could not help feeling claustrophobic there, alone in her classroom, with the echoes of those deaths—the cruelty, the malice, the evil—lingering in her mind.

She could only imagine how the students must feel. Which was why she had decided to do something to take their minds off such a grim reality. The summer term was about to begin and she had just come from a meeting with the school's principal, Mr. Yamato, who had approved her request to give her students a once-in-a-lifetime experience—they would put on a Noh play, complete with actors, musicians, and traditional dance. The club would build their own Noh stage and create costumes and props and masks.

Miss Aritomo looked at the masks again and smiled. They were just masks, after all. She had loved Noh theater since she was nine years old, when her father had taken her to a performance of The *Lady Aoi* and told her that in an earlier era, commoners had been forbidden to learn the music and dance of the Noh. Now, while she loved teaching and enjoyed all forms of art, her greatest pleasure came from her role as faculty advisor to the Noh theater club.

She studied the various masks on the wall, and felt nine years old again, studying the faces of gods and monsters.

Should they perform a realistic *genzai no*, or a more fantastical *mugen no*? After the tragic deaths of the last year, it seemed more respectful to choose a genzai no. But her Noh club would doubtless prefer some wild fantasy. It was a difficult decision.

Miss Aritomo let her gaze wander over the masks. There was Satokagura, a furious red devil with white hair and beard, and Torakumadoji, whose ivory devil face was made almost comic by the huge brushes of his bristly eyebrows. There were long-jawed gods with golden faces, dragons and elementals, and several versions of the fox-mask of Kitsune.

From the bookshelf by her desk, she plucked a thick volume that listed every Noh play included in the modern repertoire, as well as older variations that had gone out of fashion. There were fewer than three hundred to choose from, and it would be a simple matter to narrow it down now that she had decided upon some parameters.

She started to riffle through the pages, glancing at them casually. She intended to wait until the second week of the summer term to reveal her plan to the Noh club, to make certain that a few transfer students would have time to adjust to the club and decide if they wanted to remain before she sprang the surprise.

A contented smile settled upon her features as she turned

pages and thought about the effort and dedication it would require of her students. Yet she knew they would love every moment of it, just as much as she did.

Perhaps not just as much, she corrected herself, *but nearly*.

Rob would love it, though. When she had discovered that Professor Harper shared her interest in the arts, she realized that they had the potential to develop a real relationship. Yuuka had no desire to compete with the memory of his late wife, but Rob was still a young man. He had a future to look forward to, and though she knew it was much too early to be thinking so seriously, she could not pretend that she had not wondered if they might share that future together.

Don't get ahead of yourself, she thought. No matter how strong her feelings for Rob were growing, his lingering devotion to his wife created a barrier between them, and the powerful bond he shared with his daughter, Kara, meant that she would always be foremost in his mind.

That's as it should be. He's her father, Miss Aritomo reminded herself.

And yet she could not help feeling at least a little jealous.

The book fell open to *Lady Aoi*. She had read and reread the description of that play dozens of times, so it was no wonder that the binding naturally opened there, upon the first Noh she had ever seen. It would have been wonderful to do that one, but it was too grim and too fantastical, and the disturbing presence of the Hannya made it everything she didn't want for the first production of the Noh club.

First production? Her smile widened as she realized she had already begun thinking of it in this way. But she

4

told herself to slow down and focus. So much would be involved in this performance that it would be foolish to assume she would be able to do it again, or that Mr. Yamato would allow it.

A clatter came from behind her. Frowning, she turned to see that one of the masks had fallen off its hook.

"Oh, no," she said, hurrying to pick it up.

She put a finger into the book to hold her page and crouched to reach for the mask. Even as her fingers brushed its surface, she realized with a shudder that it was the Hannya mask. Knees bent, she turned it over and stared in astonishment when she saw that it was unharmed. There were no cracks, the reddish paint was not chipped, and—even more surprising—the delicate horns and metallic fangs were intact.

Yet what she felt was not relief. Her brow knitted with an unease she did not understand, and as she began to rise, a wave of disorientation swept over her. She felt cold and unsteady and her vision began to blur, and Miss Aritomo fell, book and mask both dropping from her hands.

It might have been minutes or merely seconds later that she opened her eyes and found herself sprawled on the floor. Her head ached from the impact of her fall and she felt strangely thirsty. Blinking, breathing steadily, she moved carefully into a sitting position, afraid she would faint again. She had only ever passed out once before, on a hot, humid morning when she had been a schoolgirl.

Shaken, she glanced around. The Hannya mask lay on the floor a few feet away, still intact, staring up at the ceiling with what she'd always thought of as gleeful malice. The book had fallen open a few feet from the mask, and now Miss Aritomo reached out to retrieve it.

Curious, she saw that the book had fallen open on *Dojoji*, a horrific play that, like *Lady Aoi*, also featured the Hannya. *Dojoji* concerned the spirit of a young woman who had been spurned by her lover and transformed into a demonic serpent— the Hannya—to take her vengeance.

Miss Aritomo smiled and reached for the Hannya mask. A small voice in the back of her mind objected, but she forced those concerns away and they were instantly forgotten. *Dojoji* seemed like the perfect choice for the Noh club.

Just perfect.

1
卍

Kara Harper sat in the back of the classroom, trying valiantly to stay awake. The windows of Room 2-C were open, but no breeze came off Miyazu Bay that Friday afternoon. It was the third week of August and Monju-no-Chie school had been back in session for a scant handful of sweltering days. The weather had been beautiful during the holiday weeks that separated the spring and summer terms. This far to the north of Kyoto Province, so close to the Sea of Japan, and with the school situated right on the bay, it was rare for the heat to reach brutal levels.

But now classes were back in session, and the summer had turned ugly.

Kara didn't mind so much. After the terrors of the spring, a little hot weather was nothing to complain about. She was just glad that she and her friends were all still alive to feel the heat.

During those terrifying days, she and her father had nearly decided to pack it all in and return home. Sometimes Kara wondered if they had made the right decision in staying, but mostly she was glad. It would have broken her heart to say a premature farewell to the friends she had made here—some of the best friends of her life. And though sometimes she still had nightmares, the shadows were receding.

Kara blinked. People were getting up. While her mind had been drifting, school had ended. With a grateful sigh, she stood and stretched, sticky clothes pulling away from her body. She wanted a shower, but she had hours of other responsibilities to contend with. Her calligraphy club met after school, but first came *o-soji,* the cleaning of the school, which students performed every day at the conclusion of classes. Japanese schools had maintenance staff to deal with blocked toilets and broken lightbulbs and such, but the basic cleaning—bathrooms and classrooms and garbage duty—was done by students.

The class started to head for the lockers at the back of the room. Kara's friend Miho stopped by her desk and fixed her with an odd look. She often hid behind her glasses and the long veil of her straight, black hair, but today it was pulled back with a clip on one side.

"You awake?" Miho asked.

"Barely," Kara said, in Japanese. Even with her father, she spoke Japanese nearly all the time now, to continue improving her fluency with the language. "Between the heat and Mr. Sato's monotone, I was very tempted to take a nap."

Miho smiled. "Really? A couple of times, I glanced over at you and it seemed like you had given in to temptation."

Kara arched an eyebrow. "Could be."

Since Kara had become friends with Miho and her roommate, Sakura, the Japanese girls had begun to hone their skills at American-style sarcasm. Miho had a fondness for American pop culture and she tried to persuade Kara to speak in English whenever possible so she could practice the language. She was actually starting to get pretty good at it, whereas Sakura mostly liked to learn new and different ways to say filthy things in foreign languages.

"I wish we could get out of here," Kara said.

"You don't love o-soji?" Miho asked, her expression innocent. Yes, she was getting much better at the whole sarcasm thing.

They put their things away in their lockers and then headed out through the open sliding door. In the corridor, they joined the rest of the herd of students who were getting their cleanup assignments. Mr. Sato gave Miho sweeping duty, while Kara and two other students had to gather the trash on the entire second floor.

As they parted ways, Kara noticed Mr. Sato watching her and Miho with obvious disapproval, and she quickened her pace. The man oozed irritation, and she wanted to avoid trouble. With her father a member of the faculty, Kara tried to stay on her best behavior so that she did not bring him dishonor. Honor was just as important in Japan as she had always read—maybe even more so.

She weaved her way around students who were filtering into classrooms to perform their appointed tasks, some already sweeping the corridor and stairs. Kara needed trash bags from the hall closet, but a group of students had gathered in the hall. One of them was Mai, a girl from her homeroom who Kara tended to avoid as much as possible.

In every school Kara had ever attended, there always seemed to be a group of girls who hid their cruel smiles behind their hands, putting themselves above everyone else simply by excluding others from their whispers. And for every clique of catty bitches, there was one who led the way and set the tone. When Kara had first arrived at Monju-no-Chie school, that had been a friend of Mai's named Ume. But Ume had been far worse than just some bitchy high school girl; she had been a murderer.

Or close enough. When Ume learned that her boyfriend had fallen in love with another girl, she'd followed the girl down to the shore of the bay one rainy night, a bunch of her friends in tow. Whether or not they had intended to kill her didn't really matter. They had beaten her and drowned her in the bay. The police had never found any evidence linking Ume, or anyone else, to the crime, but Kara knew Ume had killed the girl—Akane, Sakura's sister.

Ume should have been in prison, along with all of the other girls who had helped her beat Akane that night. Instead, she had transferred to another school.

Had Mai been one of the girls with Ume that night? Kara didn't know. Of all of the girls Ume had been friends with— the soccer club girls—Mai would have been the last one Kara would have imagined taking up the queen bitch crown in Ume's absence, but she had filled the role as though she'd been waiting for it her entire life. Maybe she had. The girl had even changed her name. Her real name was Maiko, but now that she was queen bitch, she had started going by the nickname "Mai," insisting everyone call her that. It had taken Kara some getting used to.

Mai took a dustpan and brush from the closet. When she looked up and saw Kara, a slanted, almost sneering smile appeared on her face.

"Bonsai," she said, exuding false charm. "Let me guess. You're on trash duty? How appropriate. Leave it to the American to know garbage when she sees it."

Kara smiled. Ume had been the one to give her the nickname "bonsai," a play on the trees whose branches were pruned and replanted to grow somewhere else. Mai and her friends used it as if it were a term of endearment, but Kara knew it was anything but.

"You're right about one thing," Kara said, pulling several plastic bags out of the closet. "I know garbage when I see it. Unfortunately, some kinds of trash are more difficult to get rid of than others."

As Mai started to reply, Kara turned and walked into the nearest classroom. The girl thrived on nastiness, and Kara had no interest in wasting another second with her. After the cleanup, she had a calligraphy club meeting, and then she was free until Monday morning. She wouldn't let Mai—or anyone else—ruin that.

Kara had never been the New-Agey, burning incense, feng-shui type. She knew a couple of girls back home in Medford, Massachusetts, who talked about their *chi* and had gotten totally into yoga as if they'd been brainwashed into a cult. Not that yoga wasn't good for you. Kara had tried it for a few months and enjoyed the sort of meditative state it put her into. But she liked her exercise sweaty and rigorous, and preferred to keep any chi-cleansing activities private, except for playing her guitar, which she also did on her own most of the time.

Calligraphy had been a kind of revelation for her. It soothed her. Using the different brushes to inscribe *kanji* characters onto the *hanshi* paper properly took both skill and artistry, both concentration and a freedom of expression that made stress evaporate.

Now that they were in the second term, the club's faculty advisor, Miss Kaneda, had begun to work more closely with beginners on the variation of line thickness and the effects of certain stylized flourishes. The fiftyish, gray-haired woman had a slow, drowsy voice that reminded Kara of the way hypnotists spoke to their patients in old movies, trying to lull them into altered states of consciousness.

Sakura sat beside Kara, occasionally whispering to their friend Ren, whose seat was in front of hers. Ren had thin, clever features, so he looked almost like a fox, and his bronze hair—which he insisted was its natural color—only added to his unique appearance. Last term, Miho had nursed a crush on Ren, but she seemed to have gotten over it, which relieved Kara and Sakura of having to break the news to Miho that Ren didn't like girls.

"Hey," Kara whispered, while Miss Kaneda was busy helping another student at the front of the room.

"What?" Sakura said.

Kara arched an eyebrow, and kept her voice low. "Some of us are trying to concentrate."

Sakura and Ren exchanged grins and then both sat up a bit straighter, adopting mock-serious expressions, holding their brushes straight, arms stiff. Good-natured snickering followed. Several other students glanced around at them, including a snooty *senpai*—or senior—named Reiko, and Sora, a girl from Kara's homeroom.

"I know where you live, Murakami," Kara warned.

But Sakura only rolled her eyes. As they had gotten to know each other better, they teased each other more and more frequently. Kara enjoyed the sparring—she'd never had a sister, but if she had, she would have been happy with two like Sakura and Miho. The two girls were opposites, but at their core they shared the best traits: loyalty, honesty, and unselfishness.

Of course, if Kara had said as much to Sakura, the girl would have feigned shock. She liked to present herself to the world as a rebel, from her hair—which was cut short in back, but in diagonal slashes in front, framing her face—to the many patches and buttons she wore inside the jacket of her sailor *fuku* uniform, turned inside out whenever she could get away with it. Sakura was proud of her status as different in a society that valued conformity so highly.

"Kara," Ren whispered.

She had just bent to her work again, and now her brush twitched the tiniest bit, ruining the line of the kanji character she had begun.

"Sorry," he said, glancing to make sure Miss Kaneda was

not paying attention. "Sakura showed me the last few pages of the manga you guys are doing. It's pretty dark stuff."

A ripple of unease went through Kara. Months had passed, but she still didn't like to talk about what had happened in April. Not that Ren had asked about that—he just wanted to know about the graphic novel she and Sakura had been working on—but Kara couldn't discuss one without being haunted by the memory of the other. The manga faithfully adapted a Noh theater play about the demon Kyuketsuki. Very few people knew that during the first term, she and Sakura, Miho, and another student, Hachiro, had encountered the real Kyuketsuki, an ancient, almost-forgotten demon spirit summoned by the violent murder of Akane, and the rage and grief of Sakura.

"The subject matter is pretty dark," Kara whispered, with a sidelong glance at Sakura. "I'm glad to be done with it."

"You mean you don't like it?" Ren said. "It's really good. Sakura's art gets better with every page, and your script is excellent. So creepy and tragic."

Kara shrugged. "It's the way the play was written. I can't take credit for it."

They had managed to stop the spirit from stepping fully into the modern world, but before it had vanished, it cursed them. In the time since, the girls had not encountered anything remotely supernatural. No hauntings, no violence, no demons. Sakura and Miho had even begun to believe that Kyuketsuki had grown so ancient that its curse no longer wielded its original power. But Kara did not feel so sure. She still had nightmares sometimes, though they were ordinary enough, not the unnatural dreams the Kyuketsuki had once created.

"Don't be so modest," Sakura said. "You did an excellent job. Even Aritomo-sensei said so, and you know how worried she was that we would disrespect the source material."

Kara wished the conversation would end. She and Sakura shared a sad and knowing look, but Ren seemed not to notice.

"So what are you going to do next?" he asked.

"Next?" Kara echoed.

"For your second manga. Sakura's getting so much better, you have to do another one," Ren said.

Kara looked at Sakura. "I hadn't really—"

Miss Kaneda cleared her throat. All three of them stiffened and looked up at the teacher, whose disapproving glance was enough to make Kara feel terribly guilty.

"I'm sorry, sensei," she said.

Miss Kaneda gave a small bow of her head. Kara returned the gesture, and lifted her brush, focusing again on her calligraphy. But as she got back to work, she couldn't seem to slide back into the peaceful, meditative state she'd been in before.

Next? They had just finished the manga about Kyuketsuki. She didn't want to think about what came next.

To Kara, the best part of summer had always been the long, golden twilight of early evening, when the day had come to an end but night had not yet arrived. On that Friday night, as the heat of the day began at last to break, she sat on a fence across the road from the tiny house she shared with her father, playing her guitar and softly singing along. It was a song about tragic romance, and though Kara had never had the kind of relationship the song depicted, she could imagine heartbreak all too well. Perhaps for that very reason, there were times when the idea of falling in love terrified her.

Or maybe you're just sending a message, she thought.

A tiny smile played at the corners of her lips, but then guilt drove it away. Her father and Miss Aritomo were inside the house, and surely could not hear her singing. Even if they could, they wouldn't have been able to make out the words. Still, she faltered, losing interest in the song, and moved on to another.

Kara had plenty of homework and she wanted to try to get as much of it as possible done tonight, because she had plans for tomorrow. But hitting the books could wait a while, especially since Miss Aritomo was inside cooking dinner with her father. The two teachers had been getting closer over the past couple of months. Though her dad kept insisting they were just friends, it was obvious to Kara—and to anyone else paying attention—that they liked each other a great deal. What was going on was more than friendship. Dating, at least. Maybe other things that she refused to think about.

At first Kara had encouraged it. Miss Aritomo taught art at Monju-no-Chie school and was the faculty advisor to the Noh theater club. While Kara and Sakura had been working on their manga, she had been a huge help.

Pretty and petite, with gorgeous eyes, Miss Aritomo had seemed to take to Rob Harper immediately. Kara had wanted her father to be happy, to smile more, and she had seen him *noticing* Miss Aritomo. She'd smiled and teased her dad to let him know it was all okay with her, had told him that her mother would never have wanted him to be alone.

Those sentiments had felt true at the time. But now that her father and Miss Aritomo were getting closer—maybe a *lot* closer—Kara was having a difficult time with it, and she refused to let her father see that it bothered her. He didn't deserve that.

So she sat on the fence across from the house and looked out over Miyazu Bay below and played her guitar. It didn't hurt that the view was considered one of the two or three most beautiful in all of Japan. A spit of land thrust out from the shore, a three-mile sandbar that had been there long enough for eight thousand pine trees to grow along its length. Ama-no-Hashidate—this finger of land—was a major tourist attraction, and Kara always smiled to see people coming to view it in the traditional way. From various vantage points, they would turn their backs to Ama-no-Hashidate and bend over, looking at it upside down through their open legs. It looked ridiculous, but she had tried it, and from that angle, the spit did indeed look like a bridge in the heavens, which was a rough English translation of its name.

Her fingers lost their way on the strings, moving almost of their own accord, jumping from song to song before finally falling still.

With a sigh, Kara stood up, holding her guitar close, and stepped over the low fence. Off to her left, in the distance, she could see Monju-no-Chie school and the welcome arch at the edge of its grounds. As she started across the street, her father opened the door of their squat little house and blinked in surprise when he spotted her.

"Perfect timing," he said with a smile.

"My stomach is psychically attuned to the precise moment of dinner's readiness," she said in English.

Her father arched an eyebrow as he stepped aside to let her in. "Hey. I thought we were supposed to stick to Japanese."

Kara laughed. "You think I can say 'psychically attuned' in Japanese? You aren't *that* good a teacher."

He gaped in false astonishment and then glared with equally invented anger. "My dear," he said in Japanese, "I am an exceptional teacher."

"And modest, too."

As they walked into the dining area, Miss Aritomo was pouring ice water into glasses from a pitcher. She smiled.

"You have a very pretty singing voice," she said.

Kara bowed her head in thanks. "I didn't realize I was singing so loud."

"Not very loud," Miss Aritomo replied. "But the window in the kitchen is open, and we could hear you while your father cooked the pork."

Kara stared at her, forgetting for a moment to put on a smile for her father's benefit. Miss Aritomo had sounded, for a moment, so much like a parent that it freaked her out. Part of her wanted to act out, to vanish into her bedroom and not come out, but that would be juvenile and it would be unfair to her father.

Instead she smiled. "Everything smells delicious."

Miss Aritomo blinked, a moment of doubt shading her eyes. She'd sensed Kara's hesitation, though Kara's father seemed clueless. Before the situation could become awkward,

Kara hurried to sit down. Dinner had already been served. There was a shiitake-mushroom rice and orange-simmered pork that really did smell wonderful.

"How was your day, Kara?" her father asked.

She smiled. "Hot."

That set the three of them off on a conversation about the terrible heat of the week, combining misery with the relief that the forecast brought. It had cooled off significantly in the past few hours, and a thunderstorm was due to sweep through overnight, pushing the last of the heat wave out to sea. They talked and ate, and her father and Miss Aritomo had some plum wine, and soon any awkwardness Kara had felt dissipated. She was glad, for her father's sake. But she couldn't stop the little twinge it gave her heart to see the two of them smiling intimately at each other, talking sweetly, and just generally behaving like a couple-in-the-making.

Get over it, she told herself, time and again. *It's what Mom would want*. And maybe that was true—she thought so—but for some reason, for once, what her mother would have wanted didn't seem to be having much influence over her. Getting over it would be easier said than done.

"Tell me about your day," her father said. "Did anything interesting happen?"

"Not really," Kara replied.

"Good," her father said, momentarily serious before his smile returned.

Swallowing a bite of pork—it was truly delicious, lean and infused with orange flavor—she gestured to both him and Miss Aritomo.

"Actually, at the calligraphy club meeting, Ren asked me and Sakura what our next manga was going to be."

"Next?" her father said. "You just finished the first one."

Kara nodded. "I know. Sakura's been drawing like crazy for months. I'm sure she's not in a rush to get started on another."

"I don't know about that," Miss Aritomo said, taking a sip of plum wine. "She's such a talented artist, and the manga has given her focus. I'm sure Sakura is already wondering the same thing. What is next for you two?"

Kara shrugged. "I have no idea. I've barely thought about it. Another Noh play, maybe. Something else creepy."

A thin smile appeared on Miss Aritomo's face and she raised an eyebrow, studying Kara over the rim of her glass. "I know just the thing."

"Really?" Kara's father said.

Miss Aritomo nodded. "I haven't told the Noh club yet, but I've decided that this term, we're going to perform an actual Noh play."

"Seriously?" Kara asked, intrigued. "Miho will love that!"

"I think they all will," Miss Aritomo said. "And it really would be perfect as a manga for you and Sakura as well. The story is gruesome and full of evil, just the way you seem to like them."

Kara forced a smile, trying to hide the way she shuddered. Such tales did make for excellent manga, but she thought *like* might be too strong a word.

2

卍

After a Saturday filled with classes and homework, Sunday morning began with a knock on her door. Kara sat at the dining table drinking a glass of juice, barely awake. She'd pulled on a pair of threadbare denim shorts and still wore the oversize T-shirt she'd slept in, and she rubbed sleep out of her eyes as she went to answer the door. Pulling it open, she found Miho and Sakura waiting on the stoop, smiling conspiratorially.

"Good morning, Kara!" Miho said brightly.

Kara leaned against the jamb, still half-asleep. "You guys aren't supposed to be here for another hour."

Sakura replied with an unusually open grin. "Change of plans. Get dressed. The guys will be here soon!"

Guys. Soon. That woke her up. Kara didn't think of herself as especially vain, and Hachiro might even think the just-rolled-out-of-bed look was cute, but if they were going out, she wanted to pull herself together, and better to do it before the guys arrived.

More focused now, she studied the girls. Sakura had added a streak of red into her hair, though she'd have to take it out by the time school started tomorrow. Miho had her hair back in a ponytail, and both girls wore loose dresses. Under Sakura's, she glimpsed the straps of a bikini. They had talked about going into Miyazu City today, having lunch with Hachiro and Ren, maybe doing a little shopping if the guys could be convinced to endure it.

"Wait, when you said change of plans . . . ?"

Miho laughed and switched to English. "Now you're awake. Yes, we're going to the beach."

It took a second for Kara to translate. She'd been speaking Japanese so much that half the time she thought in that language instead of her native tongue, and when Miho switched in the middle of a conversation, sometimes she had to catch up.

"Are we going with English today, then?" she asked.

"Of course!" Miho replied. "You promised."

Sakura made a face. Speaking English helped them both to become more fluent in the language, just as speaking Japanese helped Kara. To Miho, it was fun, almost a game, and she hoped to live in America someday, at least for a year or two, to pursue both her career and American boys, who fascinated her endlessly. But Sakura had made it plain that spending hours speaking English felt too much like homework to her.

"All right," Kara relented, still speaking English. "For a while at least."

She stepped back to let the girls in. "Have some juice or something. I need to take a quick shower and get dressed. I'll go fast. Try to be quiet, though. My dad's sleeping late."

At that, she heard a rustle of fabric from behind her and turned to find her father standing in his bedroom doorway in pajamas and a Boston Celtics shirt.

"Not anymore," he said, smiling, his face dark with weekend chin stubble. "Good morning."

Embarrassed, Miho glanced away. "Good morning, Harper-sensei," they chorused.

Sakura seemed to find the moment just as awkward as Miho, even blushing slightly. Kara smiled to herself. Sakura wanted to be different, to break the mold that society expected her to follow, and she did that, to an extent. But she wasn't the bad girl as she tried to portray herself.

Kara's father chuckled softly. "I'll stay out of your way, don't worry."

When he shuffled back into his bedroom and closed the door, Kara gestured for the girls to sit and made a beeline for the bathroom.

Less than twenty minutes later, she had showered, shaved her legs, and pulled on a black-and-white striped bikini, fretting over the way she looked in it. Living in Japan and eating Japanese food had made her thinner, which hadn't necessarily been a goal—she'd liked the way she had looked before—and from the way her top fit, it seemed like her breasts had gotten smaller. She poked and tucked and retied the top and finally gave up worrying about her appearance at all, tying her wet hair back with a rubber band. Then she pulled on a V-neck white shirt and a black cotton skirt and slipped her feet into brown leather sandals.

"Ready!" she announced, stepping into the dining room.

Sakura and Miho were sprawled in their chairs, pretending to have fallen asleep waiting for her. Kara laughed, whopped Sakura in the head, and got them moving. They went out onto the front step, leaving Kara's father to putter happily around, not worrying about who might see him in his pajamas.

"I'm surprised the guys haven't arrived yet," Miho said, still working the English, and doing a fine job of it.

As if summoned, Hachiro and Ren appeared down the street from the grounds of Monju-no-Chie school. The boys ambled along the street, Hachiro carrying a faded beach umbrella over one shoulder, and Ren burdened with what appeared to be a very full picnic basket. They were an odd pair, Hachiro tall and barrel-chested, and Ren short and thin, with almost elfin features and that stylishly ragged bronze-hued hair. Kara assumed it was dyed, despite his claims to the contrary, but apparently the school had different rules if you dyed all of your hair, versus a single streak as Sakura had.

"Good morning!" Ren called in Japanese.

"No, no," Miho corrected. "Speak English."

Ren rolled his eyes as he and Hachiro walked up to the house. "Again? Do we have to?"

"We won't answer you otherwise," Miho assured him in English, smiling.

Hachiro reached out with his free hand and clasped Kara's fingers in his. He leaned over and kissed the top of her head.

"Was this your idea?" he whispered—in Japanese—into her ear.

"Not at all," she replied in the same language. "But I indulge Miho. It makes her happy."

Hachiro pulled back, gazing into her eyes, and Kara shivered with how good that gaze made her feel. The connection between her and Hachiro had been growing stronger, but it troubled her that they had stopped putting words to it. Mostly, their rapport went unspoken. She believed he felt what she did, but he didn't talk about it much.

You're going back to America, she reminded herself. *He doesn't want to make more of it than it can be.* The trouble with that thought was that Kara couldn't turn her heart off, and she didn't think Hachiro could, either. He seemed to be trying, though, and it hurt her that he'd become so silent about what he was really thinking.

Maybe it's for the best, she thought.

But it didn't feel that way.

"All right," Hachiro said in English, turning to Miho, Sakura, and Ren. "English until lunch. That's a good compromise, okay?"

Everyone agreed, and moments later, they set off on the trek to Ama-no-Hashidate.

Though young people covered the shores in summertime, Japan wasn't really known for its beaches. Kara had been to Hawaii with her parents when she was ten years old, and Japan had nothing on the Hawaiian islands. One of the better-known beaches in the country actually imported its sand from

Australia. In many other places, the sand was more like fine gravel than the soft stuff Kara was used to from home, and she had heard that a lot of beaches were quite dirty.

But Ama-no-Hashidate was an exception. The spit of land that jutted like a finger out into Miyazu Bay boasted a variety of beauties and uses, not least of which came from the miles of white sand that lined its shore. It was known as one of the most beautiful spots in the country, and that included the beach.

Walking out along the spit, they came in sight of one of the busiest stretches of beach. Couples and some families relaxed under sun tents—the Japanese were far more wary of sun exposure than Kara was used to in America—while teenagers and twentysomethings performed the usual summer-time mating rituals. They threw one another into the water, played music too loud, tossed balls back and forth in the surf, and generally lounged around trying to look as cool and toned as possible.

Kara's friends, on the other hand, paid little attention to such things. Hachiro and Ren were just about the least self-conscious guys she had ever encountered, either at home or in Japan. They wore the big, baggy bathing shorts that most guys their age wore, but there was no evident effort to make their clothes look good. Hachiro stood out among Japanese guys due to his size—a gentle giant—and though Ren was fit enough, that seemed like a natural gift rather than an effort.

The girls, on the other hand, were totally self-aware, and going to the beach with them amused Kara greatly. The world tilted on its axis every time they got into their bathing suits. The normally demure Miho had a stunning body, and a tiny, expensive bikini that she wore because it was the only one that fit her. Still, she seemed marvelously oblivious to the looks she earned. Sakura, on the other hand, lacked Miho's natural curves, and fidgeted awkwardly any time a guy went by who might be checking them out.

The five friends relaxed on sandy mats, the guys chivalrously giving the shade of the umbrella to Miho and Sakura. Kara put on plenty of sunscreen and lay out, enjoying the feeling of the sun on her skin.

They all talked—it seemed to be what they did best—chattering about classes, about movies, about everything and nothing, and all in English. At one point, Kara felt Hachiro's fingers brush hers and she smiled, eyes still closed, as he took her hand. They lay that way on the beach for quite some time.

"Where did you get the umbrella, anyway?" she asked in Japanese. "You live in the dorm."

Miho admonished her to stick to English.

Hachiro rolled his eyes at Miho, then smiled at Kara. "I have my secrets. I am a mysterious guy."

She laughed, meaning no harm, and then laughed harder at the hurt look in his eyes. She soothed him by dragging herself over to his side and kissing him, twining together with him on the sand.

The gibes of the others finally drove them apart, but afterward, Kara relished the feeling of where his skin had pressed against hers. After a few minutes, she glanced up and found Hachiro watching her, eyes full of emotion, but he said nothing.

"Time for a swim, I think!" Sakura said, jumping up and kicking sand at Ren and Hachiro.

She tore off down the sand, shrieking happily as they gave chase. Miho and Kara exchanged a smile and rose to follow. Kara had been to the beach half a dozen times this summer, but swimming in the Sea of Japan had not lost its novelty.

Later, as they sat beneath the umbrella eating a picnic lunch of sushi and seaweed-wrapped rice balls called *onigiri*, Kara found herself in a moment of such pure bliss that she had to catch her breath. The shadows of the spring had truly been dispelled. She still had nightmares, but only of the sort that vanished upon waking.

She hadn't been so happy in a very long time.

Late Monday afternoon, after their calligraphy club meeting, Kara and Sakura went around the back of the school to the large field that separated the main building from the dormitory. On the far side of the field, toward the dorm, the girls of the soccer club were having a practice, but Kara and Sakura were there to watch Hachiro and the other boys of the baseball club. The soccer girls always seemed so much more serious, whereas the baseball club boys grinned from ear to ear. Nothing made Hachiro smile like playing baseball—not even Kara. He had his Boston Red Sox cap pulled down snugly to shade his eyes, and he waited patiently at second base for anyone to dare hit one past him.

Kara had never been a huge baseball fan, but she was a Hachiro fan, and she loved the smile he wore while playing.

"Wow," Sakura said quietly beside her. The two girls were leaning against the back wall of the school. Sakura wanted a cigarette, but agreed to forestall her nicotine craving for a few minutes.

Kara glanced at her. "What makes you say 'wow'? Nothing interesting happened."

Sakura smiled. "That's why I said 'wow.' This is actually quite boring, but you're watching with such fascination. You're falling in love with Hachiro. Or have you already fallen?"

Kara sighed and turned her attention back to the baseball game. "We're not talking about it. I can't afford to fall in love with him. I'm leaving in the spring, remember?"

"I remember," Sakura said. But she did not sound at all convinced.

Before the conversation could continue, Miho came rushing across the grass toward them, an enormous grin on her face, obviously bearing some news she could not wait to share. Kara was glad to have the interruption.

"Sakura, listen to this!" Miho cried, loud enough to draw attention. It made her blush and she turned her back to the other baseball spectators and lowered her voice. "This is going to be the most amazing few months I've ever had."

Kara noticed that Miho had barely included her, even with a glance, so the news seemed exclusively for Sakura. The two girls were her best friends now, but they had been friends, and roommates, long before Kara had come to Japan.

There would naturally be things that the two of them shared that did not involve her. Still, it stung a bit.

"What is it?" Sakura asked. "Wait, don't tell me. An American high school baseball team is coming to visit and all the boys are staying in our room while they're here?"

Miho blinked, perhaps a bit startled by the impropriety of the suggestion. Then she arched an eyebrow, face alight with mischief.

"No," she said, pushing a strand of her long hair away from her face, "but if you know a way to arrange it, I'm in."

Kara gave a low laugh of surprise. Miho didn't really mean it, in spite of her fascination with American boys, but there'd been a time when she wouldn't even have joked about it.

"All right, so what's your big news?" Kara asked.

Miho shot her a dark look, and for a second, Kara thought the girl might truly be angry with her. But then Miho's expression lightened and she reached out and gave Kara a light punch on the shoulder.

"Like you don't know. I can't believe you didn't tell me!"

Sakura glanced at Kara, who only gave a confused shrug. For a second, she wondered if this had to do with Ren, if somehow Miho had her wires crossed and had gotten the impression Ren wanted to go out with her or something, even though Miho hadn't talked much about her interest in him for months. But that didn't make any sense.

Miho huffed and rolled her eyes. "Hello?" she said, an affectation she'd picked up from Kara, who often translated her American idiom slang into Japanese. "I just got out of a Noh club meeting."

"Ohhhh," Kara said, smiling. Now she got it.

"Oh, what?" Sakura asked.

Miho grinned at her. "Aritomo-sensei just announced that this term, the Noh club will be producing and performing an actual Noh play! Everything! The acting, the music, the sets! I can't believe it. I knew she was cool, but I never thought she would let us do something like this, especially since she takes Noh theater so seriously. That she'd entrust us with an actual performance . . . it's just amazing!"

"That *is* great news," Sakura said. "Of course she trusts you all with it—the club takes it just as seriously as she does. Especially you, Miho. Why did you think Kara already knew about this?"

"On the way out of the meeting, Aritomo-sensei told me she did," Miho said, looking at Kara, once again sweeping her hair back from her eyes. "In fact, she said she'd suggested you two do the same play as your next manga."

Sakura crossed her arms. "So why am I just hearing about it now?"

Kara shrugged. "Aritomo-sensei told me about it when she came over to my house the other night. She and my father were making dinner together. That was strange enough. Anyway, she swore me to secrecy about the play until she had announced it to the Noh club, which" — she made a flourish of her hands—"she now has."

Without conferring about it, the three of them fell into step together, working their way around the baseball field, heading back toward the dorm. Kara waved to Hachiro, who grinned but kept his baseball glove down, focused on the game.

"So what is this Noh play, anyway?" Sakura asked. "Why does Aritomo-sensei think it would be a good manga for us?"

"Apparently because you've already done one gruesome manga," Miho said. "This one is a horrible story about a woman driven mad by love, who becomes a flesh-eating snake demon."

Sakura smiled thinly. "Lovely."

"It really would make a cool manga though," Miho said, a bit defensive of anything having to do with Noh. She adjusted her glasses. "The Hannya is fearsome and the story is tragic."

"Aren't they all?" Kara asked.

Sakura bumped her purposely as they walked. "So your father and Aritomo-sensei are getting pretty close."

Kara nodded. "Looks that way. But I'd much rather talk about anything else."

A look of concern crossed Miho's face. "I didn't know it was bothering you so much."

"I'll be fine," Kara said. "I want my father to be happy, and I really like Aritomo-sensei. It's just, I don't know, weird."

They reached the dorm and Sakura used her ID card to open the door. She turned to Kara. "You still want to do a new manga, though, right? This awkwardness with Aritomo-sensei won't keep you from working with her?"

Kara smiled. "Not at all. I was worried that you wouldn't want to start a new manga right away, that you might need a rest first. I've got the easier job, after all. Illustrating the pages takes a lot more time than writing them. And anyway, Aritomo-sensei knows everything there is to know about Noh theater, and almost that much about manga. She's a huge help. No, I'll adjust. The awkwardness will go away eventually."

"Good," Miho said, as they walked up the stairs to the second floor. "Because I already asked Aritomo-sensei if you two could help out for the play. Noh club will be running late, so if you want, you could come down after calligraphy club and work with us. It might help with your manga."

Sakura and Kara exchanged glances.

"I'm up for it if you are," Sakura said.

Kara nodded. "Okay." Then she looked at Miho. "I'm just surprised, I guess. Doesn't it seem a little strange that she would choose such a violent play after what the school has been through this year?"

"I had the same thought," Sakura said.

"Maybe a little strange," Miho agreed. "But, after all, it's only a play."

In Miho and Sakura's room, they looked through the finished pages of the manga Sakura and Kara had done about ketsuki, and then—as Miho told them the story of *Dojoji,* the Noh play that the club intended to perform—Sakura began to sketch what the characters might look like in a manga version. As she drew the lines that would make the demon serpent woman, Hannya, Kara shuddered. She'd had enough of monsters for a while.

With a private smile, she chided herself that she was being silly. Miho was right, after all. It *was* only a play.

Kara is at home, in her bedroom in Medford, Massachusetts. The walls are a pink wash and the curtains are sheer lace. A breeze washes through the windows, billowing the curtains, the smell of an imminent rainstorm in the air. The room is just as her mother decorated it for her, right down to the hand-painted fairies above the headboard of the bone-white sleigh bed.

They share a love of fairies, Kara and her mother.

She lies in bed, a sleepy smile on her face, turns over and settles deep into her bedclothes, relishing the cool breeze and the distant rumble of thunder. It's heaven. Her mother created this little slice of paradise for Kara when she turned seven, as a present, and painted those fairies herself. This isn't right, of course. Kara redecorated in the eighth grade, painted the walls white—too old for pink, now—and her mother even helped her brush thick, eggshell finish right over the fairies. That was not long before . . .

This isn't right, but it's perfection.

Bliss.

A soft rap comes at the door, punctuated by a crack of thunder, the rainstorm coming nearer. Sprinkles patter the windows as Kara rises on her elbow, genuinely curious.

"Who is it?"

The knob turns, the door opens a crack, and from deep inside her there comes a sense of painful longing, of fluttery, excited certainty that her mother is about to enter the room, perhaps to tell her that breakfast is ready.

But the door swings open on darkness. Green eyes—cat eyes—stare out at her from the black shadows, growing huge—a massive, bent, bestial silhouette separating itself from the deeper darkness. The face dips into the room, shadows coalescing around it, but she can see the horns and the twisted mouth and jutting fangs of Kyuketsuki, the demon whose ancient whispers spoke a curse upon her.

Terror seizes her, but all Kara can do is burrow deeper into *the bed, a little girl again. Her breath catches in her throat and she bites her lower lip, tasting blood.*

Something tumbles from the shadows, as though spilling from the Kyuketsuki's own darkness, and sprawls to the floor.

Hachiro. Dead. Limbs twisted up like some castaway doll, eyes open, dull and glassy.

Kara opens her mouth to scream, but no sound emerges.

"It's all right, sweet pea," a voice says beside her.

Hope surges through her, and love, and a kind of lightness of spirit that she has forgotten is even possible. Kara turns in bed and looks up into the face of her mother, her sandy blond hair pulled back in a ponytail, blue eyes smiling.

"It's all right, K-baby. It's only a dream. Watch."

Kara watches as her mother strides across the room, Hachiro's broken body dispersing into smoke, and closes the door, shutting out the darkness and the demon and its curse.

"There, see?" Annette Harper says as she walks back to her daughter. "All gone. Trust me, honey. There's nothing in the dark that isn't there in the light."

Kara's mother climbs into bed beside her and Kara snuggles close, wrapped in her mother's arms, her pulse slowing, relief and contentment sweeping through her. Outside the window, the rain begins to fall harder and the breeze kicks up, the curtains rising like ghosts. The storm is here now, but Kara doesn't mind at all. She has her mother . . .

And she wakes.

When Kara opened her eyes she saw rain pelting the windows, the sky gray and heavy with storm. Tuesday morning had arrived, but it was impossible to discern the time from the gloomy daylight.

In the lingering embrace of the dream, she felt emotion well up within her and tears began to slip down her face. As she attempted to brush them away, her breath hitched, and she started to cry more fiercely.

Part of the dream had been a nightmare—but, really, it was only an ordinary nightmare. She had had others. The fear and unease would dissipate, as they always did.

But to dream of her mother—her smile and the comfort and security of her embrace—and to wake to the reality that she would never see her mother again—that was an anguish that would never go away, and a weight on her heart far worse than any nightmare.

Kara thought of those fairies on her bedroom wall back home, and how her mother must have felt the day she painted them over. A small thing, really, but God, how she wished she had seen the hurt of it then, even afterward, so that she could have apologized.

If only.

The two saddest, loneliest words in the world.

3
𝄬

"A beautiful job, Kara. Keep up the good work."

Kara smiled up at Miss Aritomo and gave a little bow of her head in silent gratitude. No matter how much she wrestled with her own feelings about her father dating the art teacher, she could never say the woman was anything but sweet. Even when she had first arrived at Monju-no-Chie school, Miss Aritomo had been incredibly nice.

But as Miss Aritomo walked away, Kara grimaced. With a sigh, she brushed her blond hair away from her eyes, and then realized she'd smeared green paint on her forehead and laughed at herself, bending to pick up her paintbrush again.

"You do not seem like a girl who is having a good time," Sakura said.

Kara froze and shot a guilty glance over her shoulder, but Miss Aritomo had already left the room.

"Is it that obvious?" she asked.

Sakura nodded. "It probably helps that you've been complaining all week, but it's obvious to me. Aritomo-sensei doesn't seem to have noticed."

Kara dipped the brush into a bucket of green paint and began applying a second coat to the carved piece of wood that would eventually represent a tree in the background of the set.

"Good," she said.

"You could just tell her you want to quit, you know," Sakura said, head cocked, eyes narrowed as though Kara was some puzzle she wanted to decipher.

"It isn't that easy," Kara replied. "Miho would be heartbroken."

Sakura shrugged and went back to painting. Kara said nothing more, but she had other reasons as well. Her father had been so pleased that she had been spending this extra time under Miss Aritomo's guidance that he would be upset if she bailed on it now. Though obviously he didn't understand just how little time this volunteer gig provided for teacher–student interaction.

The previous Tuesday and Thursday afternoons, after she and Sakura had finished with calligraphy club, they had come down into the basement room where Miss Aritomo held the Noh meetings and volunteered their assistance. It had seemed like such a good idea at the time that Ren—who was also in calligraphy club—had joined them. If Hachiro hadn't had baseball club and been wholly devoted to the game, he might have done the same.

Now Kara thought that Hachiro was the lucky one. After more than a week of helping the Noh club prepare for its performance, she was racking her brain, trying to figure out some way to gracefully excuse herself from the obligation.

Sakura and Ren didn't seem nearly as bored. Noh theater had been fascinating to Kara in concept, but she had quickly learned that in execution, that fascination waned considerably. Back home in Medford, she had taken part in a couple of different school productions, including *My Fair Lady* and *A Christmas Carol.* The cast and crew would form a family unit, an easy camaraderie that created friendships between kids who might never have stopped to talk to one another in the cafeteria or the halls. Working on Miss Aritomo's pet project, she had imagined a similar arrangement, but had encountered something entirely different.

She had known, on an intellectual level, that the performers rehearsed alone. But she had not truly understood how little actual collaboration was part of the process. Kara and Sakura had been tasked with painting the background, even as other students created the various pieces that made up the traditional Noh set. Every Noh play used the same elements for its stage, and the entire platform needed to be created. But Miss Aritomo had assigned certain students to build the platform in a corner of the gymnasium that the principal had loaned them for the show, leaving Kara, Sakura, and four other students to create and paint the background.

The Noh club learned the basics for the chants and music for the play during their official meetings, but every member of the cast, including those who would be playing music, practiced alone. Kara found the discipline this required staggering to even imagine. The performers would perfect their parts in isolation, so that the play only came together as a whole story, and a singular piece of art, when they all joined their disparate elements on the stage, in front of the audience. That meant most of the members of the Noh club weren't in Miss Aritomo's room at all during "rehearsals." They weren't really even rehearsals as Kara understood the word.

Preparations, yes. Rehearsals, not so much.

Even Miho wasn't around. Like Miss Aritomo, she collected Noh masks, and so the teacher had put Miho in charge of the select group of her students who were making and painting the masks for the play. Miho seemed almost giddy with excitement. She talked about her work with the masks nonstop.

Worse yet, after volunteering mainly so he could hang around with the girls, Ren had been put on Miho's "mask squad," so they hadn't seen much of him at all.

The one bit of good news was that the weekend was coming up, and with it the Toro Nagashi Firework Festival. Kara had missed being in the United States for the Fourth of July, so she was really looking forward to the fireworks, and even more so to see the lanterns that would float in the bay. Hachiro had asked her to go with him, formally, the most official date they'd had, though they had been out together many times. All of her friends would be there, but still, it would be romantic.

"Are you daydreaming about Hachiro again?" Sakura asked.

Kara grinned.

"Well," Sakura said. "At least that earns a smile from you. And this will earn a second one."

She pointed to the wall. Kara glanced up and saw that 6:30 had arrived, and they were finally free. Happily, she poured the remains of her green paint back into the can and sealed it, then cleaned her brush. She had done her work for the day, and she thought the background for the play was coming out very well.

Kara went to a sink to wash her hands, pulling off her smock as Sakura did the same. "Come on," Kara said, wiping her hands on a rag. "Let's get Miho and Ren and get out of here."

The two girls said their good-byes to the other students who were part of their background crew and hurried into the corridor.

"Do you have a lot of homework tonight?" Sakura asked.

Kara shrugged. "What's 'a lot'? At least two hours' worth, but probably not more than that. Why?"

"I think we deserve a treat. Would you like to go into the city for dinner? We'll take Ren and Miho, and I'll show you my favorite restaurant."

"I'd love to," Kara said, shooting her a curious look. "But I doubt I can afford it, and wouldn't you and Miho get into trouble?"

Sakura scoffed. "This is me, remember?" she said in English, a line she must have stolen from a movie. Then she switched back to Japanese. "I'm inviting you to dinner, Kara. My parents only remember that I'm alive when I spend money on their credit card. Which is ironic, considering that they gave it to me so that they wouldn't have to think about me at all."

"I couldn't let you pay—"

"You're not listening. I'm not paying. My parents are. And they can afford it. As for getting into trouble, we can take the train and be back before nine. There might be a few raised eyebrows in the dormitory, perhaps even a small punishment, but we won't be suspended or expelled. Let's go. If you think your father will let you."

The taunt was obvious and explicit, but all in good fun. Sakura threw up her hands as though to ask, *what could go wrong*? Kara hesitated, then grinned. Sakura wouldn't be happy if she couldn't make a few waves now and then.

"Well, when you put it that way, how can I say no?"

They reached the room where Miho's mask squad was at work. Kara glanced inside and saw Miho painting close-up detail work on a mask representing a long-haired woman, with wide eyes meant to indicate either sorrow or fury; it was difficult to tell which. Ren stood near a rack where a couple other masks were drying, but they were the only two left in the room.

"No, no," came a voice from a room across the hall. "Like this. It must be precisely like this."

Kara frowned. She had never heard such intensity in Miss Aritomo's voice before, not even when the art teacher had been insisting that she and Sakura be faithful to the original Noh when they were adapting a play into manga.

Miho and Ren weren't quite ready, so Kara slipped across the hall and peeked into the room. A quick glance showed her Miss Aritomo working through a series of precise steps and hand motions with Otomo, one of the girls who would perform in the play.

When Sakura slipped up next to her, Kara pushed her back, and both of them went back to stand outside, waiting for Miho and Ren. Kara did not want to be caught spying.

"That's strange, don't you think?" she asked.

Sakura raised her eyebrows. "What is?"

Kara lowered her voice. "I thought all of the Noh performers were supposed to rehearse in isolation. No one's supposed to see them until the play, like the way a groom's not supposed to see his bride before the wedding. It doesn't seem like Aritomo-sensei's style to break the rules."

Sakura shrugged. "You know how seriously she takes all of this. I'm sure she just wants to make certain they do it correctly."

Kara frowned. "Yeah. I guess."

But it didn't sit right with her.

Hungry and tired, and with plenty of homework still ahead of him, Daisuke Sasaki rode his bicycle toward home, wondering what his mother had made for dinner. His parents could not afford to pay for him to live in the dormitory at Monju-no-Chie school, and anyway, they lived too close to the school even to consider it, but Daisuke didn't mind. Even on a day like today, when he had finished school only to have Noh club—and then an additional rehearsal period for the club's upcoming production—he loved the ride home.

Actually, he considered himself lucky. Many of his friends had to go to *juku,* or cram school, after finishing their regular classes for the day. But Daisuke had always been an excellent student.

He pedaled past the train station and down long streets in the warm, golden glow of the summer evening. After the rehearsal, he had lingered for a while to speak with some of his friends about the play, and then stopped at the dorm to talk baseball with several boys from the baseball club. Daisuke had an interest in Noh theater, but really only belonged to the club because it pleased his grandmother. His true love was baseball.

Still, as he rode he could not help but chant softly under his breath. He had only a small role—an old priest who warned his younger counterpart about the Hannya—but he would also be chanting several parts of the play, like many others in the club. As he had worked to memorize the chants, they stuck in his head, and now he found them as difficult to remove as the catchiest pop songs.

Daisuke rode down a short hill into a narrow street. He let the bike coast as he swung around a tight corner, and had to swerve to avoid an old man who stood in the road cradling some kind of lizard in his arms as if it were an infant.

"Be careful, young fool!" the old man shouted, and Daisuke looked back to see him brandishing a gnarled fist.

Now, that was strange. He knew from having his grandmother living in the house with him and his parents that old people could be peculiar. But the wide-eyed old man with his lizard-baby made his grandmother seem boring by comparison. *He ought to have a long, white beard. Crazy old men should all have long, white beards.*

He raced past a library and an old church, then pedaled up a winding street among apartment buildings. A shortcut brought him buzzing down a lovely road lined with small shops, a wonderful view of Miyazu Bay ahead, and then Daisuke turned left, passed a park, and headed for a dingy, more industrial area of the city, where office buildings and noodle stands gave way to warehouses nearer the waterfront.

Blinking to clear his vision, he realized that twilight had snuck up on him. An indigo haze had replaced the golden light of early evening. Night came on late this time of year, but when it arrived, it did so swiftly.

Now he began to get tired, and wished he had taken the bus today, as he did in winter, instead of riding his bicycle. Ever since they had begun working on this play, the days had been longer, and he had been up later working on his homework. Daisuke decided that tomorrow, he would take the bus for sure.

Only a mile or so from home, he put an extra effort into pedaling. The wind had shifted and, though it had been a very warm day, the breeze off the bay cooled the back of his neck. As he passed a tiny restaurant where his father often took him when the women of the house were not at home, the smell of cooking fish filled his nostrils and his stomach growled painfully.

Daisuke began to daydream about what his mother might have cooked. He hoped for tuna and some curry bread. There would simply be no way for him to focus on his homework if he had to eat tempura and pickled plums again.

The darkness gathered around him, seeming to seep in from between the buildings as he reached the crest of a short hill. With a sigh, he stopped pedaling, grateful for the rest, letting the bike coast. He sat up high on the seat, guiding the bike with only his fingertips. The wind whipped at his hair and he breathed in the fresh bay air.

Something darted into the road in front of him. Daisuke scrabbled for the handlebars, fingers latching on, and twisted to avoid the figure looming up in front of him. He thought of the old man cradling the lizard, but in the gathering darkness he could make out only a silhouette, shifting and uncertain. He had the impression of hands reaching for him, but by then disaster had already struck. He'd swerved too far. The handlebars snapped sideways, the front tire following suit, and the bike pitched him forward. He flipped through the air, arms flailing, the world turned upside down.

Daisuke hadn't time to utter a cry of panic before he struck the pavement and began to bounce and slide, pavement scouring the skin from his right arm, tearing his pants and scraping his leg. As he rolled, he struck his head, and the darkness closed in at the edges of his vision, swallowing him for long seconds.

When he opened his eyes, he lay on his side in the street, in the dark. A jagged shadow farther down the road he recognized as the wreckage of his bicycle. It hurt him just to breathe, and when he tried to shift, spikes of pain jabbed into his side and ran up his arm. Where he'd scraped the pavement, his skin sang with even more pain.

Panic seized him. The road was dark. He could hear no traffic. No one had emerged to call an ambulance for him. Someone there, in the road, had caused his accident, but he didn't hear a siren. They must have run away, maybe afraid to be blamed.

But where did that leave Daisuke?

In his agony, frightened at how hard it was to breathe, he began to cry, wondering how long it would be before his parents became worried and came to look for him. He imagined his mother in the kitchen, or sitting at the table, waiting, and the tears flowed more freely. He sobbed once, and a fresh wave of pain enveloped him, nearly forcing him again into unconsciousness.

And then he heard it—a rustle against the pavement, a scrape and hiss.

Daisuke froze. "Hello?" he managed, although even that was difficult. Maybe the person had not run away after all. Maybe they had called, and help was on the way. "Are you there?"

No reply. He tried to turn, but it hurt too much.

"Hello?" he tried again.

He heard another rustle, and a low shush, as if someone stood just behind him, breathing, watching. His pain and hope began to be replaced by fear.

Then a new sound reached him, a soft hiss, that started a few feet behind him, but swiftly came nearer, until it had become an almost intimate whisper, inches from his ear.

Kara sat at her computer, scanning through some of the photos she had taken in and around Miyazu City over the past few months. She loved taking pictures, and since Sakura often used photographic reference to inspire her art for their manga, Kara had visited some of the prettier sites in the area with her camera. Ancient prayer shrines and mountain villages always gave her a quiet sense of peace and made her feel the weight of history.

Often, her friends would come along on these jaunts. Sometimes Miho and Sakura would join her, and on others, Hachiro had been her companion. The term break had consisted mostly of exploring the area with them at her side. When classes were in session, she spent so much time at school that it had been wonderful to discover beautiful, out-of-the-way spots she would otherwise never have encountered.

She came upon a cute photo of Hachiro. They'd climbed to the top of Takigami Mountain to visit the observatory. Afterward, Hachiro had climbed onto a large, jagged rock and Kara had knelt on the ground. When he'd thrust out his arms as if they were wings, she had snapped the picture, and with the blue sky and white clouds behind him, Hachiro appeared to be flying. No Photoshop, no tweaking.

The picture made her smile.

On a whim, inspired by a burst of affection, she clicked to make the photo her computer's desktop background. As she sat back to admire the result, a wave of fatigue swept over her, and she yawned, stretching in her chair. When Miho had first asked her and Sakura to help with the Noh club's endeavor, the idea had intrigued her, but it certainly made her days seem longer. The clock on her computer screen told her that ten thirty had come and gone.

She had eaten dinner quickly and then hit the books, finishing her homework about forty-five minutes ago. Normally she read a little before bed, or played her guitar for a while, but tonight she had wanted to catch up on e-mail, check in with a few friends from home, and upload new pictures to her Facebook page. She had lost herself in the photos, and now all she wanted was to go to sleep. Facebook would have to wait until tomorrow night, or even the weekend.

With another glance at the photo of "flying" Hachiro, she got up from her chair. The room—like the house—was small, but somehow she had learned to keep it fairly neat. She cleared her books off her bed and made an orderly stack of them on the bureau. With a sigh, she glanced at her guitar on its stand in the corner, tempted to play just a little, but her bed called to her as well, and she found her pillow far more tempting than the strings of her guitar. Shaking the urge to play from her fingers, she went out into the hall.

The door to her father's room stood open, so she peeked in to find him stretched out on his bed in New England Patriots pajama pants and a plain white T-shirt. He'd propped his head on pillows and a book rested on his chest, barely held open by faltering hands. His eyes were closed, though he did not seem entirely asleep. Rob Harper had a habit of drifting off while reading, and then muttering offhandedly the next morning about having lost his place in the book.

Kara stepped quietly into the room and deftly extracted the book from his hands, freezing a moment to make sure she hadn't disturbed him. When her father's only reply was a soft exhalation that made his lower lip tremble, she gave a quiet chuckle, marked the page in his book, and set it down on the nightstand.

Stepping back, she regarded her father a moment. In those pajama pants, he looked entirely out of place in the room, with its traditional Japanese decoration and the *tatami* mats on the floor. She felt a strong kinship with him then that had nothing to do with being his daughter. No matter how well they spoke the language, or learned the customs, they would always be outsiders here. But the flip side of that coin was that, whenever they wished, they would always have a home to go to. It really was the best of both worlds.

Kara shut off his light and went down the short hall to the bathroom. With the door closed, she brushed her teeth, but even over the sound of the running water, she heard the hard knock upon their front door. A deep frown creased her forehead. Whoever might be coming to their door at a quarter to eleven probably didn't care very much about courtesy, but they were going to wake her father. Not that she could do much about it with her mouth full of toothpaste foam.

She finished quickly, rinsed out her mouth, and wiped a trace of toothpaste from her lips with a facecloth. Washing her face would have to wait. Kara pulled open the bathroom door and hurried into the living room to find her very sleepy-looking father talking to an anxious Miss Aritomo. The art teacher appeared distraught, and both of them glanced up as Kara entered.

"Dad?" she ventured, a knot of dread in her gut. "What happened? What's wrong?"

"Yuuka . . . I mean, Aritomo-sensei . . . ," he began.

"I had some upsetting news," the woman said, picking up

where her father faltered. "I went out for a walk, thinking it might ease my mind, and when I found myself passing your house, I realized that your father would want to know, and that it would be nice to have someone to talk to."

Despite her reservations about the burgeoning relationship between her father and her art teacher, Kara truly liked Miss Aritomo. Seeing her so obviously troubled, it only reminded Kara how kind the woman had been to her from the very first time they met, and she felt badly about the distance she had begun to put between them.

"Are you all right?" Kara asked, going to her, even as her father closed the front door. "What news?"

The two adults exchanged glances, a silent communication, both hesitating to tell her what had transpired. Hideous thoughts filled her head as she thought of the monstrous ket-suki, the demonic thing that had killed several students earlier in the year.

Kara started to shake her head. "Please tell me nobody's dead," she said in a tiny voice.

Miss Aritomo blinked at this, then began to shake her head as well. "No, no. It isn't that. At least, I pray that it isn't."

Kara's father put a hand on her shoulder. "One of Aritomo-sensei's Noh club students, a boy who lives on the other side of the city, hasn't come home tonight. His mother called the school. She's very upset, of course. But it's much too early to assume anything has happened to him."

He seemed to be speaking to Miss Aritomo as much as he was to Kara now, comforting them both.

"The boy might have fallen off his bike and been hurt, or he could simply be at a party. Or, worse, perhaps he's run away. But don't jump to conclusions. There's no reason to think horrible thoughts."

Kara knew her father was probably right, but she had to force herself to smile. *No, no reason at all. Unless you've been cursed.*

4

卍

There were no bad dreams that night, but Kara slept even worse than she had the night before. Wednesday morning found her tired and frayed, wiping the grit of fitful sleep from her eyes, her head aching just enough to annoy her, but not enough for her to justify staying home from school. Especially not today.

The skies were a wan gray and the air thick with humidity as she walked from her house down the street toward the campus. Off to her left, a narrow, dead-end road led partway down along the bay shore, a place for people to stop and admire Ama-no-Hashidate, or to walk down to the water and take a quick swim or skip stones. Beyond the road's end, a broad swath of the school grounds touched the shore, and then there were trees in the distance, bordering the property. Sakura's sister, Akane, had been murdered there, on the grassy shore.

The violence of Akane's murder had combined with

Sakura's grief and rage to draw the attention of the demon Kyuketsuki, who had languished in the spirit world, or in some odd limbo where old gods went to die. The demon's once-great power had withered over the centuries, diminished by time and the absence of belief. To most Japanese, it was only a story now, only a character on the Noh stage. The events of the previous fall and spring had begun to open a window for it to return, but Kara, Miho, Sakura, and Hachiro had closed that window.

Kyuketsuki had cursed them all. Despite the August heat and the humidity, Kara shuddered as she walked through the archway at the edge of the campus and up the pathway toward the school. She could still remember, word for word, what the demon had said to them.

Little remains in the world now of the darkness of ancient days . . . but what there is will come to you, and to this place. All the evil of the ages will plague you, until my thirst for vengeance is sated.

There might not be many supernatural evils left on Earth, but Kyuketsuki had basically put a bounty on their heads, marked them all for death. *All the evil of the ages* was a pretty broad statement. They'd lived in fear for the first month, and in a kind of cold, numb dread for the second.

But after a while, with no sign of any attack, or anything at all out of the ordinary, it had been easy to believe the curse meant nothing, that maybe whatever evils of the ages might still be around, they had either withered in power like Kyuketsuki, or they had better things to do.

Now this kid, Daisuke Sasaki, had gone missing.

As soon as she'd woken up this morning, Kara had asked her father if he had heard anything more, but he had not. Miss Aritomo had left after midnight—and Kara didn't even want to think about what they had been doing in the meantime, with her dad comforting the art teacher. When Miss Aritomo had finally left the house, Kara had peeked out the window, her bedroom lights off, and seen them kissing. *Erase, erase, erase.* She didn't want to think about her father kissing someone other than her mom. It had gotten under her skin, and the memory of it haunted her, but she had other concerns right now.

She needed to talk to her friends, and to find out if this Daisuke had gotten home. Kara thought she had met him a couple of times. With the way the rehearsals for the play worked—the performers practicing in isolation—it was no surprise that she didn't really know him. But Miho would.

Other students migrated toward the school, both boarders who streamed around the side from the dormitory beyond the main building and commuters who arrived by train or bus or bicycle, and even some who—like Kara—came by foot. At the bottom of the steps she paused to glance once more at the overcast sky. No distant thunder today, nor even any ominous threat of rain, just a gray shroud that looked as though it had always been there, and might never leave.

Hurrying up the stairs, she walked into the *genkan*, a large foyer whose walls were lined with cubbyholes where the students stored their street shoes. Inside the school building, they wore slippers called *uwabaki*, pink for girls and blue for boys, which always made Kara think of the way parents seemed to color-code newborn babies.

Amid the milling students, she searched for her friends. As she took off her shoes and stuffed them into a cubby, she kept glancing around, but at first saw no sign of them. Kara felt odd, her skin prickling with tension. She was in school, but felt apart from the other students. When she caught sight of bitchier-by-the-day Mai making a beeline toward her, she wished she could have been anywhere else.

"What happened to him, bonsai?" Mai said, her voice low, expression grim. She glanced around to make sure no one would overhear them. "Do you know where he is?"

A tremor passed through Kara. She knew exactly what Mai was talking about, but not *why* the girl would be asking her.

"Are you on drugs?" Kara asked, speaking loud enough to be overheard. "I don't know what you're talking about."

Mai hesitated, nostrils flaring with anger, eyes dark. Then she took a breath, and Kara could see beneath the nasty mask the girl had adopted in order to become queen of the soccer bitches. Mai had been quiet and unsure, once upon a time. That girl still lived inside this one. Kara got a glimpse of her, and realized that Mai was afraid.

"Ume told me what happened that night," Mai whispered. She leaned in close and Kara flinched. "About Kyuketsuki. So don't pretend you don't know what I'm asking you. Where is Daisuke?"

Kara glanced around, wishing her friends would appear. Where were they all? She gnawed her upper lip and then made a little shrug.

"I don't know. I mean, there's no reason to think this is

anything weird," she said. Then her eyes widened. "Unless you've heard something. Is there news?"

Mai's disappointment was plain. "No. Only that he didn't go home."

Kara felt bad for her, suddenly. Daisuke might be in Noh club, and Mai one of the soccer girls, but she clearly cared for him. "Is he your . . . I mean, are you two . . . ?"

"We're *friends*," Mai said. "Is that difficult for you to understand? I do have friends who don't play soccer, you know."

Kara had nothing to say to that. Mai had been so awful to all of them over the past few months, she couldn't quite bring herself to feel guilty, but she allowed herself to wonder if they had misjudged Mai a little. If Ume had told her what happened, perhaps Mai had been so harsh to them in order to keep them away from her. It didn't excuse her behavior, but Kara had never considered that from Mai's perspective, she and her friends might seem like the bad guys. Like trouble.

"If I hear anything—" she started.

Mai sneered at her. "You'll do what? Get someone else killed? Don't even speak to me, bonsai. You're beneath me. Beneath notice."

Kara blinked as if the girl had slapped her. Just a moment before she had been giving Mai the benefit of the doubt. Now no doubt remained.

Other soccer girls were starting to group around them, coming nearer, even as most students began to file into the corridor and walk toward the gym for the morning assembly. This time, it was Kara who stepped nearer, intimate, close enough to fill her senses with Mai's plum blossom perfume.

"Your friend Ume *murdered* Akane Murakami. For all I know, you were one of the girls with Ume that night, one of the killers. I don't appreciate the irony of you suggesting that I'm responsible for anyone dying. But, if you'd like, say that again, and I'll be happy to *hurt* you."

The soccer girls surrounded them now. If they had heard any of her whispered comments, they gave no sign of it, but Mai had heard her very clearly. Whatever part of her mask that had slipped was now repaired. Her sneering half smile showed no hint of the real girl beneath.

"I am certain your father would be quite proud of you, bonsai," Mai said.

Kara nodded slowly. "You know what? He might be. Even if it dishonored him, he would understand. So don't push me."

Several of the soccer girls began to move closer as if to do exactly that, while others glanced around to make sure they weren't observed. Mai held up a hand to forestall any scuffle.

"If you have anything to do with Daisuke being missing," Mai said, "you will know what it feels like to be pushed."

The moment went on for several beats and Kara balled her fists, ready to fight if it came to that. Then one of the soccer girls swore quietly in Japanese and stepped aside as Sakura pushed her way in among them, took Kara's hand, and led her out of the crowd.

They walked quickly out of the genkan and into the corridor, heading toward the gym for morning assembly. The soccer girls followed perhaps ten feet behind, loudly whispering rude things to them.

"*Rezu*," one of them said, taunting.

Kara glanced at Sakura, whispering, "What did they just call us?"

Sakura smiled. "They called *me* a lesbian."

"Are you?" Kara asked, arching an eyebrow.

"I couldn't say. It's sort of like cheeseburgers, I suppose."

"*How* is it like cheeseburgers?"

"I've never tried one, but when I see them in movies or on TV, I'm intrigued."

Kara let that sit for a while, trying to process it. Not that it troubled her. If Sakura eventually decided she liked girls, she wouldn't be the first lesbian Kara had been friends with. She'd always be Sakura, and that was all that mattered. What disturbed her deeply was the idea that Sakura had never had a cheeseburger.

They walked into the assembly, where the students were lined up by homeroom. In a moment, they would separate, and not see each other again until o-soji. Miho must have gotten up earlier than Sakura; she was already in line with the rest of their homeroom class. Kara spotted Hachiro with his own class and waved to him. He waved back, but she thought he looked anxious, and knew why. They all needed to talk, and soon.

"Did you hear about Daisuke?" Kara asked.

"The whole dorm heard, last night. Teachers came to ask his friends if anyone had spoken to him, or knew why he might not have come home. Now they're saying he has run away."

Kara felt a twinge of hope. "Do they know that for sure?"

Sakura shrugged. "How could they?"

"So, do you think it's got to do with . . . with Kyuketsuki?" Kara asked, whispering the last.

Before Sakura could reply, Mr. Sato snapped at Kara and gestured curtly for her to take her place in line with the other students in 2-C.

"We'll talk during calligraphy club," Sakura said, heading for her own line.

Kara got in line with her classmates, wishing she could stand with Miho. But they would have plenty of time to talk later. They needed to talk. Meanwhile, she would be spending every spare moment praying that Daisuke came home safely, for his sake and his parents', and also for hers.

Miho Baisotei had lived the first sixteen years of her life in quiet diligence. Her parents had raised her with little warmth but with a great sense of expectation that had seeped into her own sense of self. They went on with their lives, providing for her education and physical welfare, but otherwise leaving her to fulfill that expectation. When she thought of them, her heart remained mostly numb, though she had gone through long periods of melancholy. Mostly, she studied, and her effort paid off. As long as she continued along those lines, Miho would never need to attend a juku school, and she would certainly find herself in an excellent university.

And then she would escape. Years of watching Western movies and reading Western books had instilled within her a yearning to be free of the expectations, both her own and her parents'. The United States might have tarnished its reputation, but to her it still meant freedom. Her fascination with American boys sprang from the same desires. Most of the boys she knew did not seem as traditional as the adults she knew, but in America, she could be anyone or anything she wished. That was the magic and the promise of the place. Once, she had thought her parents might allow her to attend university in the United States, but they had ignored all of her attempts to discuss it, so Miho would have to wait until she had her degree. And then she would leave.

All through her schooling, she had lived her life in the balance between hope and necessity, building her life with an eye toward the future. Which wasn't to say Miho did not enjoy her studies. There had been teachers she despised and those she adored, and there were several subjects—history, biology, and, of course, American studies—that she truly enjoyed. And friends . . . she had been so lucky to be assigned Sakura as her roommate, a girl who would understand what it meant to be ignored by her parents, not to mention the desire to rebel.

Sakura didn't seem to share her desire to live in America, but when it came to breaking convention, Miho wished she had the courage to emulate her friend. How many times had she been tempted to cut and color her hair, or roll up the top of her sailor fuku skirt so that it would be scandalously short, or stay out long past curfew and come home drunk? She simply couldn't do it. Perhaps it was her natural shyness, but for now, Miho was a good girl, keeping her rebellion locked up in her heart until the day she graduated university, when she would be set free.

All that day, she sat in class, too far from Kara to speak to her except for a few words between each class and at lunch, and not daring to pass notes in class for fear that Mr. Sato would turn his stormy eyes upon her. She'd eaten lunch without really tasting it, and when she had finished and had put her *bento* box away, she barely remembered having eaten at all.

Miho could not focus that day. The teachers paraded in and out of the room for each class, and it seemed almost as if they were speaking another language. She followed hardly any of it. She took few notes, and many of those were inaccurate.

All she could think about was Kyuketsuki's curse.

Her life had been far from perfect, but it had been in perfect balance, mapped out for her. She had friends, and hopes, and a boy—Ren—who made her smile and got her thoughts spinning in embarrassing directions, despite her thing for American guys. But in April, all of her carefully constructed plans had come crashing down, and life had been thrown out of balance, not just for her, but for Kara and Sakura and Hachiro as well.

The impossible had happened. Things that she had never imagined could exist had torn down her expectations about the world, and what was real and true. Sakura had already had to deal with her sister's murder, and Miho had helped her through that as best she could. Growing up, it had never occurred to her that someone she knew might be murdered. Such things happened in movies and books. Adjusting to the truth had matured her. But the supernatural? That was the province of folk tales and Noh plays.

And now her life.

"Earth to Miho."

She glanced up to find Kara standing by her desk, and everyone else already returning their books to the lockers at the back of the classroom. The words had been spoken in English, so there was a lag time as her mind switched over from Japanese.

"I'm still on Earth, don't worry," she said, replying in English as well.

Kara did look concerned, though. "Your body's in that chair, but your brain's definitely been elsewhere all day."

Miho sighed and slid back in her seat. She rubbed her eyes and switched back to Japanese. "I'm too tired to think in two languages right now. Sorry."

The worry on Kara's face deepened. "Let's go try to talk to Sakura and Hachiro before o-soji starts," she said.

Miho nodded and stood up. The girls stashed their books in the lockers—they would worry later about what they needed to bring home for homework—and hurried out into the corridor. They did not have far to look. Hachiro stood waiting outside their homeroom, and Miho spotted Sakura just down the hall, headed their way.

"Hi," Kara said, reaching out to touch Hachiro's hand.

Hachiro's smile was sad and fleeting. "Hi."

"Are you all right?" Miho asked him. She knew Daisuke from Noh club, but he loved baseball, too.

Hachiro shrugged. "As all right as anyone. I didn't know him that well. We talked about baseball sometimes, but he didn't live in the dorm and he wasn't in my class. What really bothers me is that nobody mentioned he's missing. Not at morning assembly or during any of my classes. It's like it didn't happen."

Sakura walked up while he was talking.

"Maybe he came back," she suggested hopefully. "Maybe no one said anything because he's home now."

Neither Kara nor Hachiro said a word. Miho glanced at Sakura, who looked disheveled, and who wore several of her favorite pins—a couple of them rude—on the outside of her uniform today, as if angry at someone but unsure how to unleash that anger, or upon whom.

"You don't really believe that," Miho said.

She blinked, surprised that the words had come from her. Her friends all looked at her oddly. Her role was so often the voice of hope and reason, but she didn't feel up to it today. After months of worry, she had allowed herself to believe the curse had been only words, that it was over, and her life could go back to normal. Now she had to confront her fear that it never would.

"Daisuke *might* really have run away, you know," Kara said.

"Unless something happens to convince me otherwise, I'm going to assume that's exactly what happened," Hachiro added.

"That's not what Mai thinks," Sakura said quietly, glancing around as if saying Mai's name might make her appear.

"I don't care what she thinks," Kara said. Then she lowered her gaze, unwilling to look at any of them, and reached out for Hachiro's hand. "But I'm not as convinced as Hachiro. If this is really the . . . if it's what we think it is, I want to know, so we can at least try to protect ourselves."

"We should tell someone," Sakura said, in a tone that reminded them that she had made the suggestion before.

Hachiro shook his head. "No. Who would believe it? We would look like fools or liars. At best, they would punish us. At worst, they would contact our parents, embarrassing everyone."

Sakura stared at Kara. "Your father—"

"Not unless we know we're in danger that we can't protect ourselves from. Talking to my dad is a final option, for all of the reasons Hachiro just explained. I've caused him enough stress since we moved here, and it's difficult enough for him as a *gaijin,* without me causing him humiliation. Besides, he'll think I'm going crazy."

"Aritomo-sensei would help, if we could get her to believe us," Sakura said.

"Same problem," Kara said, lowering her voice. "Look, right now we don't know anything. We can't panic every time someone breaks curfew or runs away from home or stumbles on the stairs. There's no reason to think this has anything to do with us."

"Except we're cursed," Miho said softly.

For a moment, none of them spoke. Other students were already at work on their tasks for o-soji, sweeping and taking out the trash. Chairs were being picked up in the classroom they had just left. They'd kept their voices low, but they were getting dirty looks because they weren't helping.

"We should look into it, just to be sure," Miho said.

"How?" Kara asked.

"I'll talk to some of his friends in Noh club and find out if anyone has ever gone home with Daisuke. If they have, they would know how to get to his house. We can only guess at his actual route last night, but we could walk it. Try our best to walk the same route and see if we encounter anything . . . strange."

Hachiro cocked his head, staring at her. "You know the odds of finding anything? The police have probably already—"

"Not to mention," Sakura interrupted, "that if something's come here because of Kyuketsuki's curse, I don't want to go anywhere near it."

Miho took a deep breath and shifted her gaze back to Kara. "Don't you want to *know*?"

After a moment, Kara nodded. "Yes. Yes, I do."

Then Mr. Sato appeared, practically in their midst, clearing his throat and glaring at them all with stern disapproval. They scattered, all four of them moving off to complete their o-soji tasks, but Miho knew an agreement had been reached. If Kara agreed, then Hachiro and Sakura would go along with the plan. A tight knot of ice formed in Miho's stomach, and she recognized it as dread.

As far as she was concerned, they had only two choices—do something, or do nothing—and she couldn't simply sit around holding her breath, waiting to find out if evil had returned to Miyazu City.

5
卍

Kara stood just outside a small noodle shop, holding her breath to avoid inhaling the fumes from a battered taxi. Otherwise, she thought this street was one of the lovelier spots in Miyazu City. Despite its parks and gardens and temples, much of the city had an urban feel, and many neighborhoods were old and gray, almost the Japanese equivalent of some of the uglier areas in and around Boston, and in Medford, where she'd grown up, just minutes north of the city.

But although they called it Miyazu City, much of its heart remained the same town it had been during Japan's Edo period. Downtown there were still homes of wealthy merchants from that era, and she had even been inside one of them, Mikami-ke House, which was open to tourists.

Here on Nariai Street, it seemed a perfect blend of old and new. A small temple rose from the middle of the block, up ahead on the left, and some of the buildings had been apartments or houses at some point, while others were shops of indeterminate age. All of the older buildings had been renovated. An old woman stood with a young girl on the corner across from Kara, selling flowers, though the summer-evening light had begun to fade into dusk.

Straight ahead, down the gentle slope of the street, she could see the water of the bay, glistening with the golden sheen of twilight. This would've been a nice, even romantic, place for her to have come with Hachiro any other time.

Now she doubted she would ever be able to come here again without thinking of what brought them here this first time—not just her and Hachiro, but Miho and Sakura, and Ren, who had volunteered to join them, though he still was not one hundred percent convinced that they had not all hallucinated the Kyuketsuki incident.

According to Miho, Miss Aritomo had made only one comment about Daisuke's absence during the Noh club meeting, explaining that his parents were concerned about him, that he appeared to have run away, and if anyone heard from him, they should inform her right away. She'd made a similar plea during the rehearsal for *Dojoji*, but Kara, Sakura, and Ren had all been there for that. One kid had actually had the utter callousness to ask who would be taking Daisuke's part if he didn't come back to school. Miss Aritomo had gone cold and told the guy she would await Daisuke's return, that she was certain his parents would locate him.

Beyond that, everyone behaved as though it was business as usual. And, maybe, if things had been different, Kara would have done the same.

"This is accomplishing nothing." Sakura sighed, tromping up to stand beside her, a bit of petulance in her stance. She lit a cigarette, the pack and lighter appearing from and vanishing into her jacket pockets as if by magic.

The rest of them had changed clothes, but Sakura still wore her sailor fuku with the jacket turned inside out, all kinds of patches and pins on display, skirt hiked up too high, hair in short pigtails. This was a chance for her to act out, and she'd taken it. The Goth Lolita thing wasn't her style, but she verged on the borders of it from time to time.

"It was a . . . ," Kara began, but she didn't know how to say *long shot* in Japanese. "It was worth a try," she said instead. "Though I admit, my feet are killing me."

Sakura smiled. *Killing me* was a bit of idiomatic American slang that she'd managed to translate into Japanese and explain to her friends, and they'd quickly adopted it as their own.

They stood together, Sakura shifting slightly so that the breeze off the bay would not blow her smoke into Kara's face, and glanced back the way they had come. Hachiro had stopped to talk to a pretty woman in front of a dress shop, trying to figure out the most direct way to get from this street to Daisuke's address. Miho and Ren waited and listened, but didn't seem to be adding anything to the conversation.

"Here they come," Kara said, as Hachiro waved to the dress shop woman and the three of them started to come down the street.

"Oh, good. More walking," Sakura mumbled around the cigarette clenched between her teeth.

It wasn't just Kara's feet that hurt. Her calves ached, and

her stomach growled from lack of food. The aromas wafting from the noodle shop smelled wonderful. Kara had been concerned that her father would balk at her hanging out with her friends tonight, as it was a school night and she had homework yet to do. But when she had brought it up right after o-soji, he had been all for it. He had, he said, been thinking of taking Miss Aritomo out for a quiet dinner somewhere to distract her from her worries about the missing student, and if Kara and her friends were going out, she could fend for herself dinner-wise, and that would work out nicely.

Which all seemed fairly sensible and convenient, except that she felt sure her father and Miss Aritomo were having dinner by now, maybe even dessert, and she was famished.

"So?" Sakura asked as Hachiro, Ren, and Miho walked up. "What now?"

Miho gave a small shrug, a sheepish expression on her face. "This seemed like a good idea at the time."

"I'm not sure it ever seemed like a good idea," Hachiro said, giving her a sidelong glance. "But it did seem like something we had to do. Now, I don't know. I suppose I thought that if something happened to him, maybe we would find a clue, or some hint about where he went."

Ren pushed his sunglasses up on top of his head, longish bronze hair framing his face. "Really? The way Sakura described it, I thought we were looking for a body, or maybe his bike."

Hachiro nodded grimly. "That, too. But none of us really knows Daisuke. I talked to him more than any of you, but only ever about baseball. And if he was dead on the side of the road somewhere, the police would have found him."

Miho pointed across the street, where the flower sellers—the old woman and little girl—were packing up for the night. Twilight gathered around them. It would be truly dark soon.

"That road is the most likely one for him to have taken to get home. But it's not the only one," Miho said, shrugging again. "Daisuke could have stopped for a drink, or there might be a road that he's used to taking, a shortcut we don't know about."

Hachiro continued. "The woman at the dress shop said any of the four streets that branch off this one would lead down toward the old fishery area, and Daisuke's neighborhood is just beyond that."

Kara could see where all this was going. Sakura caught her eye, taking a drag off of her cigarette, and nodded. They were both thinking the same thing.

"It's getting dark," Sakura said, holding the cigarette down by her side as she blew out a lungful of smoke. "We won't be able to see anything."

"She's right," Kara said, glancing at Miho. This whole thing had been her idea, so she had to be the one to call it off.

Miho seemed reluctant a moment, and shifted her gaze away from them, looking down the street toward the bay. Ren and Hachiro stood on either side of her, almost protectively, though Kara could tell both of them wanted to call it quits as well. They had to be realistic about it. They didn't know which way Daisuke had gone, and weren't going to find anything in the dark.

"We really don't have any reason to think the curse has anything to do with this," Miho said.

Ren gave a short bow. "Thank you. That is what I've been saying for the past hour." He took Miho's hand and, with a gallant, courtly flourish, bent to kiss it. "Your heart is gentle, fair lady, but logic wins the day."

Miho blushed deeply. "All right, all right." She glanced at Kara. "But I hope he really did run away. This is going to haunt me until I know for sure."

Kara forced herself to smile. "Anyone up for noodles?" she said. "I'm starving."

But what she would have said, if she weren't worried about troubling Miho even more deeply, was, *Me, too*.

Mai stood in the shower, warm water sluicing down her body, pushing her fingers through her hair to rinse out the shampoo. She took a breath and placed the palms of her hands against the wall, letting the hot spray massage her shoulders, hoping it would ease the tight stress knots in her muscles. Normally she got up early and showered before school, like most of the other girls on her floor, but tonight she just needed to be out of her room and away from Wakana.

The girls had nothing in common. Mai hadn't even spoken to Wakana prior to the school year beginning in April. But Wakana had been new to Monju-no-Chie school, transferring in as a second-year student, and Mai's roommate had not returned, so they had been thrown in together. Mai had tried to make the most of it—she was still trying. She thought of herself as a good person, and it wasn't as though Wakana had ever been anything but nice to her. They were just such opposites that they had nothing to talk about, and Wakana's natural shyness would have made that difficult even if they had.

For the past twenty-four hours, though, Wakana had been insufferable. All the crying had gotten under Mai's skin so much that she could barely stand to be in the same room with the girl—which was a problem, since they were roommates. Wakana had been talking about Daisuke nonstop since May. The two of them had met in Noh club and were apparently boyfriend and girlfriend, although they never really went out anywhere, so Mai had her doubts that they could be considered a couple. If Daisuke really liked Wakana, he would have taken her to dinner, or done *something* romantic with her. At least, that was what Mai had told Wakana, over and over.

Daisuke did like to hang around, though. He commuted from home to school, but every day he seemed to linger, quietly flirting with Wakana. As her roommate, Mai saw a lot of Daisuke as well, and against her better judgment—as much as it drove her crazy how much Wakana talked about him—she ended up liking the guy. He had a cute smile and a nice laugh and a self-effacing sense of humor that charmed Mai completely.

Now Daisuke was missing. Her roommate's boyfriend. Ever since Mr. Sato and Mr. Yamato came to their room last night to ask if they had any idea where he might be, all Wakana had been able to do was cry, and Mai couldn't listen to her anymore.

She stood in the shower, the water too hot now, the spray like tiny pinpricks, her skin almost scalding, but she didn't turn it off. If she did, she would have to dry off and go back to her room and listen to Wakana cry. She wished she could stay in here until her roommate had cried herself to sleep. Mai especially did not want to go back into the room until she could stop her own tears, for she was crying for Daisuke as well.

You shouldn't be. He's not your boyfriend, she told herself. Mai knew that there wasn't anything wrong with crying out of worry for a friend's safety. But the problem was, she had started to think of Daisuke as more than a friend—her roommate's boyfriend or not. And if she went back into their room with tears in her eyes, she would never be able to hide that from Wakana.

Mai didn't want that. Acting like a bitch to that teacher's pet gaijin girl, Kara Harper, was one thing. But hurting Wakana, the most harmless person in the world, would not sit right in her heart. The other soccer girls, the ones who had worshipped Ume and were now turning that worship to Mai herself, would never understand such thoughts. They were merciless, those girls, and the only reason Mai stepped up into the queen bitch role was to prevent any of them from doing so. She had taken enough crap from Ume.

But Wakana . . . all she ever did was read, and try hard to stay out of the way. It was difficult enough for her to deal with Daisuke just vanishing, or running away, if that was really what happened. Mai just wished she would stop crying. And she wished that she could pretend Ume had never told her the crazy stories about ghosts and demons or whatever those things were back in April.

Mai hadn't really believed Ume then, and though Daisuke's disappearance had freaked her out, she didn't really believe her now. But it had been clear from the fervor in her eyes that Ume had believed, and she found that deeply unsettling.

"Stop," she whispered to herself, the word lost in the hiss of the shower. She took another deep breath. "Just stop."

The command seemed to work. She turned and let the hot water spray her face, eyes tightly shut. When she shut off the water, grabbed her towel, and ran the soft cloth over her features, her tears had ceased. Mai paused a second to make sure they wouldn't return, and then finished drying herself off before stepping out of the shower.

Clad in her robe with a towel wrapped around her head, she peeked into the hall to make sure there weren't any boys out there. This time of night, the two sides of the dorm were off-limits to the opposite sexes, but rules were made to be broken. When she saw that the coast was clear, she darted down the hall, carrying the small shower caddy where she kept her shampoo and body wash, her room key dangling from a hook there.

Mai gave the door a quick rap and tried the knob, but it didn't turn. She frowned. When she'd gone to shower, she had left it unlocked so that she wouldn't have to disturb Wakana, but the girl had actually shaken herself from her sobbing long enough to lock the door behind her?

And people think I'm *a bitch*, Mai thought.

With a sigh, she pushed her key into the lock. As she turned it, she heard a noise from inside the room—a kind of helpless, plaintive sound that was neither sob nor grunt, but something in between.

The door trembled, pressing slightly outward, and she felt

75

a cool breeze come underneath it, sweeping past her feet. As the door resettled, she turned the key and pushed it open. She entered to discover one of the two windows wide open, as far as its frame would allow, which made no sense because the air-conditioning was humming along nicely. Another gust of wind came through the window as she went to close the door, snatching the knob from her damp hand and slamming it behind her, making her jump.

The dormitory rooms were small. Two beds, tatami mats, two tiny desks, a small futon-chair, built-in closets, and a mirror.

"Wakana?" Mai said, an odd feeling creeping up her spine.

It might have been possible for her roommate to fit into one of the closets, but only barely, and not without spilling clothes out onto the floor. And then there was the question: why? Besides, Mai could feel the emptiness of the room.

Wakana was gone.

Brow furrowing, Mai glanced at the door she had just come through. Wakana must have gone out, locking the door behind her, knowing Mai had a key. It was the only thing that made any sense.

She went to the window and leaned on the sill, looking out, head cocked and all of her senses wide open. Something wasn't right. No, more than that. Many things were not right. Her heart began to beat a little faster and the skin prickled at the back of her neck. The sound she'd heard, that tiny yelp—she had not imagined it. Mai might persuade herself otherwise if she let herself, so she fixed it firmly in her memory, pinned it there, confirming for herself that it had been real. And now that she considered it, her nostrils flared as she detected the strangest aroma in the room and just outside the window. The smell was neither pleasant nor unpleasant—or, rather, it was a bit of both, like dying flowers or fruit just beginning to turn.

Mai peered out into the darkness behind the dorm, where a narrow lawn separated the building from the woods that marked the property boundary at the rear of the school grounds. The wind continued to gust, rustling leaves, but that scent remained unchanged, lingering like the spray from a skunk, though not nearly so offensive.

Somewhere far off, a bell began to ring, or perhaps had been ringing. She tried to keep count of its tolling but lost track while wondering where the sound originated. Had one of the local churches or temples gotten a new bell? She'd never heard it before.

She flinched, stepping back from the window. Down in the trees, had she seen something moving? A pale face, darting behind a tree? Her heart began to sprint, now, and Mai tried to calm down.

The clock read 10:48. Late. Too late for Wakana to have gone out. Maybe she only went to someone else's room. That had to be it. Relief washed over Mai as she grasped at this simple solution. Chuckling at herself, she let her towel and robe drop and quickly stepped into underwear and pajama bottoms and a yellow T-shirt with a cute monkey on it. She went to the door, thinking she would take a stroll down the hall, and surely she would find Wakana.

As she opened the door, a hot, humid breeze caressed her, and she remembered the open window, and the humming air-conditioner. She ought to shut the window. When she turned back to do precisely that, however, her gaze fell on something she hadn't seen before.

Wakana's keys, on the little tea table next to her bed.

Mai's throat went dry. She ran her tongue out to moisten her lips, thoughts slowing, mind a bit numb. The keys were on the inside, which meant Wakana had to have locked the door from within.

She hadn't left through the door.

Mai stared at the open window, one hand fluttering up to halfway cover her mouth as she shook her head, and thought of Daisuke. Of the police calling him a runaway.

It seemed Monju-no-Chie school had a second "runaway." Only this one had left through a second-story window.

Kara sat at her desk trying desperately to stay awake over her math homework. She spoke Japanese fluently, and could read and write it fairly well, but sometimes mentally translating the instructions on a section of calculus homework made her want to scream. It ought to have been the simplest thing, but the Japanese words describing certain formulas and mathematical theorems confused her, which led to frustration, which led—this late at night—to outrageous boredom.

It didn't help that they had walked miles tonight, both before and after their dinner at the noodle place, before taking the train back to the station near Monju-no-Chie school. It was just down the street from Kara's house, but she had not dragged herself over the threshold until nearly ten o'clock. Her father and Miss Aritomo were out later than she had expected them to be, but this, of course, was a stroke of good luck. Her father couldn't very well give her a hard time for staying out so late when he, himself, had not yet come home.

All night, she had been distracted by the question of whether or not to tell her father about Kyuketsuki. She had been emphatic about not doing so when talking to her friends, but inside she had been torn. If he believed her, he would be angry with her for not having told him the truth originally, and he might well pull her out of the school and pack them both back off home to Boston on the next flight. If he believed her.

Much more likely was option B, in which he didn't believe a word of it and was either offended or assumed she had lost her mind. In either case, he would have to do something.

Kara hated not being completely honest with her father. Their relationship had always been open, especially after her mother's death. They had drawn strength from each other, and the truth was a big part of that. But if she told him the truth, one way or another, he would have to *act* on it.

No, she had decided while reading from her biology text-book, attempting to study. If anything truly weird or scary happened, or if she had reason to believe Daisuke's disappearance had anything to do with the curse, she would tell him. Otherwise, there would be no point. All the truth would bring either one of them was stress, and unhappiness.

For what felt like the thousandth time, she tried to focus on the directions for the third section of her math homework. Her eyes felt itchy and dry and exhaustion caused her chin to start to dip toward her chest. Her lids fluttered as she struggled to stay awake.

Maybe she did actually fall asleep, just for a few minutes,

before voices outside her window woke her. Kara inhaled sharply, blinking, and for a moment only sat there, reacquainting herself with the waking world. Only then did she realize what had caught her half-conscious attention, and zero in on the voices.

Her father and Miss Aritomo were back from their dinner date at last.

Once again, she found herself in conflict, with new thoughts only adding to the mental turmoil. If she told her father, and he believed her, who would he tell? Miss Aritomo? The principal, Mr. Yamato? The police? Even if Kara could persuade her father that she and her friends had not imagined the wild things she would be telling him, once he spoke of it to others he would be subject to ridicule. No one would believe him, any more than they would have believed Kara, Sakura, and Miho. Perhaps he could convince Miss Aritomo, but in the end, it would mean dishonor and humiliation for him, and for what purpose?

Kara took a deep breath and rubbed grit from the corners of her eyes. No. She'd been right the first time. Talking to her father about any of this had to be kept as a final option. Right now, they had only their own fears to report. For all they knew, they were in no danger.

Sitting up straight in the chair, she focused intently on the instructions for the final section of her math homework. Half a dozen problems and she could go to sleep. This time, for whatever reason, she managed to decipher the directions in fairly short order. *That's all?* She smiled. This would take twenty minutes or less to complete.

But as she took up her pencil, she heard voices again and realized her father and Miss Aritomo were still outside. If they were saying good night, they were sure taking their time about it. *God*, she thought, *they're probably totally making out, right there, where anyone driving by could see them.*

Perhaps they had been, but now they were talking. For the first time that day, she managed to calm her thoughts and just listen.

"—tell you how much it's meant to me, spending this time with you," her father was saying, his voice low. Didn't he know she could hear him? Or maybe, since the only light on in her room was the little one on her desk, and she'd been so quiet . . . did he think she was asleep?

"It's been a wonderful surprise for me, too," Miss Aritomo replied sweetly.

"Ever since Annette died, I've worried almost every second. Was I doing the right thing for Kara? How could we start our lives over? Would coming to Japan make that easier, or more difficult? Always doubting myself. But whenever I'm with you, I feel such a sense of peace."

Kara smiled sadly, there in the glow of her one little lamp. If her father had really been that anxious all the time, he rarely let it show. He'd done an amazing job of keeping their world steady, and the two of them had taken care of each other. If Miss Aritomo brought him peace of mind, how could she begrudge him that?

"I'm glad," the art teacher said, voice dropping even lower. "I feel that peace, too."

A pause, a hesitation, and she knew they had to be kissing.

Kara wanted to talk, to knock something over, click off the light, do something to let them know she was there and could hear them. They were being so quiet, but not quiet enough, and she didn't want to hear, because the truth was, she did begrudge him the happiness Miss Aritomo gave him. She knew she shouldn't, but she couldn't stop it from hurting. Every longing glance or sweet word between them was a reminder to Kara that her mother was dead.

"Yuuka," her father said, his voice a rasp, obviously breaking their kiss, "I believe I'm falling in love with you."

Kara's mouth fell open, her chest tightening with grief. The pencil fell from her hand. Fair or not, hearing the words hurt her deeply. Her ears burned, face flushing, and she reached out and turned off the light.

Outside, low voices dropped to nearly silent whispers.

Ignoring the rest of her homework, Kara crawled onto her bed and pulled her knees up to her chest, staring wide-eyed at shadows. A few minutes later, when her father rapped softly at her door and spoke her name, she remained silent and did not invite him in.

6

茲

On Thursday morning, Kara's father woke her before her alarm could go off. She drew a deep breath, only vaguely aware of the conscious world, eyelids fluttering, and then she felt his grip on her shoulder, jostling her.

"Kara, get up," he said.

Even in that blurry, not-quite-awake state, she noticed the edge in his voice. Not anger, but concern—a little fear, perhaps—and she forced herself to open her eyes. Her father sat on the edge of the bed, barely seeming to weigh the mattress down, and for the first time, she noticed that he had become even thinner since they had arrived in Japan. Local cuisine didn't really allow for a lot of extra weight. Her mother had called her dad "the stork," but now he looked even more like a bird than ever. Tall and thin, sometimes awkward, he pushed his glasses up the bridge of his nose and stared at her.

"You awake now?" he asked.

"Define 'awake.'"

Rob Harper didn't even crack a smile. That was when Kara knew the morning had brought trouble. And even as that thought entered her mind, she remembered the night before, listening to her father and Miss Aritomo outside as they said good night after their date—hearing her dad tell the art teacher that he loved her. Her own smile vanished, and now they regarded each other with mutually grim expressions. Last night, he had knocked as if to ask her permission to enter, though he hadn't. This morning, it seemed any reluctance he might have felt about confronting her about her eavesdropping, and about his feelings for Miss Aritomo, had passed.

"We need to talk," her father said.

"Dad," Kara began. "It's not like I was eavesdropping. You guys were hardly even whispering, and my window is right there. I couldn't help—"

But he frowned, waving away her concerns. Anything she might have to say about the prior evening would apparently have to wait.

"You need to get up, honey. We've got to get you over to the school right away."

For the first time, Kara bothered to look at the clock, and realized he had woken her nearly an hour before she normally would have gotten up. The light coming through her window had seemed dim when she had opened her eyes, but she had assumed they were in for another overcast day. Now she realized that it was only the hour that made it seem gloomy in her bedroom.

"What is it?" she asked, searching her father's dark eyes.

"Mr. Yamato wants to speak with you," he replied.

Which was when she realized that her brain wasn't translating. She cocked her head to study him. "You aren't speaking Japanese."

He gave a small shake of his head. "Not this morning, I'm not."

Startled, she flinched. "Wait, are you angry with me for something?"

"Not now, Kara."

"I didn't do anything. I already said—"

Irritated, he sighed and stood, throwing up his hands in surrender. "Could you please just get in the shower? If you saw or heard something you didn't want to last night, that's going to have to wait until later. Right now we have more important issues to deal with."

More important than you falling in love? she wanted to say, but didn't. Obviously, as far as her father was concerned, this—whatever it might be—*was* more important. That started her thoughts churning.

Kara threw back her sheets. The sun had started to brighten outside and the breeze that came through the window felt almost too warm. Judging by the morning, Thursday was shaping up to be an absolutely brutal day.

"Fine," she snapped, climbing out of bed.

Her father blinked, a glimmer of regret in his eyes, perhaps reminded by her tone that they were supposed to be allies, not enemies.

"Sorry," he said. "It's just an ugly situation, and we're supposed to be there in forty-five minutes."

Frustrated, Kara cocked her hip, staring at him. "What is an ugly situation? You're talking in riddles!"

His expression turned darker still. "It looks like we have another runaway."

Kara froze, icy fingers closing on her heart. The shadows seemed to shift with malign intent in the corners of her room. Outside, the sky had brightened and the air felt close and thick around her.

"Who is it?" she asked.

"A girl named Wakana something. She lives in the dorm. From what Mr. Yamato said, some of the students are suggesting she was Daisuke's girlfriend, that it's likely they ran away together. Her parents live in Tokyo, but he's a local boy, and his family apparently didn't approve of him dating. I don't know. I don't have all the details, but—"

"But it sounds plausible," Kara interrupted.

"As much as anything."

For a moment, she felt relieved. There was some logic to these theories. She could imagine it happening that way, and that made her feel a little better, until she remembered that her father had said Mr. Yamato wanted to see her, specifically.

"What does that have to do with me?"

Rob Harper regarded his daughter with concern, but she saw other emotions in his eyes and wondered if any of them were suspicion.

"Wakana's roommate flipped out, apparently. She's told some wild stories. She also claims that if Mr. Yamato wants to know what happened to the missing kids, he should ask you."

Kara's mouth dropped open. It took a moment for her brain to start working again, and then she narrowed her eyes, nostrils flaring. "This roommate? Are we talking about Mai Genji?"

He nodded. "That's her."

"She's nuts," Kara said, wondering just how much detail Ume had given when she had told Mai about the events of the spring.

But her dismissive, angry tone didn't seem to influence her father. Instead, he appeared troubled by her speaking Mai's name. Then it struck her just how much damage something like this could do to his standing at the school. Simply to have his daughter called in to see Mr. Yamato was an embarrassment to her father, but if the principal thought Kara had anything at all to do with these students vanishing, it would dishonor him greatly. It might even endanger his job.

"How bad is this for you?" she asked, switching to Japanese for the first time that morning.

He hesitated before also changing to Japanese. "Go on," he said. "Jump in the shower. We'll talk more on the way over there."

Kara did as he had asked, hurrying to get cleaned up and dressed. At first, all she could think about was the missing girl, and what might have happened to her, and what Mai might have said to Mr. Yamato . . . and the trouble that might cause. But as she wolfed down the little bit of cereal that her father had poured into a bowl for her, other thoughts and feelings began to interfere, memories from the night before.

When all of this was done, another conversation awaited Kara and her father, and she wasn't looking forward to that one, either.

In the corner of Mr. Yamato's office nearest the window, a burbling fountain stood on a small round table. Loose, round stones were piled on the edges of a dozen pagoda-like levels, and the water sluiced around them, running down to the base, only to be drawn back up through the throat of the fountain and begin the course again. A single, lovely scroll hung on the wall behind the desk, bearing the image of a crane standing proud among some bamboo, and the kanji for the word "wisdom." On a simple, three-tiered black shelf sat half a dozen bonsai trees of varying sizes. A smaller shelf held perhaps a dozen books of such age that their spines were worn and cracked, and any titles long since faded.

Kara had never been in the principal's office before. In truth, she'd paid him as little attention as he had seemed to pay her since she had started at Monju-no-Chie school. Mr. Yamato had struck her from the moment she'd laid eyes on him—though *struck* certainly wasn't the right word—as totally average for a middle-aged Japanese man. Thin and well groomed, a bit of white in his black hair, fussy with his small, square glasses, he was the picture of orderliness, and thus, completely boring.

Now, though, looking around the office, she wondered if the whole boring routine was just an act. Could anyone really be this bland? This calm? The room screamed "Serenity now!" as though it had been calculated to do exactly that.

On the other hand, so much of Japanese culture was about the appearance of order and conformity and control. If Mr. Yamato's ordinariness was a facade, he had perfected it. She glanced at the bonsai trees and smiled inwardly. Her friends only ever called her *bonsai* when they were teasing her, but students who didn't know her, or the soccer girls and their circle, still used it as a derisive thing sometimes. Kara liked it, actually. She *owned* it. There could be no denying the truth—she was a bonsai—and she didn't feel the need to argue the point. The little trees were beautiful and elegant and proud.

So while Mr. Yamato glared at her through his small, square glasses, she kept the bonsai foremost in her mind, trying her best to keep her poise, both inside and outside. Otherwise, she knew she would never be able to lie convincingly . . . especially in front of her father.

"Kara," Rob Harper said, his voice tight, "Yamato-sensei asked you a question."

Pushing aside her guilt, she drew a breath and made a small bow to Mr. Yamato. The principal sat behind his desk, and her father in a chair to her right, beneath the window, but Kara had been left to stand.

"I'm sorry, Yamato-sensei. I was surprised by the question. I don't really know how to respond to it, except to say that I have never had even a single conversation with Daisuke or . . ."

Kara frowned. She couldn't think of the girl's name.

"Wakana," her father supplied.

"Right," she said, with a quick nod. "Sakura and I have

been helping out with Aritomo-sensei's Noh play after our calligraphy club meetings because we're kind of interested, and Aritomo-sensei has been so nice to us, advising us on our manga projects, and our friend Miho is in Noh club. I might have said hello to them, but no more than that."

Mr. Yamato studied her intently over the top of his glasses like a prissy librarian who took the rule of silence in the stacks much too seriously. He didn't even seem to be breathing. Long seconds ticked by before he altered his facial expression, and that was limited to a slight raising of the eyebrows. At last he shifted in his chair.

"You can think of no reason at all why Miss Genji would suggest that you might know where our two runaway students have gone?" the principal asked, his voice dry as sandpaper.

Kara blinked. Was the guy a robot? She had just answered the same question, but apparently not directly enough for the principal.

"None," she said flatly. "Except that she doesn't like me."

"Why do you say that?" Kara's father asked.

Mr. Yamato shot him a stern look, then seemed disappointed when Mr. Harper did not look duly chastened. Kara stared at her father, hoping that her patented death-glance could make him more cautious with his words, even if the principal's obvious displeasure hadn't. They had some things to sort out between them, no question, but for now, they needed to back each other up while still staying out of trouble.

"Mai and her friends have never liked me, not since my

first day of school here," Kara explained. "Maybe it's because I'm a gaijin. Or it might just be that I don't like the things that they like."

The principal nodded slowly. "They bully you, this group of girls?"

Kara shook her head. "Not bullying, exactly. But they do tease. They call me bonsai, because I've been . . ." She couldn't think of the word for *uprooted*, or one for *transplanted*. "Because I've been cut away from where I grew up and now I'm here. It's not really very hurtful. At any school, there are always going to be people you don't get along with."

Mr. Yamato glanced at her father, then back at Kara.

"Are there people who have seen the way these girls treat you?" he asked.

She shrugged. "A lot, I'm sure. My friends, and others. They've never made it a secret, though I think Mai likes me least of all. I think she blames me for her friend Ume leaving the school."

Kara had been trying to tell as much of the truth as she could without getting into trouble. Lies were difficult to keep track of. But now she realized she had made a mistake. Mr. Yamato had not mentioned Ume, but the light of recognition sparked in his eyes when Kara brought her up, which suggested that Mai had already made a connection between Ume and Kara in the principal's mind. What the hell had she told him? Could she really have told him the truth?

Wild stories, her father had said. Right now, she wanted very much to know what wild stories Mai had told the principal.

"Why would she blame you for Ume leaving?" Mr. Yamato asked.

Kara scrutinized the principal. If Mai really had told him the things that Ume had revealed to her—about Kyuketsuki, about haunted dreams and killer cats and blood-sucking things—surely he did not believe that story? Mr. Yamato hadn't brought it up yet in their conversation. That suggested he was embarrassed even to discuss it, which worked in Kara's favor.

She hated to lie, but as she felt the principal's gaze on her, glanced at her father's dark eyes, she knew the choice had been taken from her. Mai had already accused her once of having something to do with Daisuke's disappearance, and yet they still had no reason to believe anything horrible had befallen the missing. No reason to believe the curse had brought fresh evil to Monju-no-Chie school.

"I have no idea," she said firmly, meeting the principal's inquisitive gaze but not daring to look at her father. "My friends and I didn't get along with Ume at all, but we didn't drive her out of here. To be honest, though, Yamato-sensei, I am glad she is gone. She was far worse to me, and especially to Sakura, than Mai has ever been."

Kara had hoped that would be the end of it, that Mr. Yamato would dismiss her now. School would be starting in fifteen minutes or so, and he would want to prepare for the morning assembly. But he did not seem satisfied with her answer. Whatever Mai had told him, it had unsettled the man, gotten under his skin. She could almost see the thoughts roiling around in his head.

At length, he seemed to decide on another question, and Kara froze. *No*, she thought. *Don't do it. Don't ask.*

"Have you ever seen anything strange at this school, Miss Harper?" Mr. Yamato asked.

Kara glanced at her father, saw how intently he was studying her, and wondered what he must be thinking and if the principal had already explained to him what wild things Mai had accused her of being a part of.

"I don't understand," she lied, turning back to Mr. Yamato, no longer feeling an ounce of guilt. This was about protecting herself and her father and her friends. "How do you mean 'strange,' sir?"

The man opened his desk drawer and slid out a thick sheaf of paper that had been clipped together. Kara didn't have to ask what it was. The rich, dark colors of the first page of her and Sakura's manga stood out on top.

"I asked Aritomo-sensei for a copy of this manga you have done with Sakura Murakami."

Kara nodded, hoping her totally freaked-out, you've-gotta-be-kidding me smile would come off as sheer enthusiasm.

"*Kyuketsuki*. Yes, sir?"

Mr. Yamato hesitated. He swallowed, contemplating, and glanced at her father, which made Kara realize that the principal might have told him some of what Mai had said, but not all of it.

"Miss Genji claims that you and Miss Murakami based your manga on real events that took place here, at this school, several months ago."

Rob Harper apparently couldn't help himself, for he scoffed a little, then tried to cover by pretending to be clearing his throat.

Kara reached up to tuck a loose strand of her blond hair behind one ear. She'd been in a hurry this morning, and hadn't gotten the elastic quite right for her ponytail. For some reason, her sailor fuku uniform itched awfully today.

"That's true," she said.

Mr. Yamato's serenity broke then. Astonishment was the first real expression she'd ever seen on his face.

"What?" he demanded.

"We weren't trying to do anything in poor taste," Kara said quickly. "But when those students died during the last term, and then we ran across the old Noh story about Kyuketsuki, we sort of had an inspiration. I think it really helped Sakura to draw the story, too. After her sister was murdered, she had been having a really hard time, and doing the manga was . . ."

Kara glanced at her confused father and switched to English. "Dad, what's the Japanese word for *therapeutic*?"

Rob Harper supplied something Kara only barely caught. Her mind was awhirl as she spun out this alternate version of the truth. None of it was really a lie except for her pretending not to know what Mai was talking about. She had also committed major sins of omission, but she was on solid ground now. These were lies she and Sakura had told before.

"Aritomo-sensei made sure we were very careful to follow the original Noh play," Kara went on. "The manga is very faithful."

"Yes, yes," Mr. Yamato said. "But it isn't . . ."

94

He let the question trail off, looking at a loss. Kara felt sure he had been about to say *real*. But how could he ask that question without implying that he believed such things were possible, and that Mai's story was something more than either delusion or spite toward a rival. After the odd deaths in the spring, he might well believe—no matter how he conspired with the police to explain the unexplainable—but he did not dare admit it.

"I'm sorry, sir," Kara said. "It isn't what?"

Mr. Yamato took off his glasses and tiredly massaged the bridge of his nose. He set the glasses on his desk and waved the question away.

"Nothing. Nothing at all," he said, standing. He nodded to her. "You're dismissed, Miss Harper." The principal turned to her father. "Thank you, Harper-sensei."

Mai didn't attend classes that day. When Sora—the cute guy with nice eyes who sat to her right—got up to do *toban*, taking attendance, Mr. Sato did not address the silence that followed the calling of Mai's name. Sora exchanged a glance with the girl who sat in front of Kara—also, and confusingly, named Sora. Kara had often thought that if the two of them ever dated, their lives would be chaos.

As with Daisuke's disappearance, everyone already seemed to know about Wakana going missing the night before. In the breaks between classes, Kara overheard their mutterings and realized that in some ways, rather than making them more anxious, Wakana's vanishing had soothed the fears of many of her classmates. The two missing kids had been, if not boyfriend and girlfriend, at least "together." With Wakana now gone, it seemed much easier to accept that they had run away together, though no one could supply anything that sounded like a reasonable explanation as to why they might want to do so.

Kara herself said little about it, except to Miho, to whom she spoke softly during each break, telling the tale of her morning meeting with Mr. Yamato in pieces. It wasn't until lunch that they were able to discuss it at length. They retreated to a corner of the room, back by the lockers, having barely picked at the lunch in their bento boxes. Even then, they had to whisper much of their conversation. It had not occurred to Kara that Mr. Yamato might actually believe any of what Mai had told him, that the deaths caused by the ketsuki in the spring might have been mysterious enough to force him to consider a supernatural cause. Now that this seemed to be the case, should they bring what they knew to the principal?

"We have to talk to Sakura and Hachiro about it," Miho told her, glancing around to see that no one was close enough to eavesdrop. "But I don't know why you would want to discuss it with Yamato-sensei now. If there is no sign of anything . . . strange, then why should we bring it up at all?"

Kara let out a breath, nodding. "You're right. I guess I just hate carrying this around like it's some big secret." A frown creased her brow as she thought of her father the previous night, telling Miss Aritomo that he was falling in love with her. "Secrets only end up hurting people eventually, and I don't want it to hurt us."

96

Miho paused in the midst of unfastening a clip in her hair. She drew it out and let her hair fall in a curtain across her face, then stared at Kara, one eye entirely hidden.

"This isn't just about the curse, or about Yamato-sensei, is it?" Miho asked. "What's wrong?"

Kara nearly told her right then, but though no one seemed to be listening, she did not feel comfortable talking about her father's love life where any of his students might overhear.

"I'll tell you about it later," she said in English. "Just stuff with my dad."

The look on Miho's face made Kara wince inwardly. She assumed that Sakura and Hachiro would react the same way. Kara had always had such a good relationship with her father, and her anger obviously came as a surprise, especially since Miho and Sakura seemed to look at her and her father as proof that parents and their kids could actually *like* each other.

Once again, Miss Aritomo canceled the post-Noh club meeting. Apparently, progress had been made on the set by the club members, and the performers were still practicing on their own, as they were intended to. But the volunteers were told that they wouldn't be needed until the following Tuesday, which was just fine with Kara. She had been doing her homework later and later, and wanted to get an early start. More than that, however, she just wanted a little time for herself, when she didn't have to think about classes or curses or her father's feelings for her art teacher.

During o-soji, Kara and Miho had talked to Hachiro and Sakura, but the two of them had only echoed the conversation they'd had earlier. Still, as she walked the short distance home from school, Kara could not prevent curiosity from tickling at the back of her mind. Why had Daisuke and Wakana run away, and where had they gone? Where could a pair of high school kids go in Japan, without a bundle of cash, where they wouldn't be reported or discovered? The mountains? Could they have gone camping? Were they holed up in some seedy Miyazu City hotel?

Either way, their situation would turn ugly soon enough. They'd run out of money, and roughing it would lose its appeal fast. Kara's friend Paige Traficante had run away for three days freshman year to escape her parents' constant alcohol-fueled battles, but even that had not been enough to keep Paige away when her money ran out. Prostitution and drugs had seemed like things that only happened to runaways who weren't smart about their plans, and it had turned out that Paige had not been as smart as she believed.

Daisuke and Wakana would be back.

Unless, of course, something bad happened to them. With runaways, it was always a risk. Walking home in the fading heat of the August day, Kara shuddered a little, but didn't allow herself to consider what other dangers the runaways might face in Miyazu City. A chill rippled up her spine but she ignored it, and told herself she had nothing to be afraid of.

Still, she shifted her backpack from one shoulder to the other and picked up her pace, and in another minute she reached her front door. In that afternoon time of long shadows, with evening not far off, the windows seemed very dark. It would be a little while yet before her father came home, and Kara felt a tightness in her chest as she let herself in, turned on a lamp in spite of the soft light coming through the windows, and locked the door behind her.

For a moment, she considered making dinner, but there were no messages on the answering machine, and her father hadn't called her cell phone to say he would be late. If he hadn't asked, she wasn't about to volunteer. Instead, she retreated to her bedroom, and her guitar.

As she picked out the first few chords of a song, the tension she'd been feeling since her father had woken her that morning began to ease away at last. Her muscles relaxed, and soon she lost herself in the song, opening her mouth to sing.

Halfway through, she heard the front door open and her fingers faltered on the strings, making a discordant jangle that she cut off with the flat of her hand. The rush of anger that came up from within felt unexpected, but a moment later she realized she should not have been surprised. Amid the anxiety about Kyuketsuki's curse and the numb shock that came with lying to the principal's face, the real source of her anger had been simmering since the night before.

A soft knock came at her bedroom door. Last night, she hadn't answered. Now she sat up, rigid on the edge of her bed.

"Come in."

Her father opened the door and poked his head in. He looked wiped out, even a little pale.

"Hey," he said. "You doing all right?"

Kara held the guitar tightly, silenced. "Fine."

"You ready for dinner?"

"I'm not very hungry, actually."

That stopped him. He frowned, apparently trying to sort out what to say next. "That song sounded really pretty. Why did you stop?"

Kara could not think of a reply, so instead she let her fingers begin to drift over the guitar's strings again, picking up the song roughly where she left off, but she didn't sing. She hung her head, tuning him out and the song in.

"I know we need to talk," her father said, stepping farther into the room. And why the hell was he doing that, when she'd made it so obvious that she wanted him to leave? "I figured it could wait until dinner, but maybe it can't."

Kara looked up at him. "Can't what?"

"Wait."

She kept playing, the haunting tune soft, lyrics in her mind if not on her lips. She hated girls who got all drama queen over something minor like this, but couldn't help herself.

It isn't minor, she told herself.

"Kara," her father said. "Look, you need to talk to me. Nobody in the world knows you like I do. This morning, in Yamato-sensei's office . . . I know you were hiding something. You weren't telling him everything, and that scares me. Not to mention it puts me in a situation that could get really awkward. I'm not saying you've done anything wrong, except for not telling him whatever it is you know—"

Her hands fumbled a discordant note and she turned to stare at him.

"Are you kidding me, Dad? Seriously?" Kara shook her

head. "You could have prepared me better for this morning. You could have warned me. When we were in there, you could've taken my goddamn *side*! I haven't done anything wrong, not that you even care about that, and you just let him interrogate me like that?"

Her father stared at her like she was a stranger. He cocked his head.

"I did take your side, if you recall. And Yamato-sensei called me on it. I don't know what this is really about, Kara, but you can't distract me from the fact that you're hiding something by lashing out."

Kara stood up, swung her guitar around to hang across her back from its strap, and turned to face him.

"Oh, *I'm* hiding something? I guess that means I'm the one who promised we'd start over together, that we'd be a team. Wait, no, I don't think that was me after all. Just like it isn't me telling the first woman to come along that he's in love with her, but not letting his daughter in on that little detail. So much for the team supreme!"

Her father flinched. "That's what this is about?"

Kara grabbed her keys and cell phone off her bureau, stalked toward him, and faced off with her father at the threshold to her room.

"Remember what you said, Dad? You said we were doing this for Mom as much as we were for us." She gritted her teeth to keep from crying, hating the uncontrollable emotions surging up inside her but unable to put the brakes on. "So much for that!"

She started toward him and her father stepped aside, then

seemed to think better of it and pursued her down the short hall and across the living room toward the front door.

"Kara, stop. You're not going anywhere," he said, voice stern.

At the door she turned, guitar still hanging across her back. "I need some me time, Dad. But you're all *about* the me time lately, so I'm sure you understand. I'm going to go find a quiet place to sit and play my guitar."

"I'm not sure it's safe," he said. "I don't want you out after dark, Kara. Those kids—"

"It's not dark yet," she retorted, though night would not be far off. "Besides, they're runaways, remember? And I'm not running away," she said, voice breaking. "I don't have any-where else to go."

She slammed the door on her way out.

7
卍

At the rear of the dormitory, on the first floor, the students' dining room faced the narrow strip of lawn and the deep woods beyond. The boarding students at Monju-no-Chie school ate breakfast and dinner—and picked up their bento boxes for lunch—in this room, and some commuting students had special meal plans that allowed them to eat there as well if they were arriving early for school or leaving late for home.

During the day, the tall windows provided a pretty, though limited, view, and even now at dusk, the well-maintained grounds and shadowed woods had an air of quiet peace. But when the night arrived in full, the windows would turn black. Very little moonlight made it into the gap between the rear of the dorm and the thick pines behind it. Once, it wouldn't have bothered Miho at all. But now she didn't like to be down here after dark. Not by herself.

Fortunately, she wasn't alone.

"It's very sweet of you to help me like this," she said without looking up from her work. Her hand had to remain absolutely steady as she painted the eyes of one of the masks for the Noh play.

"I'm happy to help," Ren replied. "This is much more fun than homework."

Miho smiled to herself as she finished the upper line of an eye. Being around Ren made her feel flush with embarrassment. Not that she had anything to be embarrassed about. As far as he knew, Miho only paid attention to American boys—of which there were precisely zero at their school—so he couldn't possibly know she had a crush on him, unless Kara or Sakura had told him, and she knew they hadn't.

The embarrassment came from being so near him, and wanting to kiss him, which made her feel even more shy and awkward than usual. Ren always seemed so relaxed around her, so *himself*, and she envied that. He was funny and charming, didn't care what anyone else thought, and, yes, it didn't hurt that he was beautiful.

"Really," she said, going back to painting, taking a deep breath, forcing her fingers to hold steady. "When I asked Sakura at dinner, I wasn't trying to recruit you. I hope you didn't think—"

"Miho," Ren said.

She finished the line of the lower eyelid and glanced up.

Ren smiled. His bronze hair stuck up in spiky tufts. "It's really not a major thing. Sakura has a paper to finish, and I don't. You didn't drag me here in chains, I volunteered. Besides, we don't usually hang out just the two of us. I thought it would be nice."

Miho's heart raced and her skin prickled. His eyes were like copper. She nodded once.

"It *is* nice," she said. "Very."

Ren seemed to study her a moment, curiosity piqued. Miho glanced down at the mask she was working on, brain slightly frozen, and then remembered what to do next. She set about switching colors, dabbing a brush in gold paint to fill in the eyes. She would add the pupils at the end. As she worked, she wondered if he had been leading anywhere with those comments. Had he meant that he wanted to spend time with her, just the two of them, because he *liked* her? What would happen now? Would he ask her out? What would Sakura do? What, with her American upbringing, would Kara do?

Long minutes passed in silence and she couldn't stand it anymore.

Resolutely refusing to look up, turned almost completely away from him, she spoke.

"We're all going to the Toro Nagashi Festival on Saturday night, right?"

"Definitely," Ren replied.

"Maybe you and I could go together," she said, so quickly and quietly that for a second she wasn't even sure if the words had come out, if she'd had the courage to say them.

Miho stared into the single, finished gold eye of the demon mask on the table in front of her, and it stared back, and again she felt frozen.

"We *are* going together," Ren said, a chuckle in his voice. "Didn't we just establish . . . oh. Wait, you meant . . . oh."

She closed her eyes tightly, flushing now with an entirely different sort of embarrassment. Her stomach ached. Mortified, she had no idea what to say next, and then Ren touched her arm and, as though commanded by some stage hypnotist, she turned toward him.

The sympathy in his eyes almost killed her.

"Miho, I think you're wonderful. You're smart and kind and gentle, and passionate about the things you love, and you're a very pretty girl," Ren said, but as much as she ought to have been thrilled by those words, she could sense the *but* coming. "The trouble is, and don't take this the wrong way, you're really not my type."

She shook her head, backing away, wishing she could disappear into a crack in the floor or snap her fingers and just vanish. The smile that appeared on her face came from nowhere, born of anything but humor, and it felt like it would crack her face.

"No, it's . . . I understand . . . I'm—"

Ren sighed. "I really thought you knew. I can't believe they didn't tell you."

Miho blinked. "Tell me what?"

He hesitated, then turned up his hands and gave an apologetic shrug. "I don't date girls. It isn't something I talk about. I mean, we're supposed to 'fit in,' right? So only a few people know. But I just assumed the girls would have told you."

After the first sentence, her cheeks began to burn.

Backing away, she shook her head. "God, I'm so stupid. I'm sorry."

"Don't be sorry," Ren said, sadness touching his face. "That would be terrible."

Miho glanced down, realized she had taken another step away from him, and hated that he might be getting the wrong idea. But she couldn't stay. Humiliation made her want to scream.

"That's . . . that's not what I meant," she managed. And then she took another step away from him. "You are an excellent friend, Ren. I wish I could say the same for all of my friends."

"Wait," he said, getting it. "Don't blame them. I told you, it's not something—"

Miho uttered a strangled laugh. "I've got to go."

She turned and fled the dining room, leaving Ren with the masks and the paint and the mess, and knowing he would clean it all up and take as much care with the masks as she herself would have. He really was a good friend.

The soles of her shoes squeaked on the floor as she rushed down the corridor toward the front door of the dormitory. Straight-armed, she pushed it open and went down the front steps, striding so quickly that she nearly broke into a run. The large school building, with its pagoda-esque roof, stood silhouetted against the dark sky ahead. Night had finally fallen, but any anxiety Miho felt had given way to her humiliation and anger. She cut a diagonal path along the grassy expanse that separated the dorm from the school, a lawn that doubled as a sports field. The moon was bright tonight, and her shadow ran alongside her.

On the east side of the school, perhaps thirty feet separated

107

the building from the tree line, and at night it seemed a dark alley. She passed the ancient Shinto prayer shrine on the right, focused on the recessed doorway on her left. This was Sakura's favorite smoking spot, but the shadows there were empty.

Continuing around to the front of the school, she headed north across the grounds, walked the path that took her beneath the decorative arch at the edge of the property, and then a short way down the street to the little house where Kara lived with her father. A quiet voice in the back of Miho's head reminded her that it might not be the best idea to bother one of her teachers at home, but Harper-sensei had always been very kind and open, and Kara was her friend, after all.

Yes, Miho thought. *My friend.*

She made a fist, took a breath, and rapped on the door. There were lights on inside, but only a few, and it seemed very quiet. Miho fidgeted on the stoop for perhaps ten seconds before she knocked again, unable to help herself.

"Just a moment," Harper-sensei called from within.

She heard the lock click and then the door slid open. The teacher wore blue jeans and a white T-shirt. He was barefoot and his hair stuck up at odd angles like he had been asleep or reading in bed. When he saw her, Harper-sensei's eyes widened slightly.

"Miho? Is everything okay? Is Kara all right?"

She frowned in confusion. "She isn't here?"

That seemed to bring him up short. He ran a hand through his hair distractedly. "No. She went out for a walk with her guitar a while ago. I'm a little concerned about her being out after dark. You, too, for that matter."

Miho cocked her head. "Why?"

He opened his mouth to reply, but even as he did, she understood. Missing kids. Harper-sensei either did not believe Daisuke and Wakana had run away together, or he was being very cautious.

Whatever he might have said, he seemed to change his mind. Mustering a smile, he studied Miho more closely.

"You're here looking for her?"

"It can wait."

"Is everything all right?" Harper-sensei asked.

"Yes," she lied. "Thank you, sensei."

Without another word, she started to walk away, hoping it wouldn't seem too rude. Kara's father called after her, promising to tell Kara she had stopped by and suggesting she get back to her dorm before curfew, although Miho knew she had more than an hour before she would be considered late.

Time enough to keep looking, if she wanted to. But as she'd told Harper-sensei, it could wait. That part hadn't been a lie. She felt stupid and angry, and doubted any of that would have faded by morning. If Sakura wasn't already back at their room, she would be soon, and Miho would have it out with her tonight.

Tomorrow morning, it would be Kara's turn.

The northern perimeter of the school grounds stretched for quite a distance, beginning with the bay shore where Akane

Murakami had been killed. Perhaps two hundred yards west, a road began. Parking spaces were slotted along its termination point, made for people who wished to stop there and take in the scenic view of Ama-no-Hashidate. A left turn led into the school and dormitory parking lots. Traveling straight ahead, the road continued westward, away from Miyazu Bay, and a right turn led past Kara's house, to the train and bus stations, and in the distance, to the heart of Miyazu City.

Kara hadn't gone very far from home. She perched on a rock wall not far from the empty tourist parking spots at the bottom of the dead-end road. When she'd left her house, fuming at her father, she'd intended to head over to the grassy slope on the bay shore where Akane had died. It was the most beautiful part of the school grounds, after all, and if she really believed that these disappearances had nothing to do with Kyuketsuki's curse, why should she avoid it? If her father didn't want her to be out after dark, all the more reason to be in the place that would have frightened him most, if he knew what had happened there.

Instead, she had made it only as far as the dead-end, and decided she would be more comfortable on the rock wall, where she could dangle her legs while she played her guitar. That was what she told herself, anyway.

As dusk had closed in and night fell, she had kept playing, pretending that Daisuke and Wakana were not on her mind at all, and aware that she was pretending. Too many thoughts and emotions warred inside her, about her father and Miss Aritomo, about her mother and what it meant to start over, and about the way Mr. Yamato had behaved that morning.

Mostly, she kept wondering why, when there was no reason at all to think the disappearances were anything more than they appeared, she couldn't convince herself of that. No matter how many times she tried to reassure herself, that niggling suspicion remained. It didn't feel right. Perhaps that was Kyuketsuki's real curse. Would Kara feel this way for the rest of her life? Every time something bad happened, would she check the shadows for monsters?

Not long after dark, her hands grew tired and her guitar fell silent. What she wanted more than anything was just someone to talk to about this, but she felt guilty bringing it up to Miho or Sakura. Either one of them would be happy to trade their two parents for one, if that one would have cared about them as much as Kara's father did about her. But that didn't lessen her frustration with her dad, or her anxiety about where this whole thing with Miss Aritomo would lead.

Then, as she sat there, she realized who she could talk to. *Duh*, she thought. *Way to go, Harper. He's only supposed to be your boyfriend.*

Shifting her guitar to one side, she fished her cell phone out of her pocket. The breeze rustled her blond hair, which she'd left a mess when she'd bolted out of her house. The last thing she'd been thinking about was her appearance. Rippling with the wind, the water lapped against the rough ground a dozen feet below the edge of the retaining wall. The moonlight shone on the bay and glinted off small stones on the shore beneath her dangling feet, and as she slid open her cell phone, she could picture it shattering if it fell from here—or her guitar, if the strap came loose.

Kara clutched them both more tightly as she scrolled her contacts list and thumbed the button for Hachiro. It rang only twice before he picked up.

"This is a nice surprise," he said.

"Are you still dressed?" she asked without thinking. Then, blushing a bit, she backtracked. "That didn't come out right."

"It's an interesting way to start a conversation," Hachiro said. "You sound upset. Wait, what's that noise?"

"The wind," she explained. The way her head was cocked, the breeze blew against the phone and made a *shushing* noise. "I'm not upset, I'm . . . okay, maybe I am, but not with you. I had an argument with my father earlier. Now I'm a wandering . . ."

She tried to think of a Japanese word that was the equivalent of minstrel or troubadour, but could only come up with *ongakuka*, which meant "musician," so she took another tack.

"I'm out by the bay with my guitar but I don't feel like playing anymore and I'm still too upset to go home. If you're still dressed, do you want to come outside and talk? I mean, we could talk on the phone, but—"

"For you, I'll get dressed," Hachiro interrupted.

That made Kara laugh, and already she felt some of her anxiety seeping out of her. "I'll walk over and meet you in front of the dorm."

"Okay. See you in a minute," he replied, and the line went dead.

Hachiro had been sweet on the phone, but she wished he hadn't hung up so fast. It would have been nice to chat with him as she walked. On the other hand, if he really did have to put some clothes on, that would have been difficult for him. She smiled at the image that came into her mind of him trying to pull on a T-shirt while talking on the phone, and slid her cell back into her pocket.

Swinging her guitar behind her back, she stood up and gazed out at the bay. It had a different sort of beauty at night, an ethereal calm that made her want to walk out to Ama-no-Hashidate and stroll the white sands. But that would have been too far to stray from home after dark. Her father hadn't come looking for her, and probably wouldn't unless she stayed out past the school's curfew. He would want her to have some freedom, especially tonight. *Give you your own space* was how he would have put it.

But now, as she crossed the dead-end road and then started across the grounds toward the front of the school, she wanted less of her own space, not more. Despite the moonlight, the night had deepened, and off to her left, down the slope, she could see the shadows that gathered in the place where Akane had been murdered. With a shudder, she pulled her gaze away.

The way ahead of her was even darker. The school loomed ahead, a monolithic black outline silhouetted against the night sky, and to the left, where the east wall came so close to the trees, the path was nothing but inky shadows.

A little shiver went up the back of her neck and she couldn't help but turn and look back the way she'd come. She felt watched, and it was not a welcome feeling. Picking up her pace, she hurried over to the corner of the school and plunged into the darkness, just wanting to get to

Hachiro now, a part of her wondering if she should just have headed home.

Her guitar bounced a bit on its strap, clunking against her back. When she'd rushed out of the house earlier with it slung behind her, she'd felt cool, like someone out of a movie. Now it seemed ridiculous. Her guitar felt like a burden, and she didn't like that at all.

The leaves rustled in the trees off to her left and she jerked away from them, heart pounding, and let out a little yelp of alarm that sounded to her ears like a cat's yowl. She wanted to be embarrassed, but now the back of her neck felt warm and she couldn't drive from her mind the certainty that unseen eyes were watching her.

Kara brought her guitar around in front of her and held it steady, for the first time considering it a potential weapon as she hurried through the darkest part of the night.

When she emerged from that narrow space onto the moonlit field behind the school, she did not breathe a sigh of relief. Only when she had made it nearly halfway across and saw Hachiro come out the front door of the dormitory did Kara allow herself to relax, and to smile at how much she'd let her imagination get the better of her.

Afraid of the dark, she thought. *Big loser.*

But even as the words entered her mind, she dismissed them. Maybe it really had been her imagination, but she couldn't blame herself for being afraid of the nighttime.

Hachiro waved and started across the grass. Kara hurried to meet him.

She'd gotten close enough to see the smile on his face

and the gleam of his eyes, and then a scream split the night, echoing, drifting toward them on the wind.

Kara and Hachiro both spun toward the sound. It came from the school, but not the building itself. As the echoes died, Kara narrowed her eyes, pinpointing the origins of the scream. It had come from the darkness on the west side of the building, near the school's driveway and parking lot.

"Come on!" Unslinging her guitar, Kara set it on the ground and took off at a sprint.

Hachiro grabbed her arm. "Wait! We should get someone!"

"There isn't time," Kara said.

The voice cried out again—a girl's voice—but now instead of a scream there were words, a torrent of Japanese swears, and pleas to leave her alone. Blinking in shock, Kara realized that she knew that voice.

"Miho," she whispered.

This time Hachiro didn't try to stop her. They ran together across the field, barreling along a track worn into the grass by students walking back and forth. Hachiro took the lead, his legs much longer than hers, but Kara had speed and managed not to drop behind much farther.

Thoughts of missing students and whispered curses crowded her brain and she pushed them aside, focusing on Miho—smiling Miho, hair pulled back on one side, rolling her eyes heavenward whenever Sakura or Kara behaved inappropriately. Keeping that image in her mind, Kara pushed herself harder, breath coming fast, legs pumping under her.

Miho came whipping around the corner, arms outflung as she changed direction, angling toward the dorm. She slammed into Hachiro and the two of them fell in a tangle of limbs. Miho cried out in a mixture of surprise, pain, and fear, and as Hachiro groaned and tried to extricate himself from her, she began to fight him, trying to get free, perhaps to keep running. Her eyes were wide and she kept glancing back the way she'd come, into the darkness alongside the school.

"Stop," Kara said, dropping to her knees beside them and reaching for the other girl's hands. "Miho, it's okay. It's us. It's—"

Her words froze in her throat. She'd looked into those shadows as well, the darkness from which Miho had just emerged, and she'd seen something there. For just an instant, Kara's breath had caught, and she'd seen a silhouette in the shadows, swaying as though blown by the breeze, or like a snake summoned from its basket by a flute in some old cartoon. Had it been a woman? She thought so.

Yet now it was gone, the silhouette vanishing, swallowed by the deeper shadows.

"Kara?"

She looked down. Hachiro had managed to free himself from Miho's flailing arms and now the girl sat beside him, eyes frantic, gazing from Kara to the darkness and back again.

A hiss came from the darkness, and then the soft *shush* of something moving along the ground. The small hairs on the back of Kara's neck stood up and gooseflesh pimpled her skin.

"Oh, no," she whispered.

And then the sound was gone, and the shadows were only shadows.

"You saw it, didn't you?" Miho demanded. "I heard it on

the grass, coming after me. I knew it was there. I only caught a glimpse, but . . ."

She shuddered.

Hachiro stood and reached a hand down for Miho. Kara only spared a glance at them, focusing instead on the shadows.

"I saw . . . something. Kind of felt it, too," Kara replied. She thought of her fear from a few minutes earlier, the sense that someone had been watching her, but now she thought that had truly only been her nerves. What had just been here, after Miho, had weight and presence. It felt . . . the only word she could think of was *sinister*. An old-fashioned sort of word, but it fit.

"It was chasing you?" Hachiro asked.

Miho nodded. "I was coming from Kara's house."

As she offered this, her gaze darkened with some unpleasant memory, and Kara thought she saw anger there.

"Why were you at my house?" Kara asked.

"Later," Miho replied. "Right now—"

"We have to get inside," Hachiro said, as the three of them started back toward the dormitory, glancing repeatedly over their shoulders toward the place where Kara had seen that ghostly silhouette.

"I've got to get home," Kara said, suddenly realizing her predicament. To get back to her house, she'd have to pass through the very same shadows through which someone or something had just chased Miho.

"You could call your father," Hachiro said. "Ask him to come get you."

"And when he asks why?" Kara wondered.

"You tell him. Or you lie," Miho said. "But you can't walk home through that alone, and I'm not going back."

Hachiro held up a hand. "I'll walk you," he said, looking at Kara with a gentle half smile. "Let's just get Miho safely into the dorm, and—"

"No," Kara said. "Then you'd have to walk back alone. And besides, it's got to be close to curfew now as it is. I'll call him. I don't feel like asking him for anything right now, but he'll come get me."

"What will you say?" Miho asked.

"I'll say maybe he was right, that I shouldn't have gone out alone after dark, that I'm scared. The truth, basically. Only without monsters."

Miho hugged herself, glancing back at the darkness as the three of them walked across the field toward the dorm. Kara and Hachiro kept Miho between them. When they reached the place where Kara had put down her guitar, she picked it up and slung it over her shoulder.

"When you're ready, we should talk about it," Kara said.

"Not yet." Miho shuddered. "Wait until we're inside. I want lights and locked doors. I want to hide under my covers."

Kara understood, and fought the urge to try to comfort Miho with humor. Reminding her that her sheet and blanket weren't much protection wouldn't be funny right now. If ever.

"I thought I saw a girl," Hachiro said, whispering as he pulled open the door of the dormitory and stood back to let them pass. "Or a woman."

Miho shook her head. "That wasn't a woman. No matter what it looked like."

8

卍

Kara's father picked her up in front of the dorm, shooting a stern look at Hachiro as the boy escorted her to the car. It was a total *Dad* look, and Kara wanted to shout at her father. What, did he think Hachiro had caused the fight they'd had earlier? That he had done something to upset her enough that she didn't want to walk home? Stupid. She knew that all guys could be stupid sometimes, that they lost the ability to interpret what their eyes were showing them, but it still frustrated her hugely when her father turned out to be one of those men.

Yeah, Dad, she wanted to say, *Hachiro is the problem*.

Sigh.

Hachiro carried her guitar, put it into the backseat, and headed back into the dorm with about three minutes to spare before curfew. Kara sat in silence beside her father as he turned the car around and drove the almost absurdly short distance back to their house. She had figured he would assume her silence stemmed from their fight, and Kara let him go on thinking that. She wasn't ready to explain.

"Look," he said, reverting to English. That was getting to be a habit now, whenever things between them grew tense. "I should have talked to you more about what's going on between Yuuka . . . I mean, Aritomo-sensei . . . and me. But, honey, you can't pretend you didn't see this coming. You were the only one who did. I wasn't looking, and you know that. You *know* it. And you seemed to want something to happen with us—"

Kara heard the pain and confusion in his voice and knew she had caused it. Her heart gave a painful twist.

"I *did*," she admitted, sticking to Japanese. "At first."

"And now?" her father said, returning to Japanese as well, as if in reaction to her. It seemed safer, somehow, the foreign language putting distance between them.

He pulled the car in beside the house and killed the engine, then looked over at her expectantly. What did he want her to say?

Whatever it was, it would have been a lie.

"Now I need to sleep," she said. "It's been a weird night."

She opened the door and he reached over to touch her arm. Kara glanced sidelong at him. The pleading look had left his face, and now he only seemed frustrated.

He went back to English. "I'm dealing with these feelings as they hit me, honey. Same way you do. I can't consult you on them before I even know what I'm feeling."

Kara forced herself to smile. "I know that," she said, relenting by returning to English as well. "Come on, let's go in."

That seemed to satisfy him, but Kara had said it only to end the conversation. She needed time alone—time to think. The instant she was inside the house she made a beeline to her bedroom and shut her door. She'd left her guitar in the car, but no way would she be going out to get it before sunrise.

Miho lay in her bed, covers pulled tight around her, feeling vulnerable in just her T-shirt and underwear. A small fan buzzed at the end of her bed, where she had clipped it to the edge of her desk. The windows were shut tight and locked. Living on the third floor ought to have given her a sense of security, and once upon a time it had. No longer.

The small reading lamp on her desk remained lit. Sakura had known better than to protest. Especially after the whole thing with Ren. Miho had confronted them while they waited for Kara's father, and told them of her humiliation in front of Ren. Both girls had been hugely apologetic. According to Kara, Miho had "gone so quiet" about her crush on Ren that they had thought she was over him. She had been so angry at them, but that had sprung from her own embarrassment. Her friends loved her and would never have knowingly put her in a position like that. Miho knew that.

It all seemed so foolish now. In comparison to whatever had chased her out there in the dark, and the sheer *hunger* she had felt emanating from it, a little humiliation was nothing. Someday, she might even find her fumbling flirtation with Ren funny. Not tonight, though. Tonight, nothing was funny.

Miho took a deep breath and shifted under the sheet. In

the dim glow of that tiny light, she watched Sakura sleeping, grateful for her presence. She could never have stayed in the room by herself.

Mustering her courage, Miho closed her eyes and hated the darkness behind them. It took her back immediately to the hissing she'd heard in the shadow of the school, away from the moonlight, and the fear that had rushed into her heart returned. She'd been marching back to the dorm from Kara's house. Had she heard something, noticed something in the shadows? Probably. All Miho knew was that her anger had slipped away and she found herself listening intently to the darkness coalescing around her.

Something had slithered in the grass. Soft hissing began, mixed with hitching breaths that might have been quiet laughter. She'd frozen and turned, her eyes struggling to adjust to the night. Against the wall of the school she could barely make out a patch of darkness deeper than night. At first she thought it was a person, a woman maybe, from the hair, but then it moved ever so slowly, inching nearer, and turned its head, and she saw the monstrous silhouette of its face, ridged and smooth, jaws opening wide, the tiniest glint of moonlight catching on the wet, black spikes of its teeth. It *wanted* her. She felt that very keenly.

The hissing noise issued from its open mouth, and Miho screamed. Letting out a stream of swears and pleas, she had run, careening out of control along the side of the school, just above the parking lot, and then emerged into the golden glow of the moon and collided into Hachiro.

And what if he hadn't been there? she thought now, alone

in bed. *What if Kara and Hachiro had not been around? Where would you be now?*

Her eyes opened and she stared over at Sakura, who slept so soundly in her bed. Miho clenched her jaw tight, unwilling to say her roommate's name, though she longed for company, for someone to talk to. It confused and frustrated her that she felt so grateful to her friends, when the curse that nearly claimed her tonight had been Sakura's fault to begin with. If not for her . . .

That's not fair, she thought, stopping herself, biting her lip, fighting tears. She turned her back on Sakura's sleeping form. Miho loved Kara, and Sakura was her best friend in the world. It had been friendship and loyalty that led to her being cursed—to the curse upon them all—and how could she blame Sakura, when it had really all begun with Akane's murder?

With a sigh, Miho shifted her legs, trying to find a comfortable position, and closed her eyes again. She wished for her mother, and the very wishing filled her with a deep melancholy. In the spring, she had faced evil. Real, true evil. But she had been with her friends at the time, and they had survived. Never during that experience had she wished for her mother. But tonight she had been alone out there, and the thing had been chasing *her*.

Not that her mother would bother coming to visit. Miho hated to complain about her parents, since Sakura's were so much worse. They actively disliked her, and didn't want anything to do with her. The Murakamis had sent Akane and Sakura off to boarding school to be rid of them, and cared so

123

little that when Akane had been murdered, they had *left* Sakura there. Miho knew that her own parents didn't hate her, or want to be rid of her, necessarily. They hadn't put that much thought into it.

No, her mother wouldn't be coming. Until morning, at least, the only thing keeping her safe was Sakura's presence and the little light burning at the end of her bed. As these thoughts settled deeply into her mind, Miho wondered what might have happened to her, and where Daisuke and Wakana were now. They had all discussed it—she and Sakura, Kara and Hachiro—and they all hoped the two had really run away like young lovers in some teen romance manga story.

But the connections were there.

Daisuke and Wakana were part of the Noh club. They had been involved in the upcoming production of *Dojoji,* and so was Miho. Whatever had been out there in the dark, it had chosen the Noh club as its prey. But what the hell was it? Kyuketsuki had laid the curse upon them with carefully chosen words, summoning whatever remained of the supernatural in Japan to plague them. It could be anything, but then why focus on the Noh club?

Again she closed her eyes, and the hissing remained with her, like a snake.

With a sharp intake of breath, she opened her eyes. Her fingers could still remember the shape of each of the masks she had been working on for *Dojoji,* including the demon spirit who took such horrid vengeance on several of the major characters.

The serpent-woman, Hannya.

In the glow of that small light, Miho prayed.

The Hannya, Kara thought, standing in the kitchen with a glass of pineapple juice in her hand. The small window over the sink gave her a view into the street and she stared out at the house across from theirs. A quiet night. All of Miyazu City would be sleeping perfectly well tonight, except for Daisuke's parents, Kara and her father, and Miho, of course.

By now, Miho would have figured it out.

She took a sip of juice, relishing its sweetness, and listened to the darkened kitchen for sounds that didn't belong there. The hum of electricity. The creak of old wood, shifting in the wind. Nothing out of place at all. But Kara felt like a jolt of electricity had shot through her and was racing around inside her veins on some endless loop.

The Hannya. Really, it made a weird kind of sense. Unintended ritual had summoned Kyuketsuki, beginning with the murder of Akane, followed by Sakura's rage and grief and Ume's guilt. Then the curse of Kyuketsuki had called out to the lingering remnants of ancient evil in Japan and focused its attention on her, Sakura, and Miho. The curse had made them a kind of magnet. The Hannya would likely come for her and Sakura eventually, but for the moment it seemed to be following its own instincts, which was to prey upon those who'd summoned it—the Noh club. Miho met both criteria, so she was doubly in danger.

Kara set her glass down on the counter, frowning. *Those*

who'd summoned it. Miss Aritomo had chosen the play to begin with. She would be in danger as well.

Something had to be done. The trouble was that they had no proof of anything—no evidence that Daisuke and Wakana had *not* run away, or that the Hannya existed. The only reason that Kara even knew the story was because Miss Aritomo had chosen *Dojoji* for her first Noh production at the school. Even then, Kara probably never would have read the play itself except that she and Sakura had thought it would make a good manga and had started to do the research to prepare.

No one would believe them. But in Sakura and Miho's room—with Hachiro watching for her father's car down in the lobby—Kara and the girls had agreed on a course of action. Ever since, she had been trying to think of another plan, but they weren't characters in a manga—schoolgirls turned demon hunters or something. The Hannya was real, and none of them wanted to meet it face-to-face.

Just do it, she thought. *Follow the plan.*

With a sigh, she rinsed her glass and left it in the sink, crossing the darkened kitchen and living room.

Step one.

As Kara entered his room, her father looked up from making notes on a pad. He seemed surprised to see her there, and that made her sad and frustrated with him all over again.

"What is it, honey?" he asked in Japanese.

"Something happened tonight," she replied.

His eyes widened as he sat up, and she knew all sorts of unpleasant things must be rushing through his head. Had

Hachiro done something to her? Had she and the girls gotten into trouble?

"Are you all right?" he asked.

Kara smiled. Whatever else she might be feeling toward her father, she knew he loved her.

"Home safe and sound, as you can see," she said. Then she grew serious. "But Miho almost didn't make it home. After she came here looking for me, someone followed her, Dad. Somebody chased her. If Hachiro and I hadn't been out in front of the dorm, whoever it was might have gotten her."

For several seconds, his expression was immobile. Granite. Then he slid out of bed, came over to her, kissed her forehead, and held her close. Kara wanted to pull away—the two of them still had things to work out—but now wasn't the time.

"That's why you needed a ride home?"

She nodded.

"Did Miho get a look at the person chasing her?"

"Not a good one," Kara replied.

Her father took a deep breath and went to his window. From there he could see the pagoda shape of the school in the distance.

"Miho's in the Noh club," she went on. "So were Daisuke and Wakana."

"You're suggesting they didn't run away."

Kara stared at his back. "Do *you* think they did?"

"Not anymore."

Even as he turned toward her, he picked up the phone and began to dial.

. . .

For three days in the middle of August, the spirits of the dead returned to Japanese households to spend time with their ancestors—at least, according to the Buddhist festival of Obon. Kara didn't pretend to understand the significance of this, but she tried. Some Buddhists—mostly older people—seemed truly to believe that the spirits of their ancestors came to visit them, but for the most part Obon seemed to have taken on a more secular presence in local culture. In other words, to a lot of people, it was all about the pretty lights.

Not that she was making any judgments. The idea of ghosts hanging out in the house for a few days seemed creepy enough to her even before factoring in the family reunion element. Granted, she would have loved to believe that her mother's spirit could be there with her, sharing space, watching over her. It warmed her heart to think of it. But her father's mother had been a cranky, hateful old woman who complained all the time, bossed people around, and had clammy hands. She'd smelled weird, too. No way did Kara want her ghost hanging around.

On the last day of Obon, tradition required that paper lanterns be lit and floated on water, usually down a river or stream. This was called *toro nagashi*. Similar rituals were performed at other times—in Hiroshima, for instance, on the anniversary of the day the United States dropped an atomic bomb on the city. But despite the ghosts that were involved, the lantern festival was usually not such a grim affair.

Miyazu City was widely acknowledged to have the greatest toro nagashi festival in the country, complete with spectacular fireworks. For the most part, it seemed like a big party to her. Ten thousand paper lanterns in varying colors would be set adrift in the bay, floating gently out to sea as the sun set. The lanterns represented the ghosts of dead ancestors, returning to the spirit world after their three-day visit. People gathered all up and down the beach on Ama-no-Hashidate to watch. Musicians played. Kids splashed in the water. Under normal circumstances, Kara would have been happy and excited. But after what she and her friends had been through, an undercurrent of unease flowed just beneath the surface of every moment.

Her father hated the idea of her being out after dark, but just for this night, he had made an exception. For the most part, she would be on the beach with thousands of other people, and on the way home, she'd be walking with her friends, and she'd promised to be home no later than ten p.m., and earlier if possible.

But all that was for later. Right now, she sat on a straw mat on the beach, drinking flavored water and listening to the thunderous boom of the five guys who had set up *taiko* drums and were performing *kumi-daiko*, drumming as an ensemble. The sound got deep into her brain, thundered off the inside of her chest, and it made her feel remarkably there, in the moment, swallowed by Japan. Kara loved the drums, but was glad they weren't any closer. The kumi-daiko guys would have drummed her right off the beach, they were so loud.

Vendors sold sweet cakes, drinks, all kinds of noodles, fried squid, and octopus dumplings. The fried squid were a bit chewy, but the octopus dumplings were astonishingly tasty, like the best sushi.

"Maybe we should talk about the plan," Hachiro suggested as he plopped a dumpling into his mouth. A bit of something stuck to his lip and he licked it off, looking lovably silly.

Kara smiled. "Let's wait for the others. Talk to me."

"About what?" he asked, chewing.

"Anything," she said, frowning. *You're my boyfriend*, she wanted to say. *We're supposed to be able to talk.* But that would be unfair. She and Hachiro could talk about anything and nothing with equal enthusiasm, and she never felt awkward with him. Well, almost never—whenever questions arose about where their relationship would lead, things got uncomfortable.

"Sorry," he said. "It's sort of hard to think about anything else right now. When your girlfriend has a curse hanging over her head, other things don't mean very much."

Kara felt a warm happiness blossom in her chest. "Well done. Most guys can't come up with that kind of spin so quickly."

"I mean it," Hachiro protested.

"I know you do. I'm teasing. Seriously, though. Talk about baseball. How are the Red Sox doing?"

Hachiro stared at her. "You're from Boston. Aren't you the one who's supposed to be telling me?"

It was Kara's turn to shrug. "I don't care about baseball. You do."

He couldn't deny it, especially not with the Boston Red Sox cap perched firmly on his head. Hachiro seemed to think it over a moment, but then he warmed to the subject.

"They're in a slump, actually. But that happens every year after the All-Star break. People lose faith in them, and then they come back. If we're lucky, they don't let it all fall apart in the end."

Kara laughed. "Choke," she said in English.

"What?"

"In English, we would say we hope they don't 'choke.'" Then she repeated the word in Japanese.

Hachiro nodded. "Choke."

"There you go," she said, reverting to Japanese. "Now you're ready to live in Boston."

His smile vanished, confusing her a moment before she realized where her words had led his thoughts. Kara would go back to Boston eventually. Without him. That knowledge hung over them always.

Her cell phone jangled. *Saved by the bell*, she thought as she slid it open. Sakura was calling.

"Hello?"

"Where are you?"

Kara glanced around. "Exactly where we agreed. More or less."

The day they had gone to the beach together, they had sat on the seaside of Ama-no-Hashidate. Today, they needed to be on the bay side so they would be able to see the lanterns and the fireworks after it got dark, and they had decided to meet at a halfway point along the sandbar.

"No, you're not. We're here."

Kara glanced around. "They're here," she said in response to Hachiro's curious look, and he started to glance about as well. Both of them stood up, Kara turning in a circle, scanning the beach. A sea of faces looked back.

"I don't see you," she started. But then she caught a glimmer of bronze in the sun. "Oh, wait. Ren's hair!"

Smiling, she waved, and a few seconds later, Miho, Sakura, and Ren weaved their way through the crowd and began to make camp with them. Towels and mats were spread out, Miho hid under the umbrella Hachiro had already set up, and Ren opened a greasy paper bag and pulled out a wooden stick skewered with a fried piece of unidentifiable fish. He grinned happily.

Sakura laid down on her belly, feet poking up, legs crossed at the ankles. Kara thought she looked beautiful, a modern, post-Goth version of the classic 1950s beach bunny. If only she would smile.

But there was little chance of that.

"Okay, we're all here," Sakura said, glancing at Miho. Then she focused on Kara. "What do we do now?"

Kara took a breath, preparing to speak. Why were they all looking at her? How had she become the one who made decisions like this? She didn't know the answer, but it was obvious that they all needed a purpose—something to make them feel like they were doing something, instead of just waiting for the darkness to swallow them—and if she had to give them that purpose, she would.

"Step one went smoothly, as far as I can tell," she said.

Miho nodded. "I think the police believed me."

"Of course they believed you. It isn't like you were pretending to be terrified," Ren said.

Miho gave him a glance that was part grateful and part bemused. All of the awkwardness she had once displayed around him was gone now that she knew he was gay. But the moment Miho realized that the others were looking at her, she shot a blank look at Kara as if to urge her to continue.

"There isn't much more to say about step one, really," Kara said, shrugging one shoulder. "My father got Yamato-sensei worried enough to bring the police in. They're not going to say it officially, but my dad tells me the police are taking the possibility of abduction more seriously in the cases of Daisuke and Wakana."

"They talked to everyone from Noh club this morning," Miho confirmed.

"Not just from the club," Ren added, glancing at Sakura. "They talked to everyone who's been volunteering, too."

Kara nodded. She knew this already. Sakura had hated every minute of it. After the way they had handled her sister's murder, she had thought them a bunch of idiots, but when they had interrogated her after Chouku and Jiro had died back in April, Sakura had come to despise the police.

Hachiro threw up his hands, smiling, apparently sensing the tension and wanting to move on. "So, step two?"

"Step two," Kara agreed. "We turn into bodyguards."

She studied her friends, normally so open and trusting and—the attitude Sakura adopted notwithstanding—happy, and she hated to see the shadow of Kyuketsuki's curse hanging over them.

"It's a big job," Ren said.

"We can handle it," Miho piped up from under the umbrella.

Kara smiled at her. "Yeah. We can. At least while everyone's at school."

"What do you mean?" Sakura asked.

"Well, it's not as if we can follow anyone home, so after the commuters go home, we only have to worry about the members of the Noh club who live in the dorm," Kara explained. "Miho can keep in touch with the others by e-mail."

"We can't protect them all," Sakura said.

"We might not be able to protect them at all," Hachiro replied. He reached out for Kara's hand, lending her his strength and support. "But we're the only ones who know what's really going on. We have to do what we can."

"Without getting ourselves killed," Miho whispered.

Ren sighed. "That would be nice."

The taiko drums began again, startling them all. Kara hadn't even noticed that they had stopped. Her mind had been elsewhere.

"All right," she said, clapping her hands together. "Enough of that for now. Food and fireworks today. Let's 'eat, drink, and be merry.' "

She didn't bother to finish that old saying.

For tomorrow we may die.

9

Mai had always loved the Toro Nagashi Festival, and today had been the perfect day for it, hot and breezy. The beach on Ama-no-Hashidate had come alive with people. Really, she thought, it was the people who had come alive. Even the normally sedate adults had seemed to laugh more, and swim more, and play more. She'd seen mothers and fathers tossing brightly colored beach balls to their toddlers and older couples splashing in the shallows. Faces that were usually buttoned up and serious had discovered their smiles, as if everyone over thirty had sipped one glass of wine too many before coming down to watch the fireworks. It should have made her happy to see them.

And perhaps it would have, if she had been able to stop thinking about Daisuke and Wakana, or if her soccer club friends had allowed their mouths to fall silent for just five minutes. Was it so much to ask? Mai had never been the most talkative among them, but it wasn't just the talking that bothered her. They gossiped and complained, and when they weren't doing either of those things, they talked about shopping and clothes and boys, and other things of little real consequence.

I miss you, Ume, she thought.

An elbow nudged her. Mai had been sitting on the sand, knees drawn up to her chest, watching the lanterns float out on the water. Seven o'clock had come and gone and the day had begun to slip away. Dusk spread its wings across the sky. The paper lanterns were beautiful in the twilight, the lights burning within them brighter and brighter as twilight deepened.

The nudge came again. She turned and looked at Emi, who sat beside her wearing a mischievous grin. The square glasses perched on her nose made her look far more intelligent than she had ever managed to be.

"Wouldn't you like to trade places with her?" Emi said.

Beyond her, tall Kaori—probably the best soccer player in the club—snickered in agreement. The girls were focused on a twentyish couple who were chest deep in the water, wrapped around one another, kissing languorously. What had drawn their attention, no doubt, was the lean, muscular physique of the guy and the way he held his girlfriend or wife or whatever—crushed to him as though he could mold her like clay. And maybe he could. But that sort of guy had never appealed to her.

Mai smiled politely, but said nothing. Emi rolled her eyes and went back to whispering to Kaori. Mai didn't mind at all. In fact, she felt relieved. When Ume had left Monju-no-Chie school, Mai had been confused and even a little glad. They had never been the best of friends, and even Ume readily admitted she was the queen bitch of the school. She'd aspired to become that very thing. But as the reality of her departure grew closer, Mai began to realize that she would really miss Ume. Whatever else she might have been, she had been smart and confident—someone who led instead of followed.

Not that Mai wanted to be anything like her. Ume, after all, had also murdered Akane Murakami. Mai had been there. She hadn't laid a finger on Akane, but she had witnessed the whole thing and she had never spoken of it to anyone, not even the other girls who had taken part in the beating that had turned into a killing—girls like Emi and Kaori. The guilt from that night clung like a death shroud on Mai's heart. If she had stepped in, she might have been able to save Akane, or she might have been beaten or killed herself, and her fear had stopped her.

And if all the things that Ume had told her were true—about Sakura and Kara and Miho and the demon thing they had faced—then Akane's murder had been the trigger for everything that followed. Mai could have prevented it all.

She had to live with that stain on her soul for the rest of her life.

Part of her penance seemed to be listening to Emi and Kaori giggle about nonsense. As much as she wished she could just quit the soccer club and walk away from these shallow girls, she had chosen to become queen bitch in Ume's place, partially to make sure they did not get further out of control, but mostly to protect herself. The only people they treated with more venom than students they deemed less than themselves were those who'd once been their friends but no longer were.

Now she wished she could take it all back. She cared more about her roommate and Daisuke than she did about any of these girls, but she had been nasty and aloof with them a lot of the time—especially Wakana. For a while, she had comforted herself with reassurances that they would be found, that they were together, even though she had known that night when she came back to her room still wet from the shower that Wakana had not gone out the second-story window by choice. Wakana was afraid of heights.

Stop it. Stop thinking about her in the past tense.

Emi and Kaori giggled again, and she wanted to slap them. All day they had been posing when boys walked by. Now the day had cooled enough that they had closed their umbrella and even pulled on shirts and sweatshirts, but that only meant they had to find other ways to draw attention to themselves.

Mai stood up.

"Where are you going?" Kaori asked, frowning, as if Mai needed permission.

"For a walk. It's nice this time of day, and I like seeing the lanterns. Don't worry, I'll be back before the fireworks."

"We'll come!" Emi volunteered, starting to rise.

"No," Mai said quickly.

Emi blinked, obviously hurt, and she and Kaori settled back down. The other girls weren't paying any attention, focused more on the lanterns and the people wading into the water.

"I'm sorry," Mai said. "I just need a few minutes to myself."

Emi nodded once, curtly. "Of course."

Mai felt the urge to apologize again but ignored it. She wished she hadn't apologized the first time. Instead, she turned and walked away, soft sand shifting under her bare feet.

She had always loved the Toro Nagashi Festival, but she feared that after today, she would never be able to truly enjoy it again. Still, she walked and watched the paper lanterns sway on the surface of the bay, red and blue, green and yellow, pink and purple and white, and she thought about their symbolism. People took solace in the sight, and she understood why. The ritual gave her a sort of peace, now that she was away from the other girls. She could let her sadness show without the fear of being judged.

Mai went around a group of people watching the lanterns, stepping into the surf, and she enjoyed the feeling of the tiny ripples washing over her feet and ankles. She went on that way for a few minutes, wishing she knew what had happened to Daisuke and Wakana and wondering what would happen next.

In the failing sunlight, as day gave way to the dark of night, she looked up ahead, and saw a blond-haired white girl standing hand in hand with a big Japanese guy, the two of them intimately close. There were other gaijins on the beach, mostly tourists but some who lived in Miyazu City, so with the girl turned partly away from her, it took Mai a moment to realize she was looking at Kara Harper.

Her hands balled into fists.

"Do the different colors mean anything?" Kara asked.

At first Hachiro did not reply, and she wondered if it was a stupid question or if he was trying to come up with an answer. He squeezed her hand and nodded toward the bay. Night had arrived in full at last and the paper lanterns were lovely and ethereal in their pale colors.

"The white ones," Hachiro said. "I'm not sure about the others, but the white ones are supposed to represent those who have died within the past year, since the last festival."

Kara gazed out at the lanterns spread across the bay. There hadn't seemed a vast number of white ones in comparison to the others, but now that she knew their significance, there seemed far too many.

"Another thing to remind Sakura of her sister," she said.

Hachiro looked down at her. "I don't think she needs any reminders."

"No. You're right." Kara leaned against him, comforted by his solid presence.

"The fireworks will start soon," Hachiro said. "Do you want to head back and join the others?"

"Not really," she said, tilting her chin back to look up at him. "Is that horrible?"

Hachiro smiled, and for once, his grin held no trace of its familiar silliness. "Not at all. I'm enjoying just being with you. I'm glad we wandered away for a little while."

She searched his eyes. "We haven't had a lot of time alone together, especially lately. There are a lot of things I've been wanting to say to you."

He hesitated.

"We're here right now, Hachiro," she went on. "You're here, and I'm here. Maybe when this school year is over, I'll be going back to the U.S. But maybe not. With what's going on at school, your parents could pull you out of Monju-no-Chie without any notice. Then what? I've got a curse on me. A *curse*. But I'm still here. Right now, I'm here, standing in front of you, and there isn't anywhere else in the world I'd rather be. Can't you let that be enough?"

Her heart pounded in her chest, but she felt its beat pulsing throughout her body. Her face felt hot as she studied his face and she tightened her grip on his fingers. Hachiro had never looked so serious to her.

"Come on," she said, with a nervous smile. "Don't you have anything to say?"

Hachiro reached out with his free hand, brushed her hair from her face, and then cupped the back of her head as he lowered his mouth to kiss her. Kara began to protest, wanting a reply, and then his lips touched hers and she understood that this *was* his reply. He had never kissed her like this before, tender and urgent at the same time, their bodies so close, and as he broke the kiss and pulled back, she felt unsteady on her feet.

They grinned at each other.

Which was when Mai appeared, practically between them, standing ankle deep in the rippling water on the shore.

"You two seem to be enjoying yourselves," she said, her upper lip curling. Kara thought she looked like a shark on the prowl. "It's a shame that Wakana and Daisuke can't be here to watch the fireworks."

Hachiro stepped closer to Kara, as if he feared Mai might try to hurt her. "You need to leave her alone, Mai," he said.

Mai laughed humorlessly. "Of course I do. Everyone else does. Why upset the girl who knows exactly what's going on, and might be able to do something about it?"

Kara shook her head. "You have no idea what you're talking about. If I thought there was anything I could do to help, I'd do it without hesitation."

"So American, bonsai," Mai sneered. "You'd be a hero, if only you knew who to hit."

"What do you want from me?" Kara demanded.

But Mai had already looked out across the bay, at the soft colors of the paper lanterns eddying in the currents.

"The white ones are the most beautiful," Mai said. "I wonder which two are Daisuke and Wakana."

"You don't know they're dead!" Hachiro said.

"No?" Mai said, whirling on them. "Then where *are* they?"

As Kara and Hachiro stared her down, a soft *thup-thup-thup* filled the air, followed by loud pops of the first three firework explosions. Multicolored flowers blossomed in the night sky, cascading down like falling angels. Several others banged in the air, loud enough that Kara felt them in her chest, and the lights played myriad hues across Mai's face.

The crowd sighed and *ooh*ed in appreciation, and as a huge burst of blue and gold filled the heavens, Kara saw Mai's expression falter. Her anger shattered and crumbled, leaving only desperation and sadness behind.

"Please just tell me what you know," Mai pleaded.

Kara took a deep breath.

And then, in between fireworks booming thunder across the sky, she heard someone call her name. The three of them turned to see Sakura, Miho, and Ren hurrying toward them. Kara and Hachiro stepped out of the surf. Miho gave Mai a quick, curious glance, but otherwise they ignored her.

"What's wrong?" Hachiro asked as they raced up. "What happened?"

Ren's bronze hair reflected the lights of the fireworks like metal. He pushed his head between Miho and Sakura, somehow bringing them all closer together, so he could deliver his message with greater privacy.

"There's another kid missing," Ren said.

Kara's eyes went wide. She glanced at Mai, then at Miho. "Someone from Noh club?"

"It's Yasu," Miho said.

They all went quiet. The fireworks seemed to explode all around them. They all knew Yasu, a charming guy, the epitome of boy-coolness, quiet when he wanted to be enigmatic, He wore his hair longer than some of the girls, yet never got in trouble with Mr. Yamato for dress code violations. He had the lead role of Anchin in *Dojoji*.

"What do we do?" Ren asked.

Her voice almost lost in the midst of crackling fireworks, Mai spoke up. "Can I help?"

Kara could not trust her. The girl was too unstable. She

143

looked at the others. "He was here, at the festival? He vanished from the beach?"

"Just a few minutes ago," Sakura said. "When it got dark."

Kara nodded. "Good. The land is so narrow here, and
there's only one way to leave." She started hurrying up the
sand, cutting through the crowd, and they all followed, Mai
included. "Split up. Get into the woods. Let's try to stop it from
getting him out of here."

"It?" Mai said, tugging her arm. "What is *it*?"

Kara pulled her arm away, but she did look back, meeting
Mai's frightened gaze. "We're pretty sure it's the Hannya."

"But that's just a story," Mai said.

"What if it's not?" Kara asked, and then she ran to catch
up with the others.

She could not be certain over the sound of the fireworks,
their light splashing the white sand and black pines, but she
thought she heard Mai start to pray.

*I have seen many boys play Anchin, but you are more beautiful
than any of them.*

Yasu could not speak or breathe or move. His eyes bulged
and his chest burned with the need for air as its voice—*her
voice?*—wormed its way into his brain. Shadows gathered at
the corners of his eyes, but he did not think this was the ordinary darkness of the night or the black pine woods around
him. No, this was unconsciousness enveloping him, perhaps
death drawing him down into an abyss of eternal nothing.

Air. Please.

She had been there in the crowd beside him, so beautiful

and slender, her hair gleaming blacker than black, her eyes green. She wore a gossamer dress the same ebony as her hair, the moonlight hinting at delights beneath. When he had first caught sight of her, he had inhaled sharply at encountering so fine and delicate a girl. Only a few years older than himself, she had tilted her head back and thrust out her tongue as if tasting the night, and then she'd swiveled her head to return his stare, as though she'd been aware of his attention all along. When she smiled, he lost any sense of himself. In that moment, he would have been whatever kind of fool she wished.

"Come," she'd whispered, lips brushing past his ear as she took his hand.

Yasu gave no thought to his friends, or the fireworks that were about to start. He had followed her through the crowd. Somewhere, he heard the low, sonorous bong of a bell, and then they had reached the part of Ama-no-Hashidate where the beach gave way to the thick tangle of black pines that ran down the center of the sandbar.

The first of the fireworks had exploded behind them, finally breaking whatever trance Yasu had been in. He turned to look up at the beauty of the colors shooting through the night sky, and behind him, he'd heard a hiss.

The hands that grabbed him could not have been *her* hands. One folded over his mouth and nose and one wrapped around his torso, pinning his arms to his sides. But then something thick and cold and rough coiled around him, squeezing, and now he felt something crack inside of him, the darkness at the edges of his vision rushing in.

Someone came into the trees, calling his name. Other

voices shouted for him as well. The fireworks popped and thundered, throwing multicolored ghost lights among the pines.

Half-conscious, he felt himself being carried. Branches scratched his face and arms, but suddenly he could breathe again. Air rushed into his lungs. Still, he felt barely aware of his surroundings. His body swayed from side to side, still clutched by cold flesh. The touch was cold and rough at the same time. It flexed and shifted, and as awareness filtered back into his brain along with oxygen, he tried to turn his head, to get a look at the thing that had grabbed him. A single glimpse showed him red scales and dreadful yellow eyes, small black horns, wisps of white hair, and jaws opened so wide that they seemed capable of swallowing him whole. And teeth. He saw its teeth.

Yasu's first instinct was to fight, but even as he bucked his body, trying to get loose, his gaze caught on a half-dead pine tree. He thrust his arms out and grabbed hold of a branch, gouging his left wrist but adrenaline overcoming all pain. His fingers closed tightly and he tore free of the creature's grasp.

Breathing in ragged gasps, heart drumming hard, he snapped a branch off the dead pine and spun to face the thing with the yellow eyes. The woods were empty. Nothing moved. He scanned from shadow to shadow, strange colors still filtering through the branches from the fireworks high above. That single glimpse of the creature flashed in his mind and he twitched, whipped around, thought he'd seen it just out of the corner of his eye.

"Help!" he screamed. "I'm here! Help me! Anyone!"

Two seconds passed, maybe three, before he heard shouts in reply. People were looking for him. His friends, and others.

After the other kids had vanished, everyone was on guard, paying extra attention. He would be—

The hiss came from his left. He twisted, wielding the branch. Soft and low, as if just beside him, he heard the slow bong of an old bell; a church bell, a funeral bell. Something darted across his field of vision, darkness against darkness, low to the ground, and the hiss came again, to his right.

The voices were coming closer, from either side now, surrounding him. They would find him. But too late.

It rose up behind him and he felt the chill of its breath like the cold of the grave, and then its rough tongue against the back of his neck.

Yasu screamed.

Fool, it said.

Kara glanced through the trees back at the beach. Many people had come up near the tree line now, peering in from the sand, wondering what the hell was going on, or knowing, but without any idea what they could do to help. Others truly had no clue, and weren't about to be distracted from enjoying the Toro Nagashi Festival by the scrambling panic of a bunch of high school students and various adults who were lending a hand. They kept their backs turned to the trees, their eyes glued to the lanterns or the spectacle of the fireworks, and they grinned with childlike pleasure or sighed with solemn appreciation of the ritual of the lanterns.

In the woods, shouts of "Yasu!" drifted here and there, drowned out by the boom of fireworks, people yelling to be heard over one another's voices. Kara and her friends had split up. She and Hachiro picked their way among the trees, forced too many times to back up and find a new path when the pines grew thick enough to create an obstacle. Ren and Mai were a little ways off. At first she'd heard the soccer queen wincing and complaining about the scratches, but she'd quieted down quickly, and now joined the chorus of anxious searchers calling Yasu's name. Miho and Sakura were near enough that Kara could make out their voices from time to time, but she couldn't see them. There were so many people picking their way through the pines that she felt sure if Yasu was still there to be found, they would find him.

Yet Kara couldn't shake the feeling that they would find nothing, that Yasu had vanished as completely as the others. If this was the Hannya, or a Hannya, whatever serpentine spirit had been summoned up by their attempt to perform *Dojoji*, it left no trace of its victims. Either it abducted them and took them somewhere else, like a spider binding its prey to eat later, or it consumed them all without leaving a drop of blood behind.

She stopped yelling his name. Hachiro, caught up in the moment, didn't seem to notice, but Kara gave up on Yasu. She kept moving through the pines, kept searching the shadows, but she did not believe they had any hope of finding him.

And then she heard the shouting from up ahead.

"What?" she said, pushing through a scrabble of pine branches that raked her skin in order to reach Hachiro. "What was that?"

Even as he reached for her hand, he picked up the pace, pulling her behind him as they weaved among the pines.

"Someone heard him. He's calling out up ahead, or something," Hachiro said.

Kara listened carefully and thought that she could actually hear a voice crying out for help. But by then the frantic shouts for Yasu had increased to a fervent cacophony that drowned out everything but the staccato explosions of fireworks.

They ran, dodging trees, whipping through the pines, and then there were many others around them, the circle closing. She saw Mai and Ren, and behind them Sakura and Miho, and others on her left side as well.

A scream tore through the pines, rising up, louder even than the fireworks' finale, so close must they have been to its origin. They all went faster, harder, rushing, snapping branches, calling to one another now, trying to pinpoint Yasu's location.

Kara's steps faltered and she slowed. Ahead, a dozen or more searchers had come to a complete stop, forming a strange kind of half circle. An audience.

She let go of Hachiro's hand and padded forward, finding a narrow gap between two others who had participated in the search. In between them, she had a view of a small clearing in the pine woods, and of the twisted, broken, bleeding human wreckage that had been left there, a rag doll cast aside by some giant, monstrous child.

She'd been wrong, after all. They had found Yasu.

And now she wished they had not.

10

卐

Kara is drowning.

She cannot breathe, and blackness swims at the edges of her vision. Angry red spots flash in her brain. Her hearing is muffled, and as she lashes out, struggling, she feels as though she moves in slow motion. Water. I'm under water.

The realization is an epiphany. Disoriented, chest aching for air, she pushes herself in a direction she believes is upward, and her arms burst from the water. She sips at sweet relief, the air like magic in her lungs.

All around her, bobbing on the surface, paper lanterns float. Yet these don't have the variety of hues of the festival lanterns. These come only in white—white lanterns, the spirits of the recent dead, eddying around her, floating closer as though drawn to her.

Something tugs her from below the water. She tries to cry out, but no sound escapes her lips as she is dragged under once more.

No, no, no. I don't want to—

Her thoughts fall apart. The last of the air inside her struggles to be exhaled. Kara knows that if she opens her mouth she will drown. She will die. But her lungs demand air, and her thoughts are losing coherence, and she cannot stop herself.

She opens her mouth in a scream . . . but this time it is not silent.

With a gasp, she looks around. No longer in the water, she finds herself in a thick tangle of pines, and recognizes the place immediately. The black woods of Ama-no-Hashidate. Without the water muffling her hearing, the silence is gone. The air is filled with a loud hiss, layers of sound, the voices of serpents.

They hold her arms and legs, their coiled bodies emerging from the branches of the trees, more and more snakes reaching for her, tongues darting, eyes unblinking. Her throat is torn apart by her scream, her chest clenched by utter panic.

Please! she cries. *Please!*

She does not know to whom she appeals for mercy, only that mercy is her only hope.

Something grips her wrist, colder even than the skin of snakes, but not rough like the serpents. Soft. Gentle. Kara spins to see the hand on her wrist, peers into the thick bristle of darkness between two trees, and her eyes widen. Hope grows.

"Mom?"

The woman smiles. The serpents fall from Kara as though fleeing her touch, driven away. Kara blinks in astonishment and gratitude. Her mother has protected her.

Then the terrible truth crashes in from a part of her mind that cannot be deceived by dreams.

"But you're dead," she says before she can stop herself.

The sadness in her mother's face breaks her heart. The serpents return, but not for Kara. They coil around her mother's arms and legs, drape over her shoulders, and begin to pull her deeper into the trees.

"No!" Kara shouts. "Stop!"

Her mother hangs her head, hair obscuring her features, as the snakes pull her into the black nothing, and in a moment, she is gone. Kara hurls herself into the dark crush of branches that tear and scratch and jab her, lunging for her mother, but her hands close only on pine branches and shadows.

With a cry of anguish, she wakes . . .

Kara sat up, and for a moment, wasn't sure if she had really called out in her sleep. The wan light of Sunday morning came through the window, carried on a warm breeze, but though she listened for his footfalls, her father did not come to check on her. She must have cried out only in the dream.

With a deep breath, she let go of much of the fear that lingered after the nightmare. It dissipated with each passing moment. But the melancholy did not depart so quickly. Parts of the dream were already fading in her mind, but she knew it would be a long time before she forgot the worst of it. Not the snakes, though those were nightmarish. What Kara would not be able to scour from her mind was the look on her dream-mother's face when she told her that she was dead.

It had felt like a betrayal. The dream—the illusion—could have been sweet. Her mother had come to protect her, to hold Kara, to guide her, and Kara had dismissed her.

It was only a dream, she told herself now. But somehow that reassurance wasn't enough to relieve her of the strange guilt that she felt. If she had not spoken, if she had not broken the illusion, the darkness would never have claimed her mom. As foolish as it was—Kara knew dreams could not be controlled—the guilt remained.

After the events at the Toro Nagashi Festival the night before, she was exhausted. Her bedside clock revealed the time to be just before eight a.m. She could sneak in a couple more hours of sleep and she knew her father would not wake her. But Kara stretched and sat up, forcing herself to leave the comfort of her bed. Better to be awake now. If she went back to sleep right away, she might return to the same dream. It happened sometimes. This morning, she could not bear the thought.

As she'd fallen asleep the night before she had struggled with the temptation to tell her father everything, to explain what she and her friends believed was really going on. She had played out various scenarios in her mind, imagining that he would go with her to Mr. Yamato—they could bring all of the others, even Mai, in with them—and the principal would listen. She believed that part, at least, was true. The last time she'd been in Mr. Yamato's office, it had been clear that he already half-believed that something unnatural was going on at Monju-no-Chie school.

But that was where her imaginary scenario fell apart. She simply could not escape the feeling that her father, always a practical man, would think she had lost her marbles. Even when she woke up this morning, that version of events seemed so much more likely to her. He would think that fear or stress had made her snap, or that she was having some kind of break-down, or he would think she was a liar, and that was the worst scenario of all.

Things had been tense, and Kara had felt the distance growing between them. It scared her to even consider doing something that might push him further away.

She pulled on a pair of shorts and padded quietly to her door, not wanting to wake him. But when she stepped into the hallway, she paused, brows knitting, as she heard voices in the living room. Her father, yes, but he wasn't alone.

"I feel like I should be doing something," a woman's voice said.

Kara blinked. Miss Aritomo? She glanced back into her room to confirm the time. Still five minutes before eight o'clock on a Sunday morning. What the hell was the woman doing here so early in the morning?

She took a sharp breath. Had her art teacher spent the night? Had Miss Aritomo come over after Kara had gone to bed? She couldn't believe her father would do such a thing. He'd be horrified by how it might look, both to his daughter and to the school administration.

Still, Kara couldn't rule it out. Otherwise, when had Miss Aritomo arrived? Seven a.m.? Six? She couldn't imagine that, but she wouldn't let herself imagine the alternative, either. Her father was an adult, but the idea of him sleeping with any woman both disturbed and disappointed her.

"Yasu had such enthusiasm and he was so kind," Miss Aritomo said, her voice cracking. "I can't . . . even if I were to choose someone else to take his role in the play, I don't know if I could continue. I don't know if I should. Three of my students, Rob. My Noh club kids."

Kara held her breath. Miss Aritomo sounded so torn up inside that she couldn't help feeling badly. She had never given any consideration to how all of this might affect Miss Aritomo, the grief it would bring her. Could Kara really blame her for seeking some solace in her father's company?

"Yuuka," her father said, his voice soft and kind. "Look at me. You don't know what happened to those other two. It's completely possible that they really did run away together."

A few seconds passed in silence before Miss Aritomo spoke. "You don't believe that."

"No, I don't," her father admitted. "But that doesn't change anything. It's possible."

Kara walked into the living room. "Good morning."

The two of them looked up, her father in a T-shirt and pajama pants—much too comfortable dressed that way in front of this woman, his colleague—and Miss Aritomo looking tired in a pair of pants and a baggy cotton sweater. She usually looked immaculate, but this morning her hair was wild and unkempt as though she'd just rolled out of bed. And she was barefoot.

Kara checked the floor near the front door, but if Miss Aritomo had taken her shoes off upon entering, she'd tucked them away somewhere. *Yeah, like under Dad's bed.*

The thought put ice in her veins. No. He wouldn't do that. Not after the argument they had already had.

But a teapot sat on the table and it looked to have been

there for some time. Their teacups were empty. Kara's father sat up straighter, a hundred thoughts flashing behind his eyes, like he was trying to find a way to explain the cozy scenario.

"Good morning, Kara," Miss Aritomo said.

Realizing he'd not responded, Kara's father smiled sadly, apologetically. "Good morning, honey."

"Bonsai," she corrected. "It's what some of the kids call me at school. You know this. I've told you."

"Why would I call you that?" her father asked, frowning.

Miss Aritomo shifted awkwardly in her seat but continued to smile.

"It's what I am," Kara told him. She pulled out a chair and sat with them, reaching out for the teapot. A small amount of tea sloshed inside.

"Would you like me to make some more?" Miss Aritomo asked politely, beginning to rise.

"No!" Kara snapped.

Her father and her teacher stared at her. Miss Aritomo had actually flinched. Kara didn't care. This was her house, and her father's house, not the house of this woman. Wasn't she Japanese? Didn't she give a damn about propriety? Who the hell did she think she was, wanting to make tea in a place she didn't belong?

"Kara—" her father began.

She sighed. "So last night, you said you thought school would be closed for a while. Any idea how long?"

Her father hesitated, as though he wanted to go back and address what had just happened, but then he let it go. "At least three days. A lot depends on what the police are able to find out about this boy Yasu."

"About his murder, you mean?" Kara asked.

That broke Miss Aritomo's composure and her sadness returned. She lowered her head and wiped at one eye. Kara's father reached out and covered her hand with his own, and that was enough.

Kara stood up. She knew she was being a bitch, but couldn't bring herself to care. Rob Harper was her father. He should have been comforting his daughter, not this woman they'd known for only six months. Kara had been there, on the beach, helping to search for Yasu. Where was *her* comforting hand?

"I guess the police will be working overtime now, huh?" Kara said as she rose from the table and turned to go back to her room. "After what happened in April, maybe they'll need to do their jobs. With all the people who were at the festival, I don't think anyone's going to believe that 'bear attack' story again, do you?"

"What do you mean by that?" her father called after her. "Kara?"

She went into her room, closed the door, and crawled into her bed, hoping that she could fall back to sleep. Bad dreams be damned.

Shortly after one p.m., Kara walked up the street toward Monju-no-Chie school and under the archway that led onto the grounds. She had slept for several hours and woken to find the house empty. A note from her father on the kitchen table explained that the teachers were going to be at school all day, phoning parents and answering questions from the boarding students.

Her cell phone had been off while she slept, but she found two voice messages and half a dozen texts from her friends. Apparently grief counselors were coming the next day, Monday, but for this afternoon the teachers and principal would be available in their classrooms for any students who wanted to talk to them about Yasu's death or the school closure. Sakura's text messages were amusing in their fury—according to her, all outstanding assignments would be due on the first day that classes resumed. That meant Kara had to go over to the school to pick up some of her books.

Miho had left her a voice message telling her that Miss Aritomo had scheduled a special meeting of the Noh club and volunteers for 2:30 p.m., and suggested they all meet at her room in advance to discuss their next step.

Kara followed a stone path at first, then diverted from the path onto the grass. Instead of going up to the front steps of the school, where the doors were open and a uniformed security guard—a startling new addition to the campus—stood just inside, she stayed to the right of the building. Despite the sunshine and the August heat, she shivered at the thought that this was the same patch of grass—between school and parking lot—where the Hannya had come after Miho.

Picking up her pace, she crossed the field that separated the school from the dorm. On an ordinary Sunday, the field would have been full of students hanging out, studying in the sun, or playing baseball, but today there were only a handful.

One or two were alone, listening to music on their head-phones while they studied or read, but the rest were in small, anxious groups, like people gathered outside a funeral home, waiting to attend a wake.

At the door, she had to show her identification to a second security guard who had been posted at the dormitory entrance. The man seemed dubious, narrowing his gaze as he studied her and then her ID. *Yes, I'm white and American!* she wanted to shout, but managed to fight the temptation. Everyone connected to the school would be tense and frightened today, and these new security guys were no exception.

Still, the seconds ticked by. He didn't ask any questions, almost as if she weren't standing there. Just when Kara had started to think she ought to have been wearing her school uniform instead of blue jeans and a tank top, the guard handed her ID back and asked her to sign in.

Kara signed, then hurried up the stairs. She needed to see Hachiro. One of the voice messages on her cell had been from him. But Sakura and Miho were waiting for her, so she wanted to stop by their room first before they could hook up with the boys.

Several doors were open, as if to make some connection with the world outside of those rooms, but the girls inside were as quiet as they would have been studying in a library, glancing quickly at Kara as she passed in the corridor and then looking away. The building was so quiet, in fact, that the slap of her brown leather sandals on the floor made her cringe.

Miho and Sakura's door was closed. Kara gave a short,

quick knock, wanting to be out of the hall, away from the grim climate of the dorm.

"Who is it?" Miho asked from inside.

"Kara."

The lock clicked and the door swung open, revealing Miho just within. As Kara entered, she blinked in surprise, staring at the two girls who stood by the windows. Of course she had expected Sakura—she lived there, after all—but of all the guests Kara might have expected Miho and Sakura to be entertaining, Mai wouldn't even have been on the list.

"What's she doing here?" Kara blurted, so stunned she couldn't stop herself.

Sakura smiled, a bit of mischief in her eyes, and turned away from Mai, dropping down onto her bed. Overnight, she'd dyed a strip of her hair a yellow so bright that it looked like a bird's feather hanging over her face. She wore a shirt with ruffles down the middle, like it ought to go with a tuxedo, and it somehow made her chest look much bigger than it actually was. Heavy eyeliner and a black, pleated skirt—dangerously short—completed the transformation. Whatever rebellion Sakura nurtured in her heart, she had obviously decided to let it all out. Kara thought maybe this was her way of hiding from her fear. If it worked, good for her.

"She wants to help," Sakura said.

"It only makes sense," Miho added as she closed the door behind Kara, shutting the four girls in the room together. "Other than Hachiro and Ren, Mai's the only other person who knows what's really going on. Plus, Wakana is her roommate, and Daisuke is her friend. Do you really want to turn her away?"

Kara stared at Miho, who had also made a sort of transition. If Sakura found comfort in rebellion—her own little bit of chaos—Miho sought solace in order. She'd pulled her hair back into a tight ponytail, applied just a touch of makeup under her glasses, and put on pants so neat and crisp they looked new, paired with a white, ribbed top with navy blue piping that matched the color of her pants. The little gold chain around her neck only added to the impression that she had dressed for a job interview.

"What the hell?" Kara whispered in English.

She shook her head and looked at Mai. Weird as it was, the one girl in the room she couldn't stand was the only one who didn't seem to be completely freaking out. Mai looked the way she always did, uptight and arrogant, though now— as had been the case lately—with the weight of sadness in her eyes.

"You really want to help?" Kara asked.

Mai crossed her arms. "I want answers. I want to know what happened to my friends. Of course I want to help."

The corners of her mouth were pinched as if in anger, but her eyes told a different story, and Kara couldn't deny the real pain she saw there. Mai was sincere.

Kara nodded. "Fine. We needed a sixth person anyway."

"That was easier than I expected," Sakura said.

Kara glanced at Miho, then looked down at her. "If we're going to try to watch over the rest of the kids working on the Noh play, we'll have to split up. But no way is anyone going to be alone at anytime. With Mai, there are six of us; that means three teams of two."

"And how do we decide who goes with whom?" Mai asked.

"You don't," Kara said. "We do. I'm with Hachiro. Miho and Ren. You'll be with Sakura."

Sakura protested loudly. "I don't want her with me. Let her go with Hachiro. You don't necessarily have to be with your boyfriend, right? I mean, if you guys are kissing or whatever, you're not going to be able to pay much attention to the people you're supposed to be looking after."

Mai stared at Sakura. "To hell with you. I came to help." She started toward the door.

Kara held up a hand to stop her. "If you want to help, then help. Don't be a diva. You didn't really expect to show up here and have us all like you, did you? Of course not. Get over it."

Then she turned to Sakura. "You're with Mai for two reasons. First, the Hannya might be going after the kids in the Noh club for now. Maybe they disrespected it somehow, or maybe it just preys on them because they were the ones who summoned it. But you and me and Miho—we're the ones with the curse on us. If the curse has anything to do with the Hannya being here, then we're targets, too. Maybe the Noh club, the actors and stuff, they're just the appetizers. If that's true, then the three of us shouldn't be together. We partner up with someone who isn't cursed."

Mai stared at her, eyes wide. "You admit you're cursed? That this whole thing is happening because of you?"

Sakura got up off the bed, hands clenched into fists. "Don't even say that again. Yes, we have a curse on us, and maybe that's what brought the Hannya here. But it all started with your friend Ume murdering my sister. The less you remind me

162

of that, the less often I'll have to struggle with the urge to hurt you."

"That's the other reason I want you with Mai," Kara said, keeping her gaze fixed on Mai. "If she does anything that could put us in more danger, you're the only one who won't hesitate to beat the crap out of her."

Mai lifted her chin. "It might not be as easy as you imagine."

Sakura grinned, shrugging. "Hopefully we'll never know. Friends aren't supposed to fight."

"We're not friends," Mai quickly corrected.

"No," Miho agreed. "But for now, we'll have to be."

Kara nodded. "All right. Let's go get the boys. We don't want to be late for Aritomo-sensei's meeting."

11
卍

I am still committed to bringing Noh theater to life at Monju-no-Chie school," Miss Aritomo said, standing at the head of the classroom. "But I am certain that you will all understand why, for now, it is best to suspend any further preparations or rehearsals for *Dojoji*."

Kara shifted awkwardly in her seat. Several times while she was speaking, Miss Aritomo had focused on her, as though speaking directly to her. Kara wished she wouldn't do that. All morning she had been trying to erase from her mind the image of the woman sitting at the breakfast table with her father, hair unkempt, sipping tea, as though she belonged there. As though she'd woken up there.

You're not family, Kara thought now, trying to communicate the message through her gaze. Yet when Miss Aritomo did glance at her again, Kara looked away.

Muttered whispers went through the room. Normally the

Noh club would have been far more orderly and respectful, but the situation unnerved it. With members of the club as well as volunteers present, the room buzzed with voices and bulged with too many warm bodies. People stood in the back and along the side walls.

A girl at the front raised her hand. "How long before rehearsals begin again?"

Everyone had wanted to ask the same thing. Miss Aritomo smiled politely as always, and inclined her head.

"All preparations are canceled until further notice," the teacher said. "This is a time of great sadness for all of us, and of questions and cautions. We should all be reflecting upon the loss of our friend, and yet remain aware of our surroundings. Whoever killed Yasu did so on Ama-no-Hashidate, far from school. There is no reason to believe a threat exists here, but this is a reminder to us all that we must take care of ourselves and one another."

Silence fell upon the room. In the seat next to Kara, Miho fidgeted. Sakura cleared her throat a little, glancing around expectantly. Ren hadn't come in—he was upstairs with Hachiro and Mai—but if he'd been there, Kara imagined that Miss Aritomo's tone would have erased even his ever-present smile.

"Are you saying we're in danger?" one guy at the front of the room asked.

Miss Aritomo cocked her head, hesitant, as though they'd caught her saying something she hadn't meant to.

"No," she said, the lie sounding hollow. "There is no reason to think that. As I said, the attack on Yasu took place during the festival, nowhere near the school. The police are investigating, of course, but no one has suggested—"

A girl from Hachiro's homeroom raised her hand, but did not wait to be called on.

"Excuse me, Aritomo-sensei," she said, "but what about Daisuke and Wakana? I know the police say they ran away to be together, but what if they didn't? They were also in Noh club. I'm . . . I'm frightened that something might have happened to them, too. Doesn't it seem a huge coincidence that these things are happening only to students in the Noh club?"

When Miss Aritomo smiled now, her expression seemed brittle and her face had gone pale.

"I understand, Chiyoko, but it really is a coincidence. As much as we may worry about our missing friends, and grieve for Yasu—and Mr. Yamato has suspended school for these few days so that we can properly grieve—no one has suggested any connection among these cases."

Her attempts at reassuring the class were having the opposite effect, Kara thought. Miss Aritomo spoke with no conviction at all, and it was obvious that she feared the very same things, but refused to speak about them. A silence spread among the students as they recognized her fear, and Kara could see in the art teacher's eyes that she knew they had seen through her.

"For my part," she said, forging ahead, "I still look forward to working with all of you to bring *Dojoji* to life in the grand Noh tradition. To honor Yasu, and to reflect, we will simply cease work for a time, and when we resume our work, we will dedicate our efforts in his honor as well."

Kara stared at her, fascination overcoming any lingering awkwardness from the morning. Miss Aritomo had been shattered by Yasu's murder and by her fears about what might have become of her other missing students. If anything, she was more afraid than the club members about what might come next. Kara didn't think that Miss Aritomo had any inkling about what was really going on—that there was a hideous reality to her dream of bringing *Dojoji* to life—but the events of the past week obviously weighed horribly upon her.

When she dismissed the students, Miss Aritomo glanced over, but Kara pretended not to notice, standing and shuffling out of the room with Sakura and Miho. Whatever her father's girlfriend—for that's what she was now, wasn't she?—wanted to say to her, it could wait.

"What do you think?" Miho whispered to Kara and Sakura as they moved with the other students toward the stairs.

"I think she's falling apart," Sakura muttered.

They started up the stairs. Hachiro, Ren, and Mai would be waiting for them outside the front door.

"That's not what I meant," Miho said, glancing around to make sure no one was listening. "I mean, if the production is canceled, do you think it will stop now? Do we still need to follow through with the plan?"

Kara frowned. "You think it's just going to go away?"

"Well, if there isn't going to be a play—"

A ripple of unease went through Kara. She moved nearer to Miho, whispered in her ear, knowing her tone was harsh but not at all sorry.

"Have you already forgotten that thing that chased you in

167

the dark? Or the glimpse we got of Yasu's body in the woods? Hannya or not, whatever it is, it's on the hunt now. As long as it has prey, it isn't going anywhere."

Had it not been for Ren's presence by her side, Miho would never have stayed out after dark. Even with Ren there for company, she glanced nervously at the darker shadows they passed, wary for any sign of the Hannya, or even the sense that they were being followed.

For her part, the girl, Chiyoko, seemed to have no sixth sense at all when it came to being pursued. Miho and Ren had followed her from the dorm, across the grounds of the school—keeping a reasonable distance—and down the street past Kara's house and the train station, to arrive at a tiny sweet shop called Cherry Blossoms. The aromas of the candy coming through the door made Miho hungry, but she and Ren remained outside, across the road, while Chiyoko and a female friend they didn't recognize browsed inside the sweet shop.

"You do know this is hopeless, right?" Ren said, his voice low.

Miho flinched and looked at him, wondering for a moment if he meant the task at hand or the crush she'd been nurturing for him. She assumed the former, only because in the past couple of days, the awkwardness between them had begun to dissipate. In fact, now that she'd made a fool of herself by basically asking him out, only to learn that he didn't like girls, their friendship had grown much stronger. They had originally gotten to know each other because both were friends of Sakura, but now Miho and Ren had forged their own bond, thanks to her embarrassment and his kindness.

"You think we're wasting our time?" she asked.

They stood in the shadows under a tree, across the street from Cherry Blossoms. Chiyoko and her friend had been in there awhile.

Ren shrugged, still staring at the shop. Little slices of moonlight cut through the branches of the tree and made his bronze hair gleam. Miho forced herself not to think about it; he was a friend, and a friend he would stay.

"There aren't enough of us," Ren replied. He glanced at her, and she could see the worry in his eyes. "Six of us to watch out for dozens of other students? It isn't enough. We are very lucky tonight, but what about tomorrow?"

Miho took a deep breath and nodded. What could she say? They had all known the limitations of their plan from the beginning. Now that they had started to implement it, the hugeness of the task only confirmed what they had feared. Tonight, Sakura and Mai were in the lobby of the dormitory, watching out for any Noh club students who might leave the building, though most of them were too anxious to go anywhere after dark. Yasu's death had thrown a grim shroud over all of them.

Kara and Hachiro were over at the school building. A handful of Noh club kids had gone there to pack up materials they'd already completed for the stage and background. Along with the costumes, some finished and others works-in-progress, they would be carefully stored until work on the production resumed. That meant that Kara and Hachiro could watch over four of the Hannya's potential targets at one time, even as nearly all of the others were inside their dorms for the night.

Those who lived at home had departed in the afternoon, as soon as Miss Aritomo had finished briefing them. But several of the boarding students had gone out to shop or eat or on other Sunday errands, and Miho and Ren had been left with choosing who they would follow. Chiyoko had been cast to portray the Hannya itself in *Dojoji,* and so when she and her friend had left the dorm, the decision had been instant. No matter that it might leave others unwatched and therefore more vulnerable—they could only be in one place at a time.

"We had to choose," she said to Ren.

"That's my point," he replied. "What if we chose wrong? Then this is all for nothing. We can't possibly watch them all. This is wrong. We've got to tell people now, before it's too late."

Miho took a deep breath. She knew he was right. "When we get back to the dorm tonight, we'll talk to the others. Kara may argue—mainly because she doesn't want to embarrass her father—but I agree with you."

Ren gave a short nod, fixing a kind of contract between them, but then he returned his attention to the sweet shop. Chiyoko really did seem to have been in the shop a long time. Several more seconds ticked by before he took a step out from under the tree.

"Do you think we should go in?" he asked.

Just then the door of the shop clicked open and Chiyoko and her friend emerged, as though summoned by the question.

Ren retreated to Miho's side and the two faced each other, smiling and muttering bits of nothing in low voices, pretending not to notice Chiyoko at all. Miho felt silly, and not at all convincing in this ruse. Even if Ren had been her boyfriend she would not have flirted so openly and completely as she now pretended to. But Chiyoko and her friend chatted happily, thrusting their hands into a shared bag of some sort of sugary candy, and walked on by, in the general direction of the school.

"All set?" Ren asked.

Miho smiled, blushing a bit. "Feeling very silly, but yes. Let's go."

They turned, hand in hand, and followed Chiyoko and her friend. The girls meandered a bit, but as they crossed the street and passed in front of a small shoe store, Miho realized their trajectory would not lead them to the school at all. Instead, the two girls went up a small staircase into the train station.

"What now?" Ren muttered.

"Shush," Miho said, squeezing his hand.

They waited a few seconds before they followed, walking into the station as though it truly was their destination. Miho didn't understand. Chiyoko should have been scared. Nearly everyone she had spoken to had seemed at least unnerved by Yasu's death, and wanted to be cautious. But perhaps to Chiyoko, caution just meant not being out in the dark alone.

Her mind raced. Chiyoko had to be going into Miyazu City. Maybe she and her friend were meeting boys from a different school, or had some special shop to visit. Perhaps her friend didn't live in the dorm and they were going to her house for the night. That made more sense than anything, considering it was a Sunday night. They had no school tomorrow, but the rest of Miyazu City hadn't changed its schedule. Most of the shops would be closed by now, or closing soon. The city slowed down on Sunday night—there just wasn't a lot to do.

Eight other people stood on the platform, waiting for the train. Miho and Ren held back, lingering near the entrance to the platform. They could see Chiyoko fine from where they stood. Nothing could possibly happen to her there, with other train riders around. Yet something troubled Miho, making her pulse quicken. The small hairs on the back of her neck bristled and she peered around her at every narrow corner and closed-off exit. The lights on the platform were dim and flickering, and only served to make the dark places darker. Something didn't feel right.

"We should go. It would be too obvious if we followed them onto the train. They would want to know why we were stalking them. And since we don't have any idea where they're going . . . we really should just go back," Ren said, and backed up a step, looking to her to follow.

Miho grabbed his wrist. "Wait until the train comes."

"Why—"

"Please, let's just wait." She glanced around again, nudging Ren into the dome of light thrown by a wanly gleaming bulb above. Beyond the edges of that circle of light, the dark seemed to insinuate itself, moving nearer, closing in around her like the inexorable creep of the tide coming in.

The shriek of the train's brakes, so much like a scream, made her flinch. Her heart pounded. Somehow she hadn't heard the train coming.

"Are you all right?" Ren asked, squeezing her hand.

She smiled to give him a reassurance she did not feel. "Yes. I'm sorry. The tension is terrible, that's all."

As they watched, the people waiting on the platform all boarded the train, including Chiyoko and her friend. For just an instant before she vanished into the train's interior, Chiyoko glanced back and caught Miho's eyes. A flicker of recognition sparked there, and curiosity.

Chiyoko gave a little wave.

Miho waved back.

Then the train doors closed with an irritating *pinging* noise, and started to pull out of the station, airflow gusting around it. She and Ren waited until the train had departed, and then Miho felt him exhale beside her.

"That's all we can do tonight, I guess."

When Miho spoke, it came as a surprise to her. She hadn't even been aware of intending to do so until she heard her own voice.

"Ren," she said.

Something in her tone alarmed him and he turned, stepping in close, holding her shoulders and studying her face. "What's wrong?"

Miho could not reply. She stared past him, at the broad, open space where the train had just passed. Down on the tracks, something stirred, perhaps nothing more than discarded newspapers eddying on the breeze. Yet the sound whispered up to her, insinuating itself in her mind, and it seemed so much like a hiss.

With the train gone, and the station now empty, the sense

of presence ought to have departed as well. But it hadn't. Miho could feel something else there with them, and just as this thought began to form into a coherent belief, and her fear started to crystallize, she saw the shadows bunch and gather in the space between platforms, down on the tracks.

"Miho!" Ren said, his voice urgent. He snapped his fingers in front of her eyes, and then she knew she had been mesmerized, for she could not turn away.

Somewhere far off, she heard a church bell toll heavily, as though a funeral procession had passed by.

Then Miho saw her, on the other side of the tracks: a female figure in the shadows. She strode forward, picking up speed, nearly at a run, and when she reached the space between the platforms she stepped right onto the shadows and walked across as though no gap existed.

A tear ran down Miho's cheek.

Ren twisted and swore under his breath when he saw the dark figure gliding toward them. He slammed Miho in the chest with his open palm and shoved her away.

"Run!" he told her.

She started to. Wanted to. But after four steps, she could only stop and watch as Ren tried to play the hero. He stood in the path of that beautiful, ethereal creature, and the Hannya *changed*. She opened her mouth in a hiss that unhinged her jaws, spraying venom from glistening fangs. Horns pushed up through the flesh and bone of her forehead and she became, in an instant, the monstrous countenance that the Noh mask could only hint at.

Miho screamed for Ren.

The Hannya picked him up and hurled him into the coalescing shadows. He slammed against the platform and rolled off, onto the tracks below. Miho heard him grunt, and then silence.

The darkness came alive around her. She stared at the place where the Hannya had been a moment before and thought she saw an afterimage of its dreadful eyes hanging in the night air, but it had vanished.

She took a step, ready to run, mouth open to scream, and then a loud hiss filled the darkness around her like static. No, she thought, as she looked down and saw the thick, serpentine coils around her legs, felt the weight of the creature twisting around her body, tugging her arms tight against her sides, suffocating her. Miho cried out, but then the breath left her as the shadow serpent tightened her grip.

Teeth pricked her neck, she felt pressure there, suction, and a deep ache. Then the darkness crashed in at the edges of her vision and oblivion swallowed her whole.

Even before Ren reached consciousness, he felt the pain. Knives jabbed his back and twisted in the ribs under his right arm, and an iron grip clamped around the rear of his skull. Moaning, he woke and drew quick, sharp breaths, panic setting in. How badly had he hurt himself?

He lay on his side, afraid to move, each breath making his injuries throb with fresh spikes of pain. Low voices muttered nearby and he blinked to focus his eyes. At first he had thought himself lost in darkness, but now he saw that he had fallen at an angle that gave him a view of the shadows beneath an overhanging part of the train platform.

I'm on the tracks.

In the back of his mind, he had known it, but now the reality struck him. He would have to move, and soon. A sorrowful sort of fear clutched at him. If his injuries were really bad, wouldn't he only hurt himself worse by moving?

Those voices.

"Hello? Is someone there?" he said, trying to call out but managing only a painful rasp. "Hello!"

The voices up on the platform seemed to pause a moment, but then they went on. Ren took a breath. It hurt, but he realized that some of the worst pain had retreated. Perhaps he had wrenched his back, even cracked some ribs, without actually breaking anything.

Gingerly, he reached his left hand up to probe at the back of his skull. His fingers came away damp and sticky with what could only be blood, and his hair felt matted. Ren squeezed his eyes closed, pulse racing, but forced himself to continue his investigation. As he pushed his fingers through his hair, he found the cut on his scalp, but only that. His head throbbed with pain from striking it against the ground or the metal rail, but he realized he probably didn't have anything worse than a concussion.

Okay, he thought.

"Hello!" he called again, starting to sit up. The pain that shot up his back made him suck air in through his teeth, but once he'd gotten into a sitting position it wasn't as bad.

Why hadn't the people on the platform heard him? Why hadn't they come over to see where his voice was coming from?

Ren froze. His left leg lay across one of the tracks and he could feel it begin to vibrate, thrumming with the tremor and weight of an oncoming train. Only then did he hear the low groan of the train approaching. The people on the platform hadn't heard him over the rising rumble, and he could no longer hear them.

He twisted around to get onto his knees, and now he could see the lights coming around the long curve toward the station. Pain seized him, lancing into his back, but a rush of adrenaline got him up onto his feet. Cursing, frantic, Ren crossed the tracks to the platform's edge.

Air blasted past him, pushed ahead of the incoming train. Ren cried out in fear as the train thundered into the station, its roar obliterating his voice. Seven or eight people were scattered on the platform. One little girl, holding her mother's hand, turned and spotted him, pointed and said something to her mother, but her words, too, were stolen by the guttural snarl of the train.

Brakes squealed, echoing off the walls of the station.

Ren raised his hands, pain shooting through him, nearly making him falter, but then boosted himself up onto the platform, rolling out of the way with seconds to spare. The train lumbered to a hissing stop beside him. He lay on his back, still racked with throbbing pain, and stared at the ceiling of the station.

Two men in business suits bent over to look down at him. One of them asked if he was all right, but the other went off on a tirade about how stupid he'd been. Didn't he know that he could have been killed?

Ren laughed at them for a few seconds, until the adrenaline began to subside and he felt the jolts of pain that the laughter cost him. The men shook their heads and boarded the train. Moments later, it began to move again, straining to roll along its tracks like a sled dog in its traces, picking up speed.

He lay there, catching his breath, heart pounding inside his chest, and as the fear and pain subsided, he remembered how he had gotten there in the first place.

"Miho! Oh, no."

Ren reached into his pocket and plucked out his cell phone. Its face had been cracked in the fall, but the crystal display still showed a signal. Praying, he called Kara.

Kara ended the call with Ren and turned to stare at Hachiro, clutching her phone in her hand. Her eyes welled up but she bit her lip, not allowing the tears to fall. She didn't have time to cry.

"What is it?" Hachiro said, his gaze urgent. "Talk to me, Kara. What did Ren say?"

They stood in the genkan, surrounded by cubbyholes filled with blue and pink slippers. The lights in the genkan were bright, but they only made the night outside the glass doors seem even darker. Kara reached up with her free hand and pushed her hair away from her face, fingers fluttering.

"You're trembling," Hachiro said.

Kara steadied herself and reached out to grip his shoulder,

taking strength from him. "The Hannya came after Ren and Miho. It threw him onto the train tracks. He's hurt, but not badly. But Miho . . ."

She faltered, her throat closing up, and then she couldn't stop herself. Tears began to flow and she shook all over. Hachiro pulled her into his arms and held her tightly. For several seconds they stood like that, and then Kara became angry at her own indulgence. She pulled away, wiping at her tears and thrusting her phone into her pocket.

"Ren thinks he was unconscious for about twenty minutes. When he came around, Miho was gone. The Hannya took her."

Hachiro nodded. "Then we'll find her. We *will* find her."

Kara shook her head. "Not alone we won't. It's time to tell someone. We should've done this before. I've been so stupid."

"You can't blame yourself," Hachiro said.

"Sure I can. But blame can wait."

She turned and strode deeper into the school, took a right and broke into a run. Hachiro kept pace with her and when they reached the door to the basement stairs, Kara shoved it open and then they were pounding down the steps. They knew that three of the Noh club students they'd been keeping track of were still in the art room, storing away the masks and set pieces that had already been created for the play. Miss Aritomo would wait until they were all gone before locking up after them.

Kara and Hachiro rushed along the basement corridor to the art room, slowing as they approached the door. Just outside, they stopped. Kara caught her breath and glanced at

Hachiro, afraid of what she was about to do, afraid that Miss Aritomo wouldn't believe her, that her father would be humiliated, and worst of all, that it wouldn't help Miho even if they did believe her.

Please, God, let her be all right.

She stepped into the art room with Hachiro right behind her. The three students were cleaning up after themselves, one boy sweeping, another moving chairs, and a girl sitting on a table. They looked up, expressions curious.

"Hi. Sorry. Isn't Aritomo-sensei here?" Kara asked.

"She's in her homeroom," replied the sweeping boy. "She had work to do."

Kara nodded and turned away, not giving them another thought. Hachiro led the way, but they found the doors to Miss Aritomo's homeroom closed. Like those upstairs, they were the sliding doors so common in Japan. Kara knocked on the frame.

"Aritomo-sensei?" she ventured. "It's me, Kara."

They waited a few seconds. She grimaced and looked at Hachiro. He nodded toward the door.

"Try again," he suggested.

But as Kara raised her fist to knock, she paused, frowning. From within the classroom she'd heard a sound, low and insinuating and hideously familiar. Now it came once more and there could be no doubt. This was no breeze, no voice, no rustle of pages being turned. The hiss brought her back to that night in the dark, when the Hannya had pursued Miho, and she knew that it was there right now, on the other side of the thin door.

It had come for Miss Aritomo.

Ice flooded her veins. She wanted to scream, to run, but instead she reached out a shaking hand for the door. Hachiro snatched her wrist, stopping her, and she turned to see her own fear reflected back from his eyes.

Firmly, she pulled her hand away. As quietly as possible, she reached for the door and slid it open just a crack. Kara pressed her right eye to the opening. At first she saw only the light above Miss Aritomo's desk—the overhead lights were off. A dull glow of moonlight shone in the small box windows near the ceiling.

Then she saw a pale arm outstretched on the floor, beyond the reach of the desk lamp. The moment she noticed it, the rest of the dark silhouette on the floor came into sharp focus, and she saw the gentle, pretty features of Miss Aritomo. The teacher did not move, but in the gloom Kara could not see any sign of blood or injury, or even if she still drew breath.

Aritomo-sensei. The name was on her lips, but before Kara could speak, the hiss came again, now from the shadows at the back of the room. Kara had seen the masks hanging on the wall there so many times that she had barely noticed their baleful expressions back in the shadows.

Then one of them moved, and she realized that one was not a mask at all. Kara's throat went dry. Rigid with terror, she could only watch as the Hannya emerged from the shadows and knelt beside Miss Aritomo. It reached slender, clawed hands toward the petite, helpless woman, and Kara wanted to scream but could not find the courage. Hachiro touched her arm but she barely recognized the contact.

The Hannya diminished even as she watched. In the space between eyeblinks, the horned face of the demon became that of a seductive woman, and the woman began to lie beside Miss Aritomo, only to alter her form further. Demon had become temptress, and now woman became serpent, a thing of red and green so dark as to appear almost black, with tiny horns that seemed more dragon than snake.

As it slithered onto Miss Aritomo's body in a lithe, intimate coil, it shrank even further. The serpent's head prodded at the sleeping teacher's lips and Miss Aritomo's mouth opened, her head falling back.

The demon slid past her lips and down her throat, vanishing inside her.

Kara could not move. Could not breathe.

Then Miss Aritomo opened her eyes.

Kara jumped back from the door, shaking her head at the impossible. She twisted to look at Hachiro, who only looked mystified. His view blocked by her body, he had seen none of it. He opened his mouth to speak and, eyes wide with terror, she shook her head more firmly, grabbed his wrist, and together they ran.

Her mind whirled as she tried to make sense of what she had seen. All she knew was that Miho needed her. And then she thought of her father—her dad—who had fallen in love with the woman Kara had seen inside that classroom.

A woman with a demon inside her.

12

卍

Kara and Hachiro ran along a path away from Monju-no-Chie school, passing beneath the arch that always seemed to welcome students and visitors. The moment they stepped into the street, Kara felt safer, but only when she had crossed to the other side did she slow to a walk, glancing back the way they'd come. The school sat up on its slope, a monolithic silhouette against the indigo night sky. Several lights burned within, but so few and so dim as to make the building seem ghostly. Haunted.

"Are you all right?" Hachiro asked, catching his breath. No matter how much baseball he played, their flight from the school had been a hellish sprint that left them both winded.

Kara nodded. She had told him, as they ran, what she had seen in Miss Aritomo's art room. His eyes were wide and anxious now, unnerved, and that frightened Kara more than anything. Hachiro always seemed bold and confident, ready for whatever came next. Tonight, he had lost that edge.

She thought she might be in love with him.

Now they alternated between a quick walk and a light jog. Kara pulled out her phone and called Sakura, who picked up in seconds.

"Where are you?" Sakura asked. "I just talked to Ren. He said he's outside your house, waiting for you."

Breathless and halting, searching for words to express what she had witnessed, Kara explained.

"Mai and I will come over," Sakura said.

"No," Kara snapped. "No. You just stay there. Watch out for the Hannya, or for Aritomo-sensei, or whatever. After I talk to my father, I'll call you, and we'll figure out what to do next."

Reluctantly, Sakura agreed, and Kara ended the call. As she pushed her phone back into her pocket, she noticed a look of dread and sorrow on Hachiro's face.

"What is it?" she asked.

He shot a glance back toward the school. "There were a few kids still in the school. With *her*. Noh club kids. What if . . . ?"

Hachiro let the question trail off, but he didn't need to finish it. Kara felt the blood drain from her face. She had never paused to consider the fate of the kids they had left back in the basement of the school with Miss Aritomo—with the Hannya. Fear and disgust had sent her and Hachiro running.

Guilt began to grip her, but she shook it off. "We're doing the right thing," she insisted. "What should we have done? Attacked the Hannya, just the two of us? We have to get help. That's the best way to help those kids, and anyone else the demon might prey on."

As they approached the house, a figure emerged from the shadows that separated Kara's home from her neighbor's. Ren stepped nearer, and the three of them met on the edge of a pool of light cast by a nearby streetlamp. In that ghastly glow, Ren looked awful. Blood stained the right shoulder of his shirt and dappled spots all over it. His right arm was scraped and he moved gingerly, as though protecting the ribs on that side.

"Oh my God," Kara whispered in English. She quickly switched back to Japanese. "Are you all right?"

Ren did not smile. "I will be, once we find Miho. I should've been paying more attention. By the time I realized we weren't alone . . ."

The words trailed off.

Hachiro stared at him grimly. "You cannot blame yourself. We were all trying to do our best to prevent anyone else getting hurt. No one is to blame except the Hannya."

Kara felt a terrible weight forming in her gut, like a ball of cold iron. "That's not true. We're to blame. Me and Sakura and Miho. The curse is on us, not on any of you, or the school. If not for us—"

Ren stood up straight, wincing with the movement. He stared at her. "Don't say that. We've been over this. Ume and the others who murdered Akane, they were the ones who started it. But even they are not responsible for the whims of demons."

"I should have told my father sooner," Kara said.

With a sigh, Ren nodded. "Probably. But it's too late for that. We only have now."

Kara let the truth of that sink in. *Now* was all anyone ever had. She glanced at the front door of the house she shared with her father—this neat, little Japanese dwelling that she had come to think of as home—and turned to the guys.

"Wait here," she said.

"Kara," Hachiro began warily.

"No," she replied, shaking her head. "This is going to be hard enough for him to hear. Just wait for me. I won't be long."

Though she felt their eyes on her back, she didn't turn again as she entered her house and closed the door behind her. A half-empty glass of water sat on the otherwise barren coffee table. The day had been hot and the wooden beams of the house ticked as they cooled. Otherwise, all was silent within, and for a moment she feared that her father had gone out.

"Dad?" she ventured, walking through the living room.

"In here." His voice came from his small study.

Relieved, Kara hurried into the room. Her father sat behind his desk, face illuminated by the glow of his computer screen. Only a dim lamp in the corner provided additional light. His brow was furrowed as he gazed at the screen, wrapped up in work, or perhaps e-mails from home. But when she said nothing, he looked up and seemed to wake from a trance. Lines of concern appeared on his forehead.

"What's wrong?" he asked, standing quickly.

It lent her a certain comfort to know he could read her that well, but when she tried to reply, she barely managed to make a sound when her lower lip began to quiver and she had to fight to keep her tears from returning.

"Kara, sweetie, what is it?" he asked, coming toward her, reaching out to cup her cheek in his wide hand.

"Miho," she managed. "She's gone missing, too. It . . . it took her."

His expression contorted with horror. "Miho? Oh, my God. What . . . I mean, how did you hear this?"

"Ren was there. He's pretty banged up, Dad. It could have killed him, like with Yasu. And it took Miho."

She felt his hand pull away from her face. He almost seemed to shrink back from her. Hurt and confused, she looked up to meet his gaze and saw deep concern there—concern for her.

"Kara, what do you mean when you say 'it' took Miho?"

His tone alone told her how difficult the conversation was going to be. She hadn't even begun to tell him the truth, and already he had decided that she'd gone a little crazy. But the Hannya had taken Miho, and if she was still alive—*please, God, let her still be alive*—Kara had no time to waste worrying about what her father would think.

"There are things I've been keeping from you," she admitted. "And I hope you'll forgive me for that. I just never thought you'd believe me, and—"

His eyes had narrowed. "Maybe you should start at the beginning."

Kara's mouth had gone dry. She swallowed hard, went over and leaned on the edge of his desk, and started to talk. She began with Akane's murder and the longer she spoke, the more pale he became. When he took his glasses off and massaged the bridge of his nose, she thought he might be angry with her.

"So all of the things that girl, Mai, told Yamato-sensei—" he began.

"Yes," Kara interrupted. "They're all true. Or mostly. We didn't do anything wrong, Dad. All we wanted was to stop the ketsuki, and now we have this . . ."

Her eyes welled up a little but again she fought back tears, and the emotion that tightened her throat.

"You really believe you're cursed, don't you?" he asked, somewhat amazed.

Kara blinked, anger flaring. "We *are* cursed. Do you think I'm making all of this up?"

That got him. Her father blew out a deep breath and ran his fingers through his hair. "I don't know what to think, honey. What I really don't understand is why you never came to me about this before now. If even part of this is true—"

"It's *all* true!"

He held up a hand to calm her, nodding. "Okay. Give me some time to process it, will you? And if it is true, I still don't get why you never came to me before. I asked you before and after that meeting with Yamato-sensei, and you lied right to me, Kara. We just don't do that. We promised, didn't we? No lies."

Frustrated, her jaw tight, she shook her head. "This is different."

"Different *how*? If your life was in danger—"

"Stop it!" Kara shouted, pulse racing, fists clenched. "Damn it, Dad! Please, can't this wait? Can't you hold off telling me how stupid I was until we find Miho? Until I know if she's even still alive?"

Her hands were shaking, her whole body quaking. In all her life, she didn't remember being so furious with her father. Why couldn't he just listen?

"Kara—"

"This is exactly why I never told you before!"

"All right!" he said, throwing his hands up. "I'm sorry. You're right. We can argue later. We need to call the police, and Yamato-sensei. If the kids in the Noh club are all in danger—I can't believe I'm going along with any of this—I'll need to call Aritomo-sensei and try to explain it to—"

"No!" Kara snapped.

Her father flinched at the vehemence of her reaction. "Kara, come on. I know you've got issues with her, but now's not the time. You said so yourself."

"It's not that," Kara said, glancing away. "It's something else."

"What?" he demanded.

Swallowing, she stared into his eyes and told him what she had seen in Miss Aritomo's room at the school. As she spoke, his nostrils flared and his face flushed a deep red. Before she had finished, he interrupted.

"That's enough," he said, his voice cold and quiet.

"Dad, I swear—"

"I said that's enough!" he roared, and slammed his fist against the wall. He glared at her. "What did I do to you, Kara? Is it the move? Just living here? Or is it really just this thing with Yuuka? How did we get to the point where you'd go this far?"

"Dad—"

"No. No, Kara. Grow the hell up! What a stunt! How far will you go to interfere with me getting on with my life? I know you need me now, but someday you'll be gone, and I'll be alone. You're so concerned these days with what your mother would have wanted, right? Well, is that what she would have wanted? Is it?"

The words echoed in the silence of the house. His chest rose and fell as he tried to calm himself. Kara wanted to scream back at him, but she realized now that nothing she said would do any good.

"You're making a mistake," she whispered.

"Don't tell me—" he began.

They were interrupted by a loud knock on the front door. Kara whipped around, afraid for a moment, and then she realized it must be Hachiro and Ren. They would have heard the shouting and been concerned for her.

Her father seemed to deflate. Eyes dimmed by disappointment, he turned from her and strode over to the door. Kara followed a few steps, words on the tip of her tongue, ready to tell Hachiro and Ren that she was fine, that she'd be out in a minute. But when her father opened the door, instead of the guys, Kara saw Miss Aritomo standing on the threshold.

Kara's eyes went wide and she drew in a sharp breath, on the verge of a scream. The memory of what she'd seen flashed in her mind, all too vividly. She tensed, ready to lunge for her father, to protect him.

But when she met Miss Aritomo's gaze, she saw no threat

in them. The teacher looked as she always did, pretty and petite and intelligent, yet also tired and sad. She nodded hello to Kara, then focused on Kara's father.

"Rob. I'm sorry to come without calling first—"

"Not at all," Rob Harper replied, glancing at Kara over his shoulder. "Your timing couldn't be better, in fact. Come in."

He stepped aside to allow her entrance, closing the door behind her. Then, as though to make a point, he took Miss Aritomo's hand and gave her a quick, soft kiss. Kara went rigid, hair on the back of her neck bristling, and yet that was the moment that confused her the most. Miss Aritomo blinked and pulled back slightly from him, glancing shyly at the ground, obviously uncomfortable with this show of affection in front of Kara.

Where is it? Kara thought. *Where's the Hannya? Where's the evil?*

Her gaze shifted past her father and Miss Aritomo, toward the door. What had happened to Hachiro and Ren? Surely she must have seen them outside? Had she done something to them? Or did she seem so normal—so ordinary—because the demon wasn't inside her now? Was it possible that Miss Aritomo didn't *know* the evil spirit had been using her as its host?

"Anything else to say, Kara?" her father asked, obviously daring her to repeat her accusations in front of his girlfriend.

She hesitated a moment, trying to think of some way to continue the conversation. But she could come up with nothing that wouldn't explode into a major argument. Either the

Hannya was there with them right now—inside Miss Aritomo—in which case Kara didn't think the woman had any idea, or it had left her body again. Either way, Kara had no idea how to proceed. She needed to talk to her friends. They had to find Miho.

Frustration and confusion overwhelmed her, and all she could do was shake her head and make for the door.

"Where do you think you're going?" her father asked, in English.

"Out," Kara snapped, in Japanese.

"This conversation isn't over!" he called after her.

She slammed the door on the final word, heart thumping in her chest, nervous energy making her want to jump or run or scream. She had to do something. This was all insane.

"Kara?" Hachiro said, stepping from the shadows beside the house, with Ren following close behind. "Are you all right?"

"You guys could've warned me," she said, brow knitted in consternation.

"We didn't have time," Ren said, still holding his right arm stiffly against his chest. "She came walking up the street and we hid so we could watch her. We thought about just attacking her, but she seemed so normal, and . . . what if you were wrong? What if you didn't see what you thought you saw?"

Kara stared at both of them. "I saw it."

Hachiro nodded. "Okay. But even so, what were we to do? Try to kill her? We watched through the window to make sure you weren't in danger."

"You're right, I know. It's just . . . my father wouldn't listen to me. He didn't . . . he didn't believe me," she said. "The Hannya's in there with my father, and I don't know what to do!"

In the dormitory foyer, Mai leaned against the wall with her arms crossed, staring at Sakura's back. The other girl stood in front of the door, staring outside at the moonlit field that separated the dorm from the school building. The silence between them crackled with their need to be doing something, anything, with barely controlled fear, and with anticipation. Any second, Sakura's phone would ring. Kara would call. They would learn what her father had said, and what they were to do next.

"Why do you keep staring out there?" Mai asked, hearing how snippy she sounded but not caring. "The school isn't going anywhere."

Sakura didn't bother to turn around. "If the Hannya's out there, I want to see it coming. And if Kara and the others come back without calling first, I want to see them, too."

The moonlight made the red streak in Sakura's hair a deep crimson that reminded Mai of blood. Sakura had put some kind of henna tattoos on her upper arms and they almost look carved into her skin. The sight was unnerving, and Mai wished Sakura would put something over the tank top she was wearing now. The weirder things became, the stranger Sakura behaved. She made Mai's skin crawl. But maybe that was just the girl's way of dealing with her sister's murder. Whatever. Mai didn't know, and really didn't want to.

"This is crazy," she said. "We need to go to Yamato-sensei. He'll call the police. He had no proof before, because Kara lied to him. But if you come with me now, and back up what I've told him, he'll have to believe us, just a little."

That got Sakura's attention: she turned and glared at Mai with open hostility, and Mai knew Sakura had understood the part of her argument that she had not said aloud. Mr. Yamato knew that Mai was among the group of girls Sakura had blamed for her sister's murder. If *she* said Mai was telling the truth, how could Mr. Yamato argue?

"Just wait until we hear from Kara," Sakura said.

Mai sighed. "Why? Why are we waiting? Just call her and tell her we're going over to see Yamato-sensei."

Sakura's upper lip curled in distaste. Any possibility that Mai might have one day become friends with her had evaporated, but Mai didn't care.

"I understand. You don't like me," she told Sakura. "I'm not going to cry about it. I've never liked you or any of your friends very much, either. Except Hachiro, and that's only because he's cute and can play baseball."

"This is you being persuasive?" Sakura sniffed.

Mai pushed away from the wall, throwing up her hands. "This is me wanting to do something before someone else dies! Or have you forgotten the Hannya took your roommate?"

Sakura strode over, shaking her head as though ready to argue, and then slapped Mai across the face so hard that she staggered back to the steps, stumbled, and sat down.

"You bitch!" Mai snarled, one hand clapped to her cheek.

Sakura ignored her, turning away as she pulled out her cell phone. Mai's cheek stung, but her pride had been hurt even worse. Still, all she cared about right now was Wakana and Daisuke, and Sakura was making the phone call. Nothing else mattered. If she hadn't been afraid to go out after dark alone, she would have gone to Mr. Yamato's by herself. But this was better. These girls knew something, at least, about what they were facing, and something was better than nothing.

"Kara, what's going on?" Sakura asked.

Mai wished she could hear Kara's side of the conversation. After a moment, Sakura went on.

"Listen, we've got to go to Yamato-sensei. It's the only choice now. You said before you thought he believed Mai a little bit—"

Mai raised her eyebrows. That was the first she'd heard of it.

"—and we need him to believe us now, and to call the police."

Sakura paused, and it was obvious that on the other end of the line Kara was arguing with her.

"No, stop. Quiet, Kara. Listen. Mai and I are going over there, and if we have any hope of him believing us, you three have to come as well. He has to see Ren. He has to hear it from all of us. Two of us, he might think it's some kind of prank. But not all five, and not if Ren is hurt and Miho is gone . . . I know, I know, but we can't do this alone! We need help! Just meet us there!"

Sakura snapped her phone shut and put it away. She took a deep breath and started for the door without waiting for Mai.

"What did she say?" Mai said, following her out the door. "What's going on? Why was she fighting with you?"

"Kara didn't want to leave her house because Aritomo-sensei is there. The Hannya is there with her father."

A chill ran up Mai's spine and all her anger vanished. "But she's going to meet us at Yamato-sensei's?"

"She'll be there."

Mai nodded once, turned, and headed across the field with Sakura matching her stride for stride.

Miho woke to the copper scent of blood and the awful, rotting stench of death. As she grew conscious of her surroundings, eyes flickering open in the dark, the smells overwhelmed her, filling her nostrils and her throat. Her stomach convulsed and she rolled to one side, a thin stream of vomit erupting from her mouth.

Panic and revulsion brought her fully awake. She forced herself to breathe through her mouth, the stink of the room too much to take. Disoriented, she looked around, trying to make sense of what she saw.

The low ceiling above her head had a peak in the middle, and there were boxes and two old traveling chests stacked to one side. In the gloom—slices of moonlight gleaming between shutters or boards that blocked two small windows—she could make out a metal rack hung with what appeared to be old Noh or Kabuki theatrical costumes. A bare dressmaker's dummy stood beside the costume rack like some headless, limbless spectator.

The smell. Where did the smell come from?

Miho sat up and her stomach convulsed again. Bile burned in the back of her throat, but this time she managed to suppress the urge to vomit. It wasn't just the smell, she realized. The nausea and disorientation were symptoms of something else. Flashes of the conflict on the train platform came back to her. Fear flooded through her as she remembered the Hannya, its intimate hiss, and what it had done to Ren.

Oh, Ren. She squeezed her eyes tightly closed, terrible sadness gnawing at her. *Please don't be dead.*

A fresh wave of nausea hit her gut and she thought again of the Hannya. One hand fluttered up to her neck and she gave a tiny yelp at the pain as she touched the bruised, punctured skin there. Some of the blood she smelled might be her own.

It had bitten her, and the bite had poisoned her or something. It had made her sleep as if she'd been drugged, and now the effects were starting to wear off. But the Hannya would be back.

Miho took a breath, still through her mouth, but now she could taste the stink of dead flesh on her tongue. Chills shuddered through her and she looked around, eyes at last beginning to adjust to the gloom.

In a dark corner to the right of the window she saw an antique dollhouse. In the black shadows behind it lay what was left of a human body. Torn and broken, bones showing, from what she could see in the dark it looked as though wild animals had gotten to it. Hungry animals. The darker stains on the wall and on the roof of the dollhouse must have been blood.

Miho began to shake. Her eyes swam with tears.

"No," she whispered. "No, please. I haven't done anything."

Lurching to her feet, she banged her head on the low ceiling and then staggered toward the boarded window. Her fingers found purchase but she could not tear the wood away.

Miho dropped to her knees, threw back her head, and began to scream for help. She cried and she beat her fists on the boards and screamed until her throat hurt. Minutes passed before she paused to breathe, and to think.

And then a voice, little more than a dry rasp, came from behind the costume rack.

"You shouldn't bother," said the voice. "No one will hear. I've been trying for days."

13
ࠀ

Mr. Yamato sat in a rigid wooden chair, his back straight. As he listened to Kara and Sakura tell the story from the beginning, with Mai reinforcing their tale by relating again what Ume had told her and Ren showing his injuries and detailing the attack at the train station, the principal's expression did not waver. So often stern, Kara thought his face must have settled comfortably into those grim lines over the years.

"And then we came here," Kara told him. "Please, Yamato-sensei. You must believe us. I'm afraid for Miho, and for my father. More people will die if we don't do something."

The principal took a deep breath, but still his expression did not change. He shifted his gaze from student to student, studying each of them as though searching for a weak link in the story. Kara could not blame him if he thought they were all liars or lunatics, but she did not think that was the case at all. If he had, wouldn't he have thrown them out of his house minutes after they'd begun their tale? Instead, he had listened to every word, asking only clarifications.

"Please, Yamato-sensei," Mai said.

The principal's eyes narrowed further as he focused on her. What had he expected when he had opened his door to find them there? Surely not this. He had invited them inside and they had removed their shoes and sat on mats and cushions on the floor of the living room. Mr. Yamato's wife had offered them tea, but he had seen the urgency in their faces and politely asked her to let him speak to his students alone. He had apologized to them for sitting in the chair, explaining that he had trouble with his back. And then he had asked them to begin, turning to Kara as though sensing that the others also wished for her to speak first.

Now the principal shifted his gaze to Kara again.

"You lied to me that day, in my office."

She flushed but did not avert her eyes. "Yes, sensei. I'm very sorry. At that point I still hoped Wakana and Daisuke really had run away together. And I was afraid if I told you that Mai was telling the truth, you wouldn't believe any of us."

Mr. Yamato nodded, glancing at Mai. "I see. And Mai told me only part of the truth, that day."

"It was the truth as I knew it, sensei," Mai said quickly. "As told to me by Ume."

The man's eyes darkened. "Ume, who may have been a murderer."

Mai dropped her gaze.

"Tell me now, girl," the principal commanded. "Were you

one of those with Ume on the night Akane Murakami was killed?"

Kara glanced at Hachiro, Ren, and Sakura. All of them were staring at Mai, waiting for the answer. Sakura's fists were clenched, but Kara couldn't tell if the look on her face showed fury or a fresh wave of grief over the loss of her older sister.

Mai lifted her chin. "No, sensei. I swear I was not with them. Hana and Chouku were, but I know that only because Ume told me."

"How convenient that they're dead," Sakura said bitterly. "You know who else was there."

"I'd only be guessing," Mai insisted.

"Enough!" Mr. Yamato said, slicing the air with his hand. He looked at Sakura, then turned back to Mai. "We will speak about this more tomorrow. First, we must contend with the story you have told me tonight."

"Do you believe us?" Ren asked.

Mr. Yamato took a deep breath. It didn't seem possible to Kara, but he actually sat up a bit straighter in his chair.

"As a younger man, I would have dismissed such stories without a moment's thought. My grandmother loved to tell us tales of gods and demons, of spirits wearing the faces of men, and especially of tricksters who could appear to be animals. Kitsune was her favorite. I remember so many of those stories. I never believed them, but I knew my grandmother did. My father used to say the woman was crazy, and though I loved her stories, I agreed.

"As I have grown older, I have thought of my grandmother

often. In my memories, she does not seem at all insane. In all other ways, she conducted her life normally—a sweet, doting woman who made fish soup better than any I've ever had, and always kept a bit of candy hidden for me in a drawer in her kitchen. The light of faith in her eyes was ordinary belief, not madness. Many old women still tell such stories as though they really happened. Who am I to say they did not?

"Even so, I would not believe you if not for the murders in April. Jiro and Chouku had their blood taken from their bodies. The police could not explain it. No one could explain it. They came up with their ridiculous stories, lies to tell the public, and I went along with them to protect our school. We could not afford to have people thinking the students were still in danger . . . and I truly thought the danger had passed. But I knew the police were mystified, and that made me wonder. And then Mai came to me with the tale of the ketsuki, and Kyuketsuki, and a curse.

"I tried to tell myself it was impossible. But every time I did, I remembered the spark of belief in my grandmother's eyes. And now here you are, telling me a Hannya has come to Monju-no-Chie school, and I remember the story my grandmother told me of a girl named Kiyohime and the monk Anchin."

Kara felt relief washing over her. Mr. Yamato believed her. He would help! But this was all taking too long. Where was Miss Aritomo now? With her father still? And where was Miho?

"Anchin is the name of the monk in *Dojoji*," Sakura said. "Yasu was supposed to play that part."

"But who was Kiyohime?" Hachiro asked, glancing at Kara. "Is that from the play, too?"

Mr. Yamato leaned forward, resting his elbows on his knees, and Kara could not help but lean in a bit herself. She saw the others doing the same. It had the feeling of a secret about to be shared, or a story told around the fireplace.

"The story has been told in many ways. The Noh play, *Dojoji*, is only one of them. It has been performed in Kabuki theater, written as folklore, and told in songs. But my grandmother told the story of Kiyohime as something true and real, as a warning to the young boy I was that I must never mislead a girl or take advantage of affection I did not feel in return."

Hachiro and Ren shifted uncomfortably, while Mai looked confused. Sakura glanced at Kara, seeming to share her impatience, but Kara wanted to hear the rest.

"Please go on, sensei," Kara said. "Anything you can tell us about the story might help."

"Anchin lived in a temple on the banks of the Hidaka river. Once a year he visited a small village far away—I don't remember the names now—and always stayed at the same inn during his travels. The innkeeper's young daughter, Kiyohime, fussed over Anchin and during each visit he would bring her small gifts. He thought of her as a child, and never imagined that her fondness for him would turn to love. When, after several years, she confessed her passion to him, Anchin was shocked. He explained that he had taken vows of chastity and could never love her, and he returned to the temple."

Kara thought back on the play she'd read and some of the reading she'd done. "That isn't how the play goes."

Mr. Yamato shook his head. "No. It's not. Some versions of the tale claim that Anchin took advantage of the girl and then spurned her. But my grandmother's story was always that Anchin was simply blind to her growing obsession, or enjoyed it but thought it innocent enough. Kiyohime pursued the monk, and her desire for him led her to make obscene propositions. Finally, resentment turned her love to hate. By then she had begun to seek to summon spirits to help force Anchin to be her lover. Demons. She became a Hannya—a blood-drinking, flesh-eating serpent woman—and snuck into the temple."

The principal waved a hand. "The rest is much like what you've no doubt read."

Hachiro, Ren, Mai, and Sakura all looked to Kara. She nodded.

"The monks hid Anchin inside a huge bronze bell in the temple. When she discovered him, the bell came loose and fell, trapping Anchin inside. The Hannya couldn't move the bell to get to him, but it breathed fire, like a dragon, and wrapped itself around the bell, burning it with such heat that it melted the bell and Anchin inside, and incinerating itself in the process."

"No," Mr. Yamato said.

Kara looked up at him. "What?"

They were all staring at him now. The principal sat up again in his chair, fidgeting, his back obviously paining him.

"I was mistaken. If that is how the play ends, it isn't the way my grandmother told the story. In her version, there was no fire from the Hannya. It wasn't a dragon, after all. Fire makes no sense. Kiyohime tried to get to Anchin, who had hidden inside the bell. He began to beat on the iron—iron, not bronze—from within and the other monks brought out small bells hidden in their robes and began to ring them. Japanese legends are full of tales of evil being warded off by bells. The sound paralyzed Kiyohime long enough for them to burn her."

"Do you think this Hannya is actually Kiyohime?" Mai asked. "Or a different one?"

Ren glanced at her. "Does it matter?"

Sakura rose up on her knees, staring at Kara. "Aritomo-sensei's version of *Dojoji* has no bells. The monks chant . . ."

Kara's mind raced. "That can't be coincidence. The Hannya's hiding inside her, we know that, but it's obviously controlling her actions, too. At least some of the time."

"Yes, but is it just influencing her," Ren asked, "or does it take over in there? When we're talking to Aritomo-sensei, is she answering, or is the Hannya?"

"That's crazy," Mai said.

"Also the creepiest thing I've ever heard," Hachiro said. "But that doesn't mean it isn't true."

"But how did it possess her in the first place, and why her?" Sakura asked.

"The story is about jealousy," Mai said. "Who is Aritomo-sensei jealous of?"

Hachiro and Sakura looked at Kara, who immediately understood their suspicion. It made sense, in a bizarre sort of way. Miss Aritomo had taken an interest in her father, maybe wanted to get closer to him, but his first love and loyalty belonged to his daughter. It would be natural for the woman to be a little jealous of their closeness. Envious.

Would it have been enough to give the Hannya a way in? An invitation? Maybe. And they would probably never know.

Kara threw up her hands. "Look, there's no point in debating this. How it got inside her isn't nearly as important as finding a way to get it out."

"Agreed," Ren said.

Hachiro reached out and touched Kara's shoulder. She turned to see a gleam of epiphany in his eyes.

"Bells," he said.

Kara got it instantly. There were bells everywhere in the school and the dorm. Japanese culture was full of them. Students hung them on backpacks and key chains and doorknobs, though most were tiny, what they called pocket bells.

"I don't know if little ones would be enough," Sakura said.

But Kara had begun to nod. She felt the smile before it touched her lips. "Kaneda-sensei looks after the old Shinto shrine beside the school. In June she did that re-creation of an old prayer ritual, remember?"

"She does it every year," Ren said.

"And the bells she uses . . . they're on a shelf in her classroom," Kara went on. "Aren't they, Hachiro?"

Hachiro clapped his hands together. "Yes. I've dusted them a dozen times in o-soji."

"Wait!" Mai said. "If you're right about the bells . . . and maybe you are, since she didn't include them in the play . . . We can't just burn our art teacher!"

They'd almost forgotten Mr. Yamato was there. Now he slapped a hand on the arm of his chair, the sound snapping them all to attention.

206

"You will do nothing," he said, frowning deeply.

Kara stared at him. "But you said—"

"Yes, I believe you," he interrupted. "But if all you surmise is correct, Kara, your father is in no danger. He is not one of the cursed, nor is he a part of the play Aritomo-sensei wanted to stage. No, you will all stay here with me. I will phone the police. When they arrive, you will relate everything to them, just as you have to me, and I will support you."

"What?" Hachiro said, standing. "Sensei, they won't believe a word of it."

"Perhaps," Mr. Yamato said. "But the men I have dealt with know that they have not been able to unravel the mysteries that have plagued us this year. This explanation is only slightly less plausible than the wild bear story they told the newspapers in the spring. If they don't want me to make my own calls to the newspapers, they will listen to you, and then they will go to Aritomo-sensei and question her, and search her home. It may be that the missing students are there, if they are still alive—"

"Miho," Sakura said softly.

"But the police must be the ones to deal with this. I cannot allow any of you to put yourselves in further danger."

For several seconds, no one spoke. Hachiro shifted awkwardly on his feet. Sakura whispered Kara's name, a question, and then all of them were looking at her.

Kara stood, shaking her head. "No. I'm sorry, Yamato-sensei. That will take too long. We'll go to her house ourselves. If the others are there, we'll rescue them. And if Aritomo-sensei is there . . . we'll have the answers we're looking for. I only hope you're right about my father."

She and Hachiro turned to leave and the others started to rise to follow them. Kara's thoughts were already running ahead, wondering how quickly they could gather the bells they would need, and thinking also about the story of *Dojoji*, about the monks, and the role that masks played in Noh theater.

"Stop!" Mr. Yamato barked. "I forbid you to leave. You will wait for the police."

Kara held the door open for the others. As they filed out, she turned to the principal. "I'm sorry, sensei. This is ancient evil. We don't have time to wait for the modern world to believe in it."

Miss Aritomo lived a mile or so from the Harpers, in a house that had been built long before World War II. Once upon a time it had been one of a handful of larger homes beyond the outskirts of the city, but Miyazu had grown over the years and sprawled outward around it. There were offices nearby, as well as a handful of shops, a sushi bar, and a laundry, but the neighborhood had gone downhill of late. The doctor's office next door had been abandoned, a realtor's sign in the window.

"It must have been beautiful once," Mai said, studying the front of the house.

Sakura frowned. As far as she was concerned, the art teacher's house had not lost any of its beauty. If anything, the ugliness of its surroundings only enhanced its elegance, though she understood why some people wouldn't see it that way.

She and Mai stood in a small alley beside the laundry. Its

windows were dark and the building silent, but the streetlights were bright and they did not want to be seen if anyone should look out the window of Miss Aritomo's house.

Kara, Ren, and Hachiro had gone to the school. It would be locked up, but they had passed the point where locks would stop them. The police would be on their way to Mr. Yamato's house by now, but by the time the principal explained to them what he thought was going on—or some version of the truth, at least—it might be hours before they did anything about it. Sakura thought Hachiro and Ren might balk at breaking a window to get into the school, but she knew Kara wouldn't hesitate. Not now. But she knew that if they did that, alarms would go off, summoning the police, and those explanations would also take too long.

Fortunately, they wouldn't have to break any windows. Sakura spent some time every day in the shadowy recessed doorway on the east side of the school. It was her quiet spot—her smoking spot. She contemplated life during those cigarette breaks, thought about the past and about the future, about her sister and their hollow, loveless parents, and the hopes and dreams she never dared discuss in detail, even with her closest friends.

She also worked to pry the lock open on the door.

It had been forgotten, that door. Locked for years, it had been painted over and ignored, an emergency exit from a time before the renovations to the school created new ones at the rear of the school and out through the gym. In fiddling with it one day, Sakura had found out that the school's present alarm system was not wired to that door, that any wires were antiquated, and connected to nothing. All they'd need to get in was a fork or knife, anything to pry the lock.

That was the easy part.

"How long do you think it will take them?" Mai asked.

Sakura glanced at her, biting back a snippy retort. "I don't know. If they get lucky, they'll find enough bells right away. If not . . ."

She didn't have to finish the sentence. Mai sighed and nodded, shifting her weight from one leg to the other.

"I can't stand just waiting here," Mai said.

"Patience has never been one of my virtues," Sakura replied. "But what other choice do we have? If we have any hope of stopping the Hannya—or even just getting our friends back—we need some kind of advantage."

Mai scowled. "And you think bells will give us that advantage?"

Sakura shrugged. "I don't know what to think. But so far, the old stories have proven to have truth in them. We can only hope that this is one of the true parts. And besides, you said yourself it didn't seem like coincidence that Aritomo-sensei left the bells out of the play."

They fell grimly silent after that, no trace of friendship or even camaraderie between them. Sakura had given her the benefit of the doubt a few times, but despite Mai's denials, she would never be able to shake the feeling that the girl knew more about Akane's murder than she admitted—that she might actually have been there that night. At the very least, she had known more than she told the police. If she had told the truth, Ume might be in prison now.

Sakura frowned and glanced sidelong at her, there in the dark alley beyond the golden glow thrown by the streetlights. Maybe it wasn't too late. Could she make Mai talk to the police now, after all these months? Given what the girl had said in front of Mr. Yamato, she probably could.

The thought made her happy, and for several minutes she stood and stared at the dark facade of Miss Aritomo's house, fantasizing about what would happen if the police arrested Ume. Sakura had been forced to let go of much of her grief and anger in order to defeat the ketsuki in April, but that did not mean that her heart had healed. She still wanted justice.

They waited on. Cars and scooters flew by, and people on bicycles, but there were not very many, and no one seemed to notice the two girls in the alley. The house remained dark and silent. Sakura tapped her front left pocket, where she kept her cell phone, and then her right pocket, where her cigarettes were nestled away.

"I would love a cigarette right now," she whispered, becoming jittery. "I need a smoke."

Mai shot her a dubious look. "Why don't you have one, then?"

Sakura sniffed, rolling her eyes. "You're not very sneaky, are you? If there's anyone in the house, they might see the match, never mind the cigarette burning."

Affronted, Mai raised her chin, half-turned away. "You say I'm not sneaky as though it's an accusation. Is being sneaky an admirable trait?"

"That was me being polite," Sakura replied. "By 'sneaky,' I mean clever. Which you're not."

That ended any further discussion, and Sakura was glad. She fidgeted, both with impatience and with a craving for nicotine. Thirty or forty minutes went by without her exchanging another word with Mai. Fewer cars passed. After a while, all Sakura could think about was how idiotic she had been to take up smoking, and how she really needed to quit the habit.

In a way, that was good. The less she thought about the house across the street, the better. Whenever she let herself focus too much on Miss Aritomo's lovely old place, she wondered if Miho might be inside, and if she would still be alive when they went in after her. Those thoughts made her want to scream.

Craving a cigarette helped keep the fear bottled up.

Mai stiffened beside her. "Did you hear that?"

Sakura frowned, edgier than ever. "What? I didn't hear anything."

They both stood frozen in the alley, necks craned, concentrating on the sounds of the night around them. There were no cars driving by now, and no distant roar of motorcycle engines or rumble of a passing train. In that moment, the neighborhood was probably as quiet as it ever got.

Sakura cocked her head. Had she heard a muffled cry in the distance?

"There it is again," Mai said, turning to stare at her, eyes wide with hope and terror. "You heard that."

Sakura bit her lower lip, thinking for a moment before replying. "I heard *something*."

Anger flickered in Mai's eyes. "That was a voice. Someone's screaming for help inside that house."

Sakura stared at the house, listening intently. Mai fumed, but when she seemed about to speak, Sakura hushed her. Nearly a full minute passed before Sakura heard the sound again, and this time she could not deny that it sounded like a person calling out, though she could decipher no words and the voice seemed so distant.

Still, it might have been coming from the house.

"I don't know. It could be some woman three streets away yelling at her kids."

Mai threw up her hands. "You know that's not what it is!" she snapped, taking a few steps out of the alley, into the pool of illumination thrown by the streetlight.

"What are you doing?" Sakura demanded.

Mai turned to stare at her with a how-stupid-are-you? look on her face. "I'm not just going to wait here. If our friends are still alive, that could be them calling for help. I'm not waiting another second."

Sakura grabbed her wrist. "Don't be stupid. Kara and the boys will be here soon—"

"And what if it's not soon enough? It was one thing when we weren't sure, but someone's in there. In the dark." She yanked her arm away. "I'm going in. Are you coming with me?"

"Not a chance," Sakura replied. "Someone has to be here to explain why you're either dead or a prisoner in that house. You don't have a weapon, or anything else to distract the Hannya aside from your incredible stupidity."

Mai shot her a furious, withering glance, spun on one heel, and raced across the road. Sakura receded once more into the shadows of the alley and watched Mai run up alongside Miss Aritomo's house and then disappear around the back.

Guilt filled Sakura as she worried what might happen to Mai, or what the Hannya might do to Miho and the others when Mai broke in, if they really *were* imprisoned within those walls. But she stayed put. Without the bells, on her own, she'd be no help to anyone.

Only after the heavy potted plant left her hands did Mai fully consider the danger she might be in, but by then it was too late. The pot shattered the window with a terrible crash, followed by an almost musical noise as broken shards hit the floor inside. She backed up, glanced around, and hid behind a tree that grew in the stone and flower garden that Miss Aritomo must have spent all of her free time grooming.

Mai held her breath and waited, but no lights went on inside the house. Faintly, she thought she heard that voice from inside, but somehow it seemed even more muffled back there.

Her mouth had gone dry and her whole face seemed to throb with every beat of her skittish heart, but at last she bent to pick up a small, decorative stone and went to the window, where she used the stone to knock out the fragments of glass that jutted from the frame. Without hesitation—for she knew if she hesitated again she would never go in—she boosted herself up onto the window frame, swung one leg over, and stepped inside.

The glass crunched beneath the soles of her shoes as she crept through what appeared to be a sort of artist's studio, complete with canvases stacked against the wall and a fresh one atop an easel, covered with a sheet. Tempted by the urge to unveil the painting, to see what a woman possessed by a demon might paint, she pressed on instead, wanting to search the house and be gone before Miss Aritomo came home. But with every step, she regretted not having looked at that painting, and knew she would always wonder what image the canvas might have revealed.

Though it was not a small house, it was sparsely furnished, and it took Mai only a few minutes to peek into every room on the first floor and make her way to the second. While she moved swiftly through the art teacher's immaculately neat bedroom, she heard a thump above her head. And then another. Stopping to listen, Mai heard a voice again, and this time there was no mistaking it as anything other than a cry for help.

She raced to the end of the hall, where narrow back stairs led up to what could only be an attic. Mai's own house had no such space—most modern homes did not—but they'd be more common in an old prewar building like this.

The narrow landing at the top of the steps was dark, and she wished she had searched for a switch before coming up. She tried the door, found it locked tight, and threw her weight against it. Again someone shouted from within. Was there a note of new hope in that voice?

"Wakana?" Mai cried, throwing herself against the door again. But that was getting her nowhere.

Carefully, she hurried back down the steps, hands searching for a light switch. When she found it, a dusty old fixture flickered to life up on the landing. Heart pounding, aware every second of the possibility of Miss Aritomo's return, she hurtled up the stairs and stared at the door.

Two locks. One was simple enough, a deadbolt, which she threw back instantly. But the other required a key.

Mai sagged backward, racking her brain. The heavy lock would not be easily forced.

"Think, think," she told herself. Frustrated, she slapped the wall.

Something jangled right next to her. She turned to see a hook, upon which there hung a key. Mai grinned at the luck. The old metal key might have hung there for years, even decades, with Miss Aritomo having little need of it.

Now she snatched it up, pushed it into the lock, twisted it and heard the tumbles fall. With a surge of hope, she shoved the door wide. The light from the old fixture on the landing spilled into the pitch-black attic.

Something moved in there. Mai blinked, waiting for her eyes to adjust, and recoiled at the horrid odors that wafted from the attic.

"Who is it?" said a weak, rasping voice.

"Wakana?" Mai said, crouching slightly to step into the dusty, low-ceilinged room.

Then she looked deeper into the attic, trying to make out the strange shape that had been revealed by the shaft of light from the open door. A dollhouse. And behind it, broken pieces of something that must once have been her friend.

Mai had to scream, needed desperately to release the shriek of horror that seemed to catch in her throat. She staggered backward and struck her head on the door frame. The impact jarred something loose within her, and then she did scream, loud and long.

Kara ran along the street, passing through illumination from a streetlight above. Her legs felt heavy, and the backs of her calves burned, reminding her that she hadn't been getting enough exercise lately. She slowed to a walk, catching her breath, and glanced over her shoulder to see Hachiro and Ren hurrying after her. Ren had a small box clutched to his chest, while Hachiro carried a sack made of rough cloth over his shoulder.

They had run most of the way to the school from Mr. Yamato's, but it had taken much too long to pry the lock on the side door and then locate the items they were searching for. The route from the school to Miss Aritomo's house had started as a kind of mad dash, but all three of them had needed to slow down several times. Passing her own house, Kara had seen lights on inside. Her father's little Honda remained parked in front, and Miss Aritomo's bicycle was still locked to a lamppost nearby. Kara had been torn between relief that the Hannya had not gone home yet, and fear for her father, that he was still with her.

But if the Hannya was keeping Miho and the others in Miss Aritomo's house—and Kara and her friends hadn't been able to think of any other possible places—then this might be their one chance to find out. And if Miho and the others *weren't* in the art teacher's house, Kara feared they must be dead after all.

So she had kept running, and the guys had raced along behind her, each carrying his burden. Now they were almost there. Hachiro and Ren caught up to her, then they both slowed to a walk as well, out of breath. The street came to an intersection, where the main road jogged left and a narrow avenue ran off to the right, newish homes clustered all along it. They kept to the main road, bearing left beneath the gleaming dome of another streetlight.

Kara jumped a little at the sudden vibration in her pocket. With a soft, self-deprecating chuckle, she pulled out her cell phone, which she'd silenced when they had been breaking into the school. Sakura was calling.

"Hey," Kara answered.

"Where are you?" Sakura demanded, her voice low.

"Almost there."

"You'd better hurry. We heard something, maybe someone calling for help. Mai panicked. She went around the back and I think she's breaking in."

"Shit," Kara muttered. "Be there in a minute."

She hung up and as she slid the phone back into her pocket, she glanced up at Hachiro. "We've got to hurry."

"What do you think we've been doing?" Ren asked, still trying to steady his breathing.

Hachiro took Kara's hand and squeezed it. He gave her a quick kiss. "Let's go."

Ren held up a hand. "Wait, wait, please! Just give me a minute."

Kara smiled and grabbed his hand, now locked between the two guys. "Sorry."

Then they were off and running, the two of them dragging Ren along despite his wheezing protests. In moments they came in sight of Miss Aritomo's house. Veering to the right, they hid as deeply in the shadows of the buildings as they could manage.

"Sakura!" Kara called in a rough whisper.

"Why are you being quiet?" Hachiro asked, frowning. "Aritomo-sensei is not home."

Ren hit his arm. "Think. Just because Aritomo-sensei isn't here, that doesn't mean the Hannya is also gone."

Kara shivered, remembering all too clearly the sight of the evil spirit transforming and then vanishing inside Miss Aritomo's prone body.

When she called out a second time, Sakura emerged from beside the building on their right, a darkened laundry, and beckoned them to her. Kara, Ren, and Hachiro hurried over, and Kara felt vulnerable and exposed under the glow of yet another streetlamp. She exhaled as they stepped into a darkened alley beside the laundry, where Sakura had apparently been hiding.

"Did you get everything?" Sakura asked.

"We think so," Ren told her, patting the box in his hands. "It's just so strange to think that any of this will make a difference. We should have guns or knives or something."

Hachiro nodded. "A baseball bat."

Kara looked at him.

"What? It worked before."

"The baseball bat helped, but it wasn't what got rid of the ketsuki, or kept Kyuketsuki from coming into the world.

The rules of things like this are very peculiar, and sometimes don't make any sense, but the secrets are all in the stories themselves. If the monks destroyed the Hannya with the sound of bells, and Aritomo-sensei purposely left them out of the play . . . Look, maybe this will work and maybe it won't, but if it doesn't, I don't have another plan, and a baseball bat isn't going to help."

Ren cocked his head, looking across the street at the darkened house. "It might."

The sound of an approaching car made them step deeper into the alley and they fell silent as they turned to watch it pass. But the car did not drive past. The engine rumbled and the vehicle slowed, and a moment later the headlights turned left, casting an ugly yellow light onto Miss Aritomo's house as the car pulled into the drive. A moment later, the headlights went dark and the engine silent, but not before Kara saw the open trunk, and the bicycle jutting out of it.

"Oh, no," Ren said.

"Kara, it's your father," Hachiro whispered.

She barely heard them. Staring, wondering how the teacher had persuaded him to drive her home, and if it had been Miss Aritomo or the Hannya doing the talking—how did that work, having a demon riding inside your mind?—Kara started out of the alley.

Sakura grabbed her shoulder. "Wait."

Kara shook her off and took one more step before Ren lent a hand, he and Sakura preventing Kara from going any farther. Hachiro stepped in front of her, blocking Kara's view of the house. Her pulse raced, gaze darting around. Her skin prickled with frenzied thoughts and fears, and she looked up into Hachiro's eyes.

Car doors slammed. Her father would be taking Miss Aritomo's bike out of the trunk now.

"Why would she bring him back here?" Kara demanded. "I thought . . . I don't know if Aritomo-sensei knows the Hannya's inside her, and my dad's got nothing to do with the play, so I hoped he would be safe. But if she's bringing him here, I have to stop him from going inside."

"No," Hachiro said firmly. "We have to stick to the plan. Just a couple of minutes and we'll go in. He'll be all right."

At the sound of Miss Aritomo's front door closing, anger flashed through Kara. "You don't know that."

She pulled away from her friends, stepped past Hachiro, and stared at the house. A light had come on downstairs.

And then, from higher up—from the attic, it seemed to Kara—there came a piercing scream that rose and arced and then died out, leaving horrible silence behind.

"Mai," Sakura whispered.

Kara spun, grabbed the box from Ren's hands, and tore it open. She looked up at her friends, who were staring at her.

"Hurry!"

14

卍

Kara and Hachiro stood just outside Miss Aritomo's house. She cocked her head, trying to get a glimpse of her father through a window, but despite the inside light, nothing seemed to be moving within. The sickle moon cast a dim yellow gloom over the buildings and the street. Kara glanced at Hachiro, swallowed hard, and nodded.

"That should be long enough," she whispered.

Sakura and Ren had gone around the back of the house, following Mai's path. However she had gotten in, they would as well. Which only left the front door.

"Ready?" Hachiro asked softly.

Kara nodded, and he reached into the cloth sack that he had taken from the art room and withdrew one of the Noh masks that Miho had made, handing it to her. Kara stared at it. The visage seemed almost genderless, a white-haired, grimly pale expression permanently fixed upon it. A villager or a monk, she thought. As she watched, Hachiro pulled a second mask from the bag, this one with a thin tangle of beard marking it as male. Surely it must be one of the monks.

Hachiro donned his mask, fitting the string behind his head. Kara took a deep breath and did the same. Ren and Sakura had taken their masks with them. There were two others in the bag—the one they'd brought for Mai to wear and another that Kara feared might have been a mistake to bring along. That fear gnawed at her, but they would know soon enough.

Kara looked at Hachiro, hating the way the mask obscured his features, but his eyes were still there, soft and kind. She nodded and pointed at the door.

"Let's go."

Hachiro took a deep breath. He had the sack grasped in one fist and in the other he clutched a small iron bell. Kara reached into her pocket and pulled out her own bell, two fingers inside it to keep it silent until the right moment.

This is insane, she thought. They didn't really know if any of this would work. It was all pure conjecture. But in her time in Japan, reading folklore and Noh plays—and from their brush with Kyuketsuki—she had learned that somehow, over time, the stories themselves seemed to have rejuvenated some spirits. The supernatural beings that survived in Japan were no longer worshiped, and so drew their remaining vitality from the stories and plays about them. The stories had reshaped them, in some way.

And if the stories could shape them, then wearing the masks of the monks who destroyed the Hannya in *Dojoji* would give them a certain power over the creature. It would almost expect them to defeat it, and that would give them an advantage.

Or so Kara now believed.

In moments, she would discover if there was any truth to that theory.

The bells, though, were different. There were so many instances in Japanese legend of the sound of bells warding off or weakening evil, even destroying it. The masks might give them an advantage, but the bells could actually be a weapon. If they were lucky. If they were right.

Hachiro stepped up to the house and slammed his foot against the door, just beside the knob. Grimacing, he launched another powerful kick, striking the same spot. In quick succession, he struck the door twice more, and the lock gave way with a splinter of wood. The door swung inward and Hachiro didn't hesitate. He burst into the house, and Kara followed.

Her father and Miss Aritomo were standing at the bottom of the steps. It looked like they had been about to go up, belatedly responding to the scream from the attic. Rob Harper had a heavy lamp in his hand, apparently to use as a weapon, and Miss Aritomo held a long kitchen knife. They both looked startled, and if Kara had not seen the Hannya slipping into the art teacher with her own eyes, she would never have thought that Miss Aritomo was anything but terrified at that moment.

At the sight of her and Hachiro in the masks, Miss Aritomo screamed. Kara's father came toward them, wielding the lamp.

"Dad, wait!" Kara said.

"Kara?" he muttered, too confused to be angry yet.

"Get away from her, Harper-sensei!" Hachiro barked, sliding away from Kara, watching Miss Aritomo closely.

Maybe the Hannya's not here, Kara thought. *That could be, right? It's not in her now.*

"Hachiro, it might be in the attic. That's why Mai was screaming."

"Mai? What is Mai doing in my attic?" Miss Aritomo asked. "What is going on here? Why are you wearing those masks? You have a lot of explaining to do!"

Sakura and Ren appeared from a hall that led toward the back of the house. They moved slowly into the living room, fanning out so that the four students had Miss Aritomo surrounded, with the stairs to the second story her only route of escape. They had also donned their masks, and clutched iron bells in their fists.

"Shut up, demon!" Sakura snarled at Miss Aritomo.

"No, Sakura," Ren said, staring at their teacher. "Look at her. I don't think she knows it's in her."

Kara thought he was right. The expression on Miss Aritomo's face made it clear—she really didn't know. Somehow the Hannya had gotten into her and used her body as a host. Perhaps it influenced her from within, but she had no idea she had been possessed. When it left her body to prowl the world, it somehow lulled the teacher into unconsciousness, as Kara had seen with her own eyes.

Her father put the lamp down on a small table and stared at his daughter. He spoke in low, measured tones. She had never seen him so furious. "Kara, you've gone much too far now. This is ... it's too much. It's going to change everything."

Guilt and doubt surged up in her and she started to flush, averting her eyes. For several seconds, she almost crumbled under his gaze. What could she do? Call it off and apologize? Run from the house?

No.

"I know what I saw, Dad. This is real. We've been to Yamato-sensei. He believes us. He's talking to the police right now. But if you won't believe your own daughter—if you really think I'd take it this far on some crazy whim—all you have to do is go up to the attic and find out what Mai was screaming about."

He hesitated, obviously confused, and Kara knew she'd finally gotten through to him. Her father turned to look at Miss Aritomo, but even as he did, the art teacher's eyelids fluttered and she began to collapse. He caught Miss Aritomo before she could fall, but she lay limp in his arms, arms akimbo, like a puppet whose strings had been cut. The kitchen knife she'd been holding fell from her hand and skittered across the wood floor.

"Yuuka?" her father said, alarmed. He knelt down, laying her gently on the floor, still cradling her head and upper body. "Yuuka, what's wrong? Wake up!"

He twisted to look at Kara. "Call an ambulance."

"They're not going to be able to help," Hachiro said.

"Please, Harper-sensei," Sakura began. "Get away from her."

226

He glared at her, then at Kara.

"Move back, Dad," she said. "You don't understand."

"Call an ambulance, goddammit!" he snapped, then turned back to Miss Aritomo. He slapped her lightly on the cheek. "Yuuka. Yuuka!"

With a scowl of frustration, he cradled her head with one hand while, with the other, he fished out his own cell phone.

"Dad!" Kara shouted. "Get back!"

For Miss Aritomo's head had lolled back in his grasp. Her mouth opened wide and a darkness formed deep in her throat. Yellow eyes peered from the inside of her distended lips, and then the serpent slid out, all rippling shadows and hateful glare. It hissed, the sound filling the room until it seemed to come from every corner and from beneath every piece of furniture.

Rob Harper must have heard the noise, for he turned to look. At the sight of the Hannya emerging from its host, the woman with whom he was falling in love, he dropped his cell phone with a clatter on the floor, and yanked his hand away from Miss Aritomo. Her skull thunked down and he tried to scramble away, but too late.

The serpent darted toward him, fangs sinking into his wrist.

"Dad!" Kara cried once more.

Her father tried to stand, but already the demon's venom began to slow him. It blossomed from horned snake to horned demon, growing in an eyeblink into the hideous visage that hung on the wall in Miss Aritomo's classroom. But this was no mask. The Hannya wrapped its arms around Kara's father and hauled him upward until his feet were dangling several inches above the floor.

Its tongue flickered out in a long hiss and its flesh shifted again, becoming a snake-eyed woman of exotic beauty. The Hannya whispered a hiss into Rob Harper's ear and, staring over his shoulder from behind, grinned at Kara with the twin glint of two sharp teeth.

"Remember, later," the demon said, in a quiet, almost dainty voice, "that he didn't have to die. Know that I killed him because you interfered."

Miho could still feel the effects of the Hannya's venom. Her bones were stiff and her muscles ached and her head felt stuffed with cotton. But she was alive, and thanks to Mai—of all people—she thought she might get to stay that way. When the girl had first come through the attic door and seen the ruin of flesh and bone that had once been Daisuke, of course Mai had screamed. Miho whispering to her from the shadows only startled her into screaming louder.

But when Mai saw Wakana, she had begun to calm down, and to think. Miho had moved to block both girls' view of Daisuke's corpse as Mai fussed over the bruises and cuts that Wakana had acquired in the attic. Wakana had not told Miho much—she was so disoriented and weak herself—but it seemed she had hurt herself trying to force her way out of the attic, and that more than once the Hannya had bitten her, filling her blood with that paralyzing venom.

For several minutes, Wakana and Mai had embraced there in the attic, with the door yawning wide just beyond them. Miho tried to be as respectful as she could, to give them that time. It was obvious that they both had cared deeply for Daisuke, and grief shook them both as they wept quietly in each other's arms. But then she could not wait any longer.

"We need to get out of here," Miho said. "While the house is empty, before it—before *she* comes back."

Mai kept her eyes shut and squeezed Wakana to her tightly. With a deep breath, she released her. Wakana swayed to one side, barely able to remain standing, so Mai steadied her, then turned toward Miho and nodded.

"I just want to . . . to say good-bye to Daisuke," Mai said.

Miho had shaken her head. "No you don't. Not now."

"She's right," Wakana said. "Daisuke isn't here anymore. We'll remember him properly when all of this is done."

Reluctantly, Mai relented. She put an arm around Wakana and helped the girl toward the door. Miho had gone ahead of them. Even as she put her foot on the landing, there came a crash from far below, on the first floor.

"What was that?" Wakana asked, eyes wide.

Miho and Mai exchanged a glance. "The front door?" Miho said.

"I think so. Your friends are all coming to help us. It must be them," Mai replied. "But if they're willing to break in like that—"

"The Hannya must be coming," Miho finished. "Either that or it's already here."

Wakana whimpered, sagging, forcing Mai to bear even more of her weight.

"She should wait here," Miho said. "If we have to defend ourselves—"

"What? No!" Wakana said, her words slightly slurred as though she'd been drinking.

Mai glared at Miho. "I will not leave her here. If we have to make a run for it, Wakana would be alone. We'll make it out together, or not at all."

All Miho could do was shrug. Voices carried from downstairs, shouting at one another. She led the way, hurrying down to the second floor, with Mai helping Wakana descend behind her. Miho hesitated only a moment, glancing around to make sure they were alone on that level of the house, and then she started down to the first floor. Now she could hear the voices more clearly—Kara's, her father's, Hachiro's, and Sakura's—and the words chilled her.

Halfway down the steps, she paused, holding her breath. Kara shouted at her father, who then began to scream at them to call for an ambulance. Something had happened to Miss Aritomo. But didn't they know that she was the Hannya? Wasn't that why they were here?

Miho crept down a few more steps, light from the living room spilling into the stairwell. Something touched her arm and she gasped and turned to find Mai beside her. Despite her fears for Wakana, she had left the other girl at the top of the stairs. That was good. Something awful had begun to unfold in the living room and Wakana would only be in more danger if they brought her into its midst.

Mai nodded to Miho, a signal for them to continue, and Miho obliged. They went down several more steps together, clinging to the walls, and now Miho caught sight of the Hannya wrapping itself around Professor Harper. And it spoke.

"Remember, later, that he didn't have to die. Know that I killed him because you interfered."

Miho reached out and grabbed Mai's wrist. She stared, unable to breathe, as the Hannya opened its mouth—the dark beauty of its female guise giving way to grotesquerie as its jaws unhinged—and bent its head as though to tear out Professor Harper's throat.

"No!" Miho cried.

She and Mai lunged as one and grabbed the Hannya's arms, their weight and momentum helping them tear the demon away from Kara's father. Its hiss of rage and frustration filled Miho's ears, but she heard another noise—a shout of triumph—as Sakura threw herself at Professor Harper, practically tackling him as she forced him across the room, away from the Hannya.

As the demon hissed in their grasp it thrashed against Mai and Miho. Staggering backward, Miho stumbled over the unconscious Miss Aritomo, and then she and Mai were both falling in a tangle of limbs, dragging the Hannya down on top of them.

Mai screamed in pain and Miho flinched as tiny flecks of the other girl's blood spattered her face. The Hannya writhed in Miho's grip, flesh shifting as it twisted round, and once again it wore the face of the demon. This close, Miho saw it looked very little like the mask on Miss Aritomo's wall, or the one she herself had tried to create for the staging of *Dojoji*. Its eyes had huge black slitted pupils, limned with sickly yellow, and nictating membranes slid over those gelatinous orbs. The demon's wiry hair looked like dried, blackened cornsilk, and its leathern skin consisted of a million diamond-shaped scales.

"Get it off her!" someone shouted.

Sakura called her name.

Miho saw, just a few feet away, a long kitchen knife gleaming on the wooden floor where someone had dropped it. Bells began to ring, and the Hannya flinched, tensing and hissing. Miho took that moment to lunge for the knife, but the Hannya shrugged as though shaking off a blow and caught her before she could reach the blade. As it dragged Miho closer, its forked tongue darted out and struck her cheek and she cried out, but already a terrible numbness spread across her face and down her spine.

Mai wrapped an arm around the Hannya's throat, preventing it from lunging any closer to Miho, but the demon grabbed hold of Mai's left hand and twisted hard enough that the snap of breaking bone was clearly audible.

Mai screamed. The Hannya thrashed her off and came at Miho again. She tried to block its attack with her hands, even as she grew disoriented once more. Her palm caught on one of the Hannya's horns, puncturing the skin and drawing her blood.

It darted in, so much like a snake, and bit her with a quick strike before pulling back. Those dreadful eyes studied her and the Hannya smiled.

As darkness began to swim in around the edges of her vision, Miho heard the ringing of the bells grow louder and more insistent. Then her senses began to fail her entirely, except that she could still smell Mai's blood.

. . .

In the moment when the Hannya had been about to kill her father, Kara had frozen. Unable to breathe, unable to move, she could only stare as the impossible unfolded before her. It couldn't be happening. Inside her head, she could hear herself screaming, but no sound came from her lips. The Hannya had locked eyes with her, pinning her with its gaze, but she knew that even if she hurled herself across the room she would never reach the demon in time to save him. She felt herself suffocating inside the Noh mask that covered her face.

Then Miho and Mai had surged from the shadowy stairwell and attacked the Hannya. As Kara gaped at their courage, Sakura ran at her father and practically tackled him, dragging him to the corner of the room, away from the chaos erupting at its center.

Hachiro and Ren began to shout. Mai screamed in pain. Kara saw blood. Sakura called out for Miho. Then Hachiro began to ring his bell and at last Kara snapped out of whatever momentary trance had paralyzed her.

She rang hers as well, and in a moment Ren and Sakura were doing the same. Leaving Kara's father in the corner, Sakura moved in closer. Ren and Hachiro hurried to place themselves as evenly as possible around the Hannya and the three bodies that lay on the floor. Kara saw it all through the strange eyes of her Noh mask. Miss Aritomo remained unconscious, but Mai moaned, cradling her left arm, blood soaking into her shirt from a long gash in her face and a wound on her shoulder.

Miho fought weakly against the Hannya, beginning to go limp in its grasp. Just a few feet from them, the kitchen knife

Miss Aritomo had fetched earlier lay on the floor. Kara wished she could get it and use it, but feared it might be useless against the Hannya.

"Louder!" Kara shouted.

She held the bell high and took a step closer, then another. The iron grew strangely warm in her hand and the smell of hot metal began to fill the room, and then she knew that all of their conjecture had been right—the bells were the weapon they needed.

Sakura, Ren, and Hachiro took her cue and they began to close the circle. It might only have been Kara's imagination, but the voices of the bells seemed to join in a chorus so pure they became almost one sound, ringing together, loud and bright.

The Hannya shrank down upon itself as though to protect itself from attack. It hissed, but the sound of the bells contained the demon's hiss, swallowed and silenced it. The shadows on the floor began to coalesce and the corners of the room grew darker, but Kara shook her bell harder, ringing it even louder, so that her fingers felt scorched by the heat of the metal. The others followed suit, and soon the shadows were only shadows, with none of the demon's influence.

Its skin rippled, jaws opening again to reveal those needle fangs, and now its flesh seemed trapped between monster and serpent. It bulged and pulsed, shifting as if the Hannya were attempting to control its shape and failing.

The demon turned and reached for Miho, tongue darting out, jaws opening wide.

"Never!" Ren shouted, and stepped nearer.

The Hannya grinned up at him, fixing him in its yellow serpent's gaze. But Hachiro, Sakura, and Kara matched Ren's step, holding the circle firm, somehow caging it there.

Kara saw its gaze shift toward the prone form of Miss Aritomo and immediately she understood its intent.

"Hachiro!" she shouted. "Throw me the bag!"

Confusion filled his gaze, but he trusted her and did not hesitate. Hachiro tossed her the cloth sack that still contained two of the masks Miho had made for *Dojoji*. Kara dropped to her knees, still ringing her bell, and shoved her free hand into the sack. The first face she touched had horns, and she knew that wasn't what she wanted. She yanked the other free of the cloth.

The Hannya started to move, but Kara leaped to Miss Aritomo's side, covering her teacher's face with the mask of Anchin, the monk who had resisted all of the Hannya's attempts at seduction, and who had burned to death rather than surrender to it. Miss Aritomo had always said that the masks of the Noh had power, that they were imbued with such tradition that they could help transform the wearer into the character they played. Noh theater was more than just acting, it was inhabiting the legend, and letting the legend inhabit the actor. But the old demons and spirits were equally influenced. With no one left to worship them, they were controlled by the tales people still told about them—things like Noh theater.

To the Hannya, Miss Aritomo was now Anchin, and Anchin had never feared it.

It had lost its host.

The Hannya shrank back from Miss Aritomo and looked up in confusion. The demon hesitated, then shrieked in fury and lunged for Kara. She thrust the bell nearly into its face, ringing it loudly. This close to the Hannya, the metal grew so hot that she could barely stand to hold it, but she dared not drop the bell.

"Damn you!" the Hannya said, its voice a damp, slithery thing. It had become more serpent than woman or monster now, and rose up on its thick snake's body, swaying in front of her.

It pointed at Miss Aritomo. "She summoned me here! And you dare to—"

"Liar!" Kara's father shouted, springing away from the wall.

"Dad, stay back!" Kara snapped.

She needn't have feared. Her father was an intelligent man. He kept well away from the circle that the four of them had created with the ringing of their bells and the power of the Noh masks—the Hannya saw the people of the temple who had destroyed it once already, heard the bells of the monks.

"It lies!" Rob Harper shouted. Then he sneered at the Hannya, pointing at Miss Aritomo himself. "Yuuka never summoned you, she *honored* you. And this is how you repay her?"

Its voice weak and ragged with pain, the Hannya laughed.

"You are right, of course, teacher. But this woman you love opened the window for me to enter."

Kara watched as it diminished further, shrinking to become the ebony, horned serpent—part flesh and part smoke—that she had seen before.

"Louder!" she told her friends. "Close the circle!"

And they did. She saw the pain in their faces and knew that the iron bells must have been searing their skin just as hers did, but they did not hesitate. The serpent twisted and coiled in upon itself, then it whipped around and stared at Kara herself, those hypnotic serpent's eyes locking with hers.

"I won't be the last, girl. You know that. You all do. My sister Kyuketsuki put her curse upon you and it calls to the rest of us like the scent of fresh prey. Worse things than I will come for you, and you and all that you love will die."

Movement to her left caught Kara's attention and she risked a glance, only to see Wakana stumbling into the circle. For a heartbeat, she was too astonished at seeing the girl alive, and too busy trying to put together how she came to be there—that Mai must have freed her from the attic along with Miho—that she didn't even have a chance to cry out to warn Wakana.

Then she saw the kitchen knife glinting in Wakana's hand and realized she had picked it up off the floor.

"Some of us have already lost what we loved," Wakana said, tears streaming down her face.

The serpent twisted round to face her, but too late. Wakana slashed the blade through the air and sliced the horned serpent's head from its body.

It flopped to the floor in two pieces, a final hiss rising from it—though, this time, of steam. A horrible stench filled the house, a smell of sickness and death, and the shadows puffed up from the serpent like smoke, drifting away.

"What the hell?" Kara muttered in English.

She kept ringing her bell and the others did the same as they moved closer to it. But the iron had gone suddenly cold in her hand and the thing on the floor showed no signs of its horns. All that remained of the Hannya were the head and body of a small garden snake.

"Kara!" her father snapped.

She turned to see the cloth bag containing the final Noh mask burning up. Flames rippled across the fabric, which quickly blackened. Her father raced to it and stomped on the bag until all that remained were tattered, scorched bits of cloth. Of the mask inside—the face of the Hannya—nothing remained but a coppery-hued dust.

The bells fell silent.

Sakura and Ren pulled off their masks and ran to Miho's side. Wakana knelt by Mai, speaking softly to her. Hachiro stomped on the snake to make sure it was dead.

Kara removed her own mask and looked up into her father's eyes, surprised to find fear there. At first she didn't understand, and then she realized what she saw was his fear of losing her.

"Dad . . ."

"Quiet," he said, pulling her into his arms and kissing the top of her head over and over. He held her face in his hands and kissed her forehead. "I'm so sorry. So, so sorry. I should have believed you."

Kara shook her head. "No. You shouldn't have. How could you?"

But he wouldn't accept her forgiveness. "I'm your father. That's how."

Again he kissed the top of her head, and then he turned toward Miss Aritomo. The teacher had begun to stir. Kara's father went to her, crouched down and slid the mask of Anchin off her face, revealing once more the beauty beneath. Kara watched the way her father looked at Miss Aritomo, the gentle way he brushed the hair from her eyes, and though she wished she could have pretended otherwise, it still hurt her, even after all they had been through. She missed her mother.

But she found now that she could find room in her heart for both the sorrow of her mother's absence and the happiness of her father's new hope for the future. The two emotions would not sit easily together, but for now, it would be enough.

In the distance, police sirens wailed.

Otherwise, Miss Aritomo's house had fallen silent.

EPILOGUE

They met, strangely enough, at Kara's house. She thought that perhaps Mr. Yamato had decided he didn't want to talk about demon spirits in his own home, and he certainly couldn't have held the gathering at his office without people asking questions he would be unwilling to answer.

The house proved a better choice anyway. Miss Aritomo obviously felt more comfortable there, which was no small thing, considering how traumatized she was. The woman sat primly on the love seat beside Kara's father, and he held both of her small, birdlike hands in his own. She didn't look up often, and had spoken not a word from the moment Mr. Yamato had arrived. Kara's father had told her that Miss Aritomo had spoken to the police, but that otherwise she had said little in the days since the horror that had unfolded in her living room.

It hurt her heart to look at Miss Aritomo, and to think of how hard she had made it for her father to fall in love with someone who wasn't her mother. Kara regretted all of that now. Miss Aritomo had always been kind to her, and now the woman had gone through a terrible ordeal, her body violated by something awful. Something . . . evil. Kara felt awkward even thinking the word, but there could be no denying the Hannya's nature.

Miss Aritomo needed someone to hold her now, and Kara found herself glad that her father could be that person. It would still be hard to share him, but she knew that she and her father would get through it all together. They needed to have their own lives, but they had to support each other, too. If they didn't, who would?

"You can't be serious!" Mai snapped, staring at Mr. Yamato.

The principal's eyes narrowed and his lips formed a tight little line. "You are upset, girl, so I will forgive your insolence."

But Mai only shook her head in amazement and turned to Wakana. The roommates stood with their arms linked together not far from the door, as though they might flee the house at any moment. Wakana still looked drawn and pale, though her bruises and scratches were fading. Mai, on the other hand, had a long recovery ahead of her. Doctors had put a cast on her broken arm and she wore it now in a sling. Of greater concern was the long gash on her right cheek, which had been stitched closed as deftly as her surgeon could manage. Even with plastic surgery, the scar would be significant.

"I don't want your forgiveness, nor do I need it," Mai said, turning back toward the principal. "We are not in school, Yamato-sensei—"

Mr. Yamato's eyes blazed with quiet fury. "But you are still a student of Monju-no-Chie school, girl. For the moment."

Kara knew she had to step in. She took a deep breath, glancing around the room at her friends who had gathered there. Sakura sat with a bandaged and bruised Miho on the floor. Ren had pulled a chair over from the dining table and taken a seat, while Hachiro stood behind him, hands on the back of the chair. The way he stood, he seemed almost to expect trouble. He kept glancing at Kara, checking over and over again to make sure she was all right. She liked the way those protective glances made her feel, and discovered that the instinct had become mutual. Later, when the meeting had broken up, they would go for a walk together and talk about what the future held for them. She had a feeling there would be lots of walks for them, many places they would wander together. But not by the bay. The time had come to make a new path, together. They would ramble in the hills and mountains around the city, explore the other beauties that Miyazu had to offer.

Soon. It was a promise she had made to herself.

"Please, stop," Kara said, holding up her hands.

They all looked at her. Even Miss Aritomo lifted her sad gaze to see what Kara had to say. Mr. Yamato turned to her with the same glare he'd given Mai.

Kara gave the principal a small, informal bow. "Yamato-sensei, you must realize that it is not for our own sake that we argue. If you go along with the story the police have concocted—the latest in a series of ridiculous lies—no one will ever know what really happened."

Her father cleared his throat. "Kara, honey, that's the point. That's what we want."

She shook her head. "No, Dad, it isn't." Again she glanced around at her friends. Hachiro and Miho both nodded to urge her on. "People need to know so they can be on guard."

"On guard against what?" Mr. Yamato shouted. "It's over!"

Miss Aritomo flinched and shifted closer to Kara's father, the loud noise troubling her.

"But what if it isn't?" Ren asked quietly.

"'What if?'" Sakura said, throwing up her hands. "We know it isn't over!"

"You don't know that," Kara's father said. Mr. Yamato started to speak up, but Rob Harper raised a hand to forestall any interruption and kept talking. "I know, I know. The curse. But you've said yourselves that Kyuketsuki told you there were few . . . what, demons? Ancient spirits? Old gods? Whatever they are. You said there weren't many left in the world. How do we know any others will ever make their way here? It took the Hannya months, and even then, it might never have found the entry point it needed if Miss Aritomo had not had that mask on her wall. She—"

"Sssssshhhh," the art teacher said, putting a finger to his lips. "Please. Don't."

A flicker of pain crossed his face and then Kara's father fell silent. Miss Aritomo didn't like to talk about the Hannya. Kara couldn't blame her.

Mr. Yamato cleared his throat. "Months. Harper-sensei is correct. There is no way to predict what might happen. It is possible no other . . . entity will ever trouble you again."

Hachiro glanced at Kara, hope lighting his eyes.

"Is it?" Ren asked, glancing over at Sakura and Miho. "Is that possible?"

Miho shrugged. "I suppose, but what are the odds? This curse is real. None of you should let yourselves forget it, no matter how much you may want to."

Wakana spoke then, her voice quiet but carrying the power of condemnation. Firm and unwavering.

"So no one will ever know how Daisuke died? Or Yasu? We all pretend to believe the lies the police are telling?" she demanded.

Fed up, Mr. Yamato stood from his own chair, arms crossed, staring at Wakana and Mai with stormy eyes.

"What you call 'lies' are a service to the public," the principal said. "The truth would either cause utter panic, or it would be discarded as absurd, and no one would take the Miyazu City police seriously. No one would believe."

Kara stared at him, trying to figure out how the story the police had created sounded any more believable than the truth. The cops had not only fabricated a story to explain the two boys' deaths, but one that made them look competent at the same time. Yasu and Daisuke had been murdered by a man who had been part of the crew of a freighter that had been docked in Miyazu Bay for nearly a week. He had stalked Miss Aritomo and had killed two of her students, leaving Daisuke's body in her attic as a way to torment her. Only when the smell of death began to permeate the house did she realize something was wrong, but at first she had thought some kind of animal had died up there.

Then, at a meeting Miss Aritomo had held at her home to discuss the future of the Noh club, Rob Harper had gone upstairs to seek out the source of that smell, only to find that the killer had broken in and was hiding in the attic. His ship had been scheduled to sail that night, and he had intended to rape and probably kill Miss Aritomo before departing. A fight had ensued, with the killer using a knife from the teacher's kitchen, but the man had gotten away, at which point Miss Aritomo had called the police. While waiting for officers to arrive, Kara's father had found Daisuke's remains.

The killer, according to the official police report, had left port that night aboard the freighter upon which he served as a deck hand. But the ship had been bound for Osaka, and Miyazu City police were working closely with Osaka police, who were especially intrigued because the man fit the description of a suspect they were seeking in four similar cases in their own city.

The story was convoluted, which made it the worst sort of lie—one that would be difficult to keep track of. It was what her friends from home would have called "one hundred percent, grade-A bullshit." But the police were the police. The lie belonged to them. Kara had been told, along with her father, her friends, Mr. Yamato, and Miss Aritomo, to rebuff any inquiries by explaining that the police had asked them not to talk about it for legal reasons, as it was an ongoing investigation. Miraculously, the dodge had worked so far. Kara thought that, in spite of its audacity, the police lie was somewhat ingenious. By blaming the killings on an outsider—someone who was not only not from the community but who had already left the area and become the responsibility of the police department of a major Japanese city—they had created the implication that the case was, for all intents and purposes, solved and closed.

It troubled Kara that the cops could lie so well. She also had to wonder how much of the truth about what had happened in April they really knew. Had they spun lies about Jiro and Chouku's deaths because they didn't want people to be afraid, or because they knew something supernatural had killed them and were purposefully covering that up? And if the latter were true, what else did the police know? What other secrets and mysteries were they hiding from people?

Something to think about, Kara realized. *But not today.*

A deeply awkward silence had come over the room. Mr. Yamato still looked angry, but now his expression softened a bit.

"I know this is frightening, and I know it is difficult," he said, glancing around at each of them in turn—Kara, Hachiro and Ren, Sakura and Miho, Kara's father and Miss Aritomo, and Mai and Wakana. "But it is *necessary*."

When none of them replied, the principal stood up from his chair.

"You will not speak of this to anyone. I would prefer you not even discuss it among yourselves, though I know that would be next to impossible. The school would suffer terrible embarrassment if it became known."

"Embarrassment?" Wakana asked. "The school would be destroyed. No one would send their children here ever again. That's more than embarrassment."

Mr. Yamato sighed and looked at her, shaking his head sagely. "You don't listen. Yes, that is what would happen if people believed such things were true. But they will not. The police will lie. I will lie. It would seem nothing more than a wild story made up by a group of students . . ." He glanced at Miss Aritomo and Kara's father. "Or by dishonorable faculty members wishing to draw attention to themselves. It would be considered a hoax, and that would be an embarrassment."

The principal began to walk toward the door, but paused to look at Kara. "If anything else happens, if there is any sign of supernatural presence at all, come to me and I will do whatever I can to help. The police will help as well. But unless such a presence appears, this *is* over. It is ended."

Mr. Yamato went out the door, pulling it firmly shut behind him as he left.

Kara glanced at Mai, then searched the eyes of her friends, and finally looked at her father, who was holding Miss Aritomo close to him on the love seat, whispering soft assurances in her ear.

They all knew that it wasn't over.

Kara feared it would never be.

AUTHOR'S NOTE

Though Miyazu City is a real place, and I certainly recommend that you visit it someday and take in the beauty of Ama-no-Hashidate, I have taken certain liberties in creating its fictional counterpart for The Waking. Shh. I won't tell if you won't.

ACKNOWLEDGMENTS

I would like to thank super-editor Margaret Miller, as well as Melanie Cecka and the whole Bloomsbury team. Thanks to Allie Costa for all of her work on behalf of these books, both in making sure I don't screw them up and in helping to get the word out. Thanks again to Jack Haringa for his keen eye and helpful feedback, and, as ever, to my family for their love and laughter.

All the evil of the ages will plague you,
until my thirst for vengeance is sated . . .

A WINTER OF
GHOSTS

Read on for a sneak peek!

1

卍

Winter had come to Miyazu City, yet instead of the silence and darkness it so often promised, it had brought Kara Harper happiness and renewal. Most people making their way through the shop-lined streets of downtown Miyazu seemed trapped in a long, grim hangover now that the holidays were over. The city had to return to business as usual. In two days, school would start again and Kara would have to do the same, but she was looking forward to it.

A new year. After the nightmares come to life that had plagued her first two terms at Monju-no-Chie school, she relished the idea of a fresh start.

"Hey, lovebirds, wait up!" she called in English, hurrying to match stride with her father, Rob, and his girlfriend, Yuuka Aritomo.

Her dad and Miss Aritomo were both teachers at Monju-no-Chie, a private school on the outskirts of Miyazu City, where he taught English and American Studies, and she taught art. Their relationship had taken Kara a lot of getting used to—her mother, Annette, had been dead only two years—but she had come to accept it.

It helped that Kara had also fallen for someone. After all that they had endured, it seemed so improbable that she and her father would both be so happy at the same time, but she never spoke about that unlikeliness of their good fortune because she did not want to jinx it. Kara had definitely had enough of curses to last her a lifetime.

"Here we are," Kara said, guiding them into the shop.

"How much are these boots, anyway?" her father finally thought to ask.

Kara gave him an innocent look. "Dad, they're lined and waterproof. Can you put a price tag on keeping your loving daughter's feet warm and dry?"

He gave a good-natured sigh. "That much, huh?"

Inside the shop, where several customers were lined up at the register and others milled about trying on winter coats and boots, Kara stopped and batted her lashes at him.

"Not that much, but . . ."

"But?"

"There's this jacket you're going to love just as much as I do. White and gold and puffy—"

Her father turned to Miss Aritomo and hung his head. "Save me."

The art teacher laughed and nodded to Kara. "Go on. Show us these boots."

. . .

After persuading her father that the white coat with the fake fur around the hood was an absolute necessity—with a little help from Miss Aritomo—Kara waited in line with him to pay. Someone had apparently gone on a break and left an old woman with a cranky, pinched face as the only clerk. Kara dared not complain about the wait. Instead, she leaned her head on her father's shoulder.

"Thanks, Dad."

"It's okay," he said. "I don't want my little girl's toes freezing off."

"Yuck. Me either."

"So everyone's due back tomorrow, right?" he asked.

Kara smiled. By "everyone," he meant her two best friends, Miho and Sakura, and Hachiro, but he tried not to pry too much into her feelings for her boyfriend. She didn't mind talking about Hachiro with her father, actually, but he seemed very wary about seeming too curious, which was probably for the best. As long as she was happy and Hachiro was treating her well, he didn't need to know any more than that.

Despite what her mother had always said, boyfriends were the one area where fathers didn't always indulge their daughters.

". . . That's terrible," Miss Aritomo said. "How did she die?"

Kara and her father both turned to see the teacher talking to a short, fiftyish man whose glasses were too big for his face. His expression was grim.

"She got lost on the mountain during the first snowstorm we had last month," the man said, shaking his head slowly, mouth set in a thin line. "They searched for her after the storm, but two days passed before they found her. She had frozen."

Kara flinched at the word. "God," she whispered, in English.

Miss Aritomo expressed her sorrow at the news and the man with the big glasses—who Kara now realized was an employee here, but also someone the teacher knew—nodded again. Or perhaps they were small bows, accepting her condolences.

The conversation went on, but Kara had had enough.

"I'm going to look at gloves," she said, forcing a smile.

"You already have gloves," her father said.

"I didn't say 'buy.' I'm just looking," she replied, and then she was off, heading over to a circular display where what seemed hundreds of pairs of gloves hung.

Things had been going so well. They were happy. Kara had had enough of death and ugliness and did not want to hear about any more of it.

As she searched for a pair of gloves that would match her new jacket, not really intending to ask her father to buy them, but curious, she heard soft voices whispering behind her, and then one of them spoke up.

"Well, hello, *bonsai*. Happy New Year."

Mai Genji had seemed like her nemesis for a while. She had inherited the position of queen of the soccer bitches when the reigning queen, a girl named Ume, had been expelled during the spring term. Ume had told Mai about the impossible, awful things that had happened in April of last year—about the curse that the demon Kyuketsuki had put on Kara and Sakura and Miho—and for a time Mai had blamed Kara for Ume's expulsion and for the horrible things that had followed it, during the autumn term.

Now Mai knew better, and she had a long, thin white scar on her right cheek that would remind her every time she looked in the mirror. It had all started with Ume, whom they suspected of having murdered Sakura's sister, Akane.

Kara's first year in Japan had been long and strange and sometimes awful. And though the curse still lingered, and she worried that it would draw even more evil to her and her friends, she wanted to focus on the new beginning that the winter term offered.

So she smiled at the queen of the soccer bitches, and at her roommate, Wakana, who had nearly been killed herself back in the fall.

"Happy New Year," Kara said.

"Your father and Aritomo-sensei look very happy," Mai said, an edge to the words that seemed on the verge of mockery.

Kara bristled. No way would she put up with anyone saying anything about her dad and Miss Aritomo.

"They *are*," she said.

To her surprise, both girls smiled. They looked at each other and then back at Kara.

"They're really cute together," Wakana said.

"We're glad for them," Mai added, and then her smile vanished. "I'll see you in homeroom."

"Yeah," Kara said. "I'll see you."

The two girls turned and meandered off through the racks, whispering to each other in a way that she should have assumed meant they were gossiping about her. But she didn't think they were. They had lives, just like she did. Families. They had probably enjoyed the holidays with the people they loved, and now it was a new year.

No, they would never be friends.

But maybe it really was a new beginning for all of them.

Hachiro had seen a lot of impossible things since Kara had come into his life, but never a ghost. The one on the train back to Miyazu City to begin the winter term was his first.

Late that Monday night, just a couple of days after New Year's, he sat aboard the busy train, head lolled against the window, lights strobing across the dark glass as the express shot through some commuter station without slowing down. His parents had struggled trying to decide when to drive him back to school and who would take him, so Hachiro had suggested they let him take the train back to Miyazu. At first they had balked, but he had appealed to reason. He knew they loved him, but they both worked and he could take care of himself. Logic triumphed, and now he found himself returning to Monju-no-Chie school a day earlier than he'd planned.

The early return would be a pleasant surprise for Kara, so he had not told her. And Hachiro had quickly discovered that he did not mind traveling alone. A couple of hours on a train had offered myriad options. He could have played a video game or read baseball magazines or manga. Instead, he listened to music and read from *To Kill a Mockingbird* in English. Professor Harper had assigned it over break, and explained that the subject matter would be addressed in his American Studies classes and that it would be a challenge for his English-language students. Hachiro had read it twice. Kara's Japanese was excellent, and he wanted to surprise her by improving his command of her language.

Now, though, as nine o'clock came and went and the long winter night was well under way, he could not help closing his eyes. He drifted in and out of wakefulness, barely aware of the murmured conversations around him, of the old couple attempting to retain their composure while their grand-daughter exhibited a wild imagination and bursts of laughing energy, of the rock star–cool university guy with two giggling girlfriends fawning over him. They were all just vague back-ground as he dozed.

The train slowed a bit as it rattled onto older tracks, and so he knew they were not far from Miyazu City. The ride would not be as smooth from here on in, but still he rested his head against the window, skull juddering against the glass. Sleepy as he was, Hachiro could not fall into a full slumber because he knew that once he arrived in Miyazu he would have to change to the local train that would take him out along the bay to the station just down the street from Monju-no-Chie school.

The little girl let out a mischievous squeal, forcing her grandmother to snap at her. Drifting, Hachiro listened, and felt badly for both the girl, who only wanted to play, and the old woman, who could not help being embarrassed by what she would see as improper behavior.

Eyes closed, head jouncing against the window, he lis-tened. The too-cool university guy whispered things to his female companions that were doubtless far more improper than anything the little girl's grandmother could even imagine.

There were giggles and more whispers, and Hachiro began to drift off again.

A cold draft caressed his face and slipped like a scarf of silk and snow around his neck. He opened his eyes, wondering where the breeze had come from. Had someone opened a door that let the winter in?

He glanced around at the windows, then at the doors at either end of the car, but saw nothing that could have been the source of the draft. Only when he lowered his gaze, shifting in his seat, did his mind process what he had just seen. A familiar face, spiky black hair, bright eyes. A face he knew very well.

Hachiro's heart raced and a tentative smile touched his lips. Impossible. He was sleepy, half in a dream. There were plenty of teenaged boys with spiky hair, and the kid was half-turned away from him anyway. He could be anyone.

Curiosity driving him, that chill caress running up the back of his neck, he turned again and looked toward the back of the car. The kid had his chin down, almost as if he were dozing off as well, but his eyes were open and he stared at the floor. The lights in the train car flickered, and in each lightless moment it almost seemed that the darkness outside the windows was trying to get in.

Jiro.

But it couldn't be Jiro, of course. Jiro had been murdered on the shore of Miyazu Bay, his body found drained of blood, his shoes missing. Hachiro had been there when they hauled his corpse out of the water. He could still feel the hollow place inside where his friendship with Jiro had once been.

The resemblance was uncanny. Hachiro wanted to look away, but he couldn't stop staring. The train rumbled over a rough section of track and outside the windows he saw the lights of shops and offices—they would be arriving at Miyazu station in moments.

The wan, yellow luminescence inside the train car flickered again, off and on, off and on, off for several long seconds, and then on again. The kid had not moved.

Hachiro leaned forward to get a fuller view of the kid, slid almost off his seat so he could see past briefcases and small suitcases and outstretched legs. Then he froze, ice racing through his veins. His breath came in tiny, hitching gasps and he slowly shook his head.

The kid had no shoes on. His feet were so pale.

He turned to look at Hachiro, not in some random fashion but in a slow, sad glance that said he had been aware all along of being watched. And when he smiled wistfully and gave a tiny nod of acknowledgment, Hachiro could not lie to himself anymore.

Jiro.

The train began to slow. Hachiro could not breathe. He locked eyes with the ghost—for what else could it be?—and felt all of the sadness of his friend's death return. He wanted to speak, to ask questions, to say that Jiro had been missed. He wanted to run, to hide, to nurture the fear that rose in him. The lights flickered again, and now, for the first time, he realized that Jiro had faded, his presence thin as delicate parchment, the shapes and shadows of the floor and the seat and even the window visible through him.

The conductor's voice filled the air. The train lurched three times in quick succession, but the third was the worst, rocking Hachiro forward, breaking his eye contact with Jiro. He had to put a hand out to keep from being thrown from his seat as the train came to an abrupt halt.

As he turned, the doors shushed open and people rose, grabbing their bags, chatter erupting as they began to herd out.

"No," Hachiro said, grabbing his bag and standing.

He thrust himself into the flow of disembarking passengers, searching the crowd for that spiky hair, that familiar face. He caught a glimpse of a silhouette he thought might be that of the ghost.

"Jiro!" he called.

Several people gave him disapproving looks, but most simply pretended not to hear him. Hachiro called out again, fear and confusion warring within him, and he pushed through the crowd and stepped off the train.

On the station platform he stopped and looked around. Hachiro was tall and broad shouldered, so he stood his ground and peered over the heads of the other passengers. He called Jiro's name again, but already his hopes were fading. Someone bumped him from behind and he staggered two steps forward.

People streamed away, reuniting with family and friends and lovers and then vanishing from the platform. Only stragglers were left when the train hissed loudly and the doors closed and it began to glide away.

Jiro stood just inside the doors, staring out at Hachiro as the train pulled away. He hadn't been there a moment before.

The ghost watched him with sad eyes, and as the train rattled out of the station he faded from view.

Gone again.

Hachiro stared along the tracks for a long time after the train had gone, frightened and glad all at the same time, and he wondered if, perhaps, he should never have come back to Miyazu City. To Monju-no-Chie school.

To Kara.

ABOUT THE AUTHOR

THOMAS RANDALL is the author of the popular children's fantasy series Adventures in Strangewood. He lives in Tarrytown, New York, and frequently vacations in places that exist only inside his head.

www.thewakingbooks.com